The Critics Do a Doub
Double D<

"As the years separate the 1960s from the present, **the value of** *Double Double,* **Yglesias's tongue-in-cheek depiction of this turbulent decade, continues to increase** . . . Through Yglesias's skillful use of interior monologues, the reader comes to know Seth [the protagonist] very well, and, more important, comes to experience **the excitement, the energy, the confusion, the hypocrisy, and above all the naïve innocence that characterized the 1960s** . . . This euphoric time in American history was destined to come to an abrupt and violent end. *Double Double* . . . **is a highly original re-creation of an era** both defined and destroyed by the unbalanced interplay between idealism and realism."

—Richard Keenan in *The Critical Survey of Long Fiction*

"A **compelling** blend of the personal and the socio-political . . . Yglesias unfailingly discovers, happily or unhappily for his characters, parallel moral crises between the generations. This aspect of his work reaches its finest, albeit pessimistic, fruition in his fourth and least ethnic novel, *Double Double* . . . Four well-realized aspects of *Double Double* make it **Yglesias's best work. The plot is the masterstroke.** From this emanates **an astute psychological rendering** of [protagonist] Seth Evergood's character, **a brilliant unfolding** of how the limitations (if not the sins) of the father are revisited upon the son, **and a lucid vision** of the deadly serious ramifications of political dissent."

—David M. Heaton in *Contemporary Novelists*

(Please turn the page for more about Jose Yglesias)

Books by
Jose Yglesias

Fiction

Break-In
Double Double
The Guns in the Closet
Home Again
The Kill Price
The Old Gents
One German Dead
An Orderly Life
Tristan and the Hispanics
The Truth About Them
A Wake in Ybor City

Non-Fiction

Down There
The Franco Years
The Goodbye Land
In the Fist of the Revolution

Double
Double

Jose Yglesias

Arte Público Press
Houston, Texas
2000

Double Double

Jose Yglesias

Arte Público Press
Houston, Texas
2000

This volume is made possible through grants from the National Endowment for the Arts (a federal agency),the Lila Wallace-Reader's Digest Fund and the City of Houston through The Cultural Arts Council of Houston, Harris County.

Recovering the past, creating the future

Arte Público Press
University of Houston
Houston, Texas 77204-2174

Cover illustration and design by James F. Brisson

Yglesias, Jose.
    Double double / Jose Yglesias.
    p.   cm.
    ISBN 1-55885-272-7 (pbk. : alk. paper)
    Nineteen sixties — Fiction. 2. Politicians — Fiction.
3. Radicals—Fiction. I. Title.
PS3575.G5 D68   2000
813'.54—dc21   00-025944
                                    CIP

0 1 2 3 4 5 6 7 8 9   10 9 8 7 6 5 4 3 2 1

to Helen

Chapter 1

There were raised fists at the end of Seth's lecture. Laughter followed almost immediately. It started down front in the auditorium and traveled up to the balcony: an ironical acknowledgment that raised fists were something of revolution at Harvest College—it *was* founded by Quakers. Seth moved to one side of the podium and took a step forward—he always did this whenever he meant to arouse his audience—and the applause and the laughter paused. "Are we a *petite minuscule?*" he asked the students, holding up his own fist. In the first row the chairman of the History Department, who had handed him his $500 honorarium before the lecture, looked down between his knees and shuddered. *Yes, yes,* the students yelled. Hands held up the paperback edition of Seth's book, *Paris Spring: 1968.* Seth hugged his middle and bent slightly forward, smiling, to show he enjoyed their response, but straightened attentively when an enormous, bearded young man stood up. "We are free!" the young man called, and whirled and repeated it to the balcony. *Free, free,* the audience answered. Free, Seth thought, of my wife and my shrink. He jumped from the low stage to the floor of the hall as if to join them all the more quickly, and decided, when he saw the students spring toward him, that tomorrow he would finally make the break. He would start life anew.

The chairman of the department waved to him from the fringe of students and disappeared; but the young history instructor appointed to squire Seth on campus struggled to his side. "Listen, everybody," the instructor announced, and his voice quavered with the desire not to sound authoritarian. "Mr. Evergood has one hour to make his bus."

"One hour!" a boy moaned.

1

"Well, why the shit did you keep him with the faculty before the lecture?" asked a girl. Immediately more students pushed toward Seth, and the instructor was drawn from his side by the tidal movement. "Leave him to us now. We'll take him to the bus."

Seth was shorter than everyone around him, and the enormous young man cut off his view of the girl and the instructor. "Evergood, think it over," the young man said, leaning over him. "Do you have to leave?"

"No, no, not Evergood," Seth said. "It's Seth."

"Right on, brother," the young man said, and placed an arm around Seth's waist and drew him to his side. The motion lifted Seth off his feet, and the instructor reappeared in Seth's sight before the young man returned him to the floor. The instructor looked alarmed. He held up an envelope. "I've got his ticket," he cried above the noise, and shook the envelope to get attention. Another wave of students carried him out to sea. The envelope disappeared from his hand, and the instructor called, "Evergood! Evergood!"

"I've got your ticket," the girl shrilled an octave higher, and the others let her get to Seth.

"Evergood?" the instructor pleaded, his face red.

"Lift me up again," Seth said to the bearded student. The boy crouched, grabbed Seth's knees, and brought him up on one shoulder. "I'm OK!" Seth shouted as soon as he saw the instructor. "They'll take me to the bus." The instructor nodded and tried to adjust his face into a good-humored expression, but the last look Seth got of him before the bearded student lowered him to the floor showed that the poor instructor felt pained and left out. Seth thought he knew what the instructor suffered: he was snubbed by the older faculty and ignored by the students. Too bad, Seth decided, he can make his existential choice as I have.

"I'm sorry for what's-his-name," Seth said to the bearded youth. "He wanted to talk about publications and publishers. . . ."

Smiling faces answered him. "Him? Don't be sorry for him!" Seth could not be sure who said that, but the girl with the bus ticket was now at his side and she added, "What the world does *not* need is one more dumb-ass Ph.D. thesis."

"My briefcase," Seth said. "I left it on the stage."

A boy wearing a beaded headband said, "I've got it."

"Don't you lose it," Seth said. "It's got a shirt, shorts, socks, all dirty."

They moved up the aisle, the bearded youth with his hand on Seth's right arm, the girl with the bus ticket hugging the other. Behind them another student said, "Did you hear that? He's groovy!"

"Seth, Seth, you sure you got to catch that bus?" the boy said. "We were counting on getting you to our pad. Rap some, smoke a little. We'll put you on the morning bus to New York. Lots of things to discuss, what do you say?"

Seth hesitated; it sounded cozy. At less isolated colleges the students did not so readily make him one of their own. He looked at the girl at his side. She was small, his size, and her eyes were all acceptance, not a tense line on her face. She did not tower over him like his wife, Mathilde.

She said, "Lots of things to ask you we couldn't in front of the faculty. We got to turn this college around. Reforms, reforms, that's all we've gotten and everybody's losing interest. Can you blame them? It's still the same uptight little private liberal arts college. In New York they can fight for open admissions—but here? We got a Third World studies program and a say in curriculum and discipline and all that shit but—"

"Wow, look at that moon!" the boy with the headband said. They were on the green now, some twenty-five in all, and the group looked up at the shining three-quarter moon. "You won't sleep on that bus."

"I've got to, I've got to," Seth said, in a voice that asked them to commiserate with him. "I go straight to a meeting from the bus station in New York."

"Then you can't groove?" the bearded boy said.

Seth paused until all the students listened. "I leave it to you to decide, brothers." Then waited again. "OK? But first let me tell you what the meeting's about."

They were all admiration; Seth knew he was not being fair. "It's about Regis Debray," he began. "We're sending three men to Bolivia to talk to the government and we've got to decide on tactics. Do we announce it to the press? How? In an open letter to the Bolivians announcing the delegation?"

"Are you going?" the girl asked.

"But you were thrown out a year ago," the bearded boy said, "when you got fired from the AP."

"Right, the time the Bertrand Russell Foundation sent me," Seth replied. "But now the nationalist generals are in power and there's more of a chance."

"Dyno," the girl said.

"That's heavy," a boy with blond curls like a nimbus said. "That Russell Foundation, man."

"No, no, not them," Seth said. He reached out and touched two of the students nearest him, as if to say, Listen to this. "The Mackey Committee. Mackey, the Pittsburgh millionaire. He fancies himself another Bertie Russell!"

"Take his bread, Seth," the bearded boy advised. "That's no rip-off—"

"That's a *good* rip-off," the girl insisted. "So you're going?"

"I don't know, I don't know," Seth said. "That's the kind of thing we have to decide tomorrow." He exhaled and looked around at the group. Beautiful, he thought, and felt an undirected sexual excitement.

"Wow, man, let's take him to the bus station," the boy with Seth's briefcase said. "He can't stay here just to rap."

Seth looked at him and then at the others. He thought of his friend Gary who was head of the Mackey Committee, and felt a momentary panic that someone might know he was lying. Gary had asked him to call but said nothing about Bolivia or a meeting. Finally, he said, "But I'll stay if you decide."

They walked him off the campus, became hushed through the sleeping residential streets lined with rows of little houses, and began to talk again when they reached the main street, called Main Street, where all the shops and the one pizza parlor were dark and shut. "That was our slum back there," the girl said.

"Blacks?" Seth said.

"In this Pennsylvania mountain town!" she said. Someone laughed. "All these people work for the college—the jobs stay in the families for generations."

"Conservative, man!" the boy with the headband said, and swung Seth's briefcase with joyous desperation.

"No industry," the bearded boy explained soberly. "If you don't get a job in the college, you try at the rug factory thirty miles away. Weekends they get in their cars with six-packs and drive around, avoiding the one state trooper for three counties. And the big social-minded activity of the high school kids is to go around with plastic bags picking up the beer cans their big brothers threw out of their cars."

"You can't reach them," the girl said. "No way for us to break out of the campus."

Seth thought: all the borders are made of marshmallow. He must remember that for his notebook. He said, "How'd they feel about your strike?"

"They were for the administration, of course," the girl replied.

"What did they do?" Seth asked.

"Do?" she said.

"Nothing," the bearded boy said. "After all . . ."

A voice behind Seth called out, "Say it, baby."

"We're the rich kids and they don't like us," the bearded boy admitted. "We *are* the rich kids, after all, and they won't touch us."

"Poor old Marx," the boy with the briefcase said.

Seth laughed with the students and quickly reminded himself that he must read Marx. He must read. For a year now he could not sit down and read; he barely scanned the newspaper headlines. He got by on six quotes from Marx, a couple from Sartre—a shorthand everyone responded to. He discovered he was frowning, his breath coming in that alarming way, and he thought of the time, six months ago, when Mathilde informed him, with much care, making sure that he was sitting down and had taken sips of his bourbon . . . informed him that she had made an appointment for a cardiograph. It was all in his mind, he knew that, but he still couldn't read. He thought: I'll start tomorrow, yes.

"It's a problem," the bearded boy was saying, and Seth realized that he thought Seth was pondering what they were telling him. What were they telling him? He made an effort and brought back enough of the phrases they had used to put it together: he was good at that double attention. It had saved him as a newspaperman, but because of this agility he did not think any thought through. I lack depth, he said to himself, and remembered Amelie, his French nanny, saying, "You worry too much, *mon Seth*—you drown in much too little water."

Harvest College had dropped ROTC, imported a black scholar to head a black studies program, had entirely revised its grading system for students past the freshman year. The cardiograph had shown nothing, and Mathilde, such a proper middle-class girl despite all, suggested, as if it were a victory won over herself, the shrink. There were no Defense projects at the university to attack, no local community clamoring for open admissions. The shrink was the ideal person, like a surrogate French nanny, to get him out of his marriage, but after the blessed release of the first session, he began to improvise for the shrink too. The breathlessness continued and the pains that ran up and down his left arm, and headaches that radiated from a knot of anxiety at the back of his neck. The bearded boy said, "The college has to be turned completely around, become an actively anti-imperialist college—the training ground for cadres for the revolution!"

Seth had made no comment. He felt them waiting. *"L'audace, toujours l'audace,"* he said finally, and here, at last, they were at the bus station. "In France it began as university reform—the kids were sitting on the windowsills for lectures, you know the whole thing."

There was no one else at the station. The doors were open, the lights on, the floors swept, but it was closed for business. "Nothing to rip off," the bearded boy said. "A small-town tradition."

They flopped on the two benches that faced each other in the middle of the narrow room, and others sat on the floor. "So what do you think?" asked a new girl whom Seth had not noticed in the dimly lit streets. She hunkered on the floor between the benches. Jeans and a tank top that breathed with her, and delicate bare feet, dirty at the toes from walking the streets and pink and mother-of-pearl white at the ankles. She rubbed one hand up and down the calf of her right leg, and Seth leaned forward involuntarily. I am thirty-six, he thought, but I look ten years younger.

"You adjourned the school for a week of discussion on the war during Kent State and you did the same for Bobby Seale's trial," Seth said. "One has to know your situation better, be closer to it than I am, but wasn't Harvest College a stop on the underground railroad before the Civil War?"

"Don't think they haven't told us," said the boy with his briefcase, now hugging it between his knees and chest. "Big deal."

"Well, why can't you make it a sanctuary for draft resisters?" Seth said. He brought his hands together in a clapping motion and clasped them, the way he had seen French public speakers do when they were struck by a new idea. "But not secret, not even as a stop on the way to Canada—announce it and let them bring in the police, the works."

He heard the bearded boy's exaggerated intake of breath beside him, and the students across from him leaned toward him with approval. "Wow!" said the boy with the headband.

"Oh man, man, we got to rap about this," the bearded boy said. He threw an arm over Seth's shoulder and slowly exhaled. The thin smoke hung between them. That sweetish smell of marijuana. He thought of Mathilde leaving parties as soon as she smelled it. "Seth, take me home," she said, already in her coat and his on her arm. "I'm tired and there's the baby-sitter. . . ." And as at those parties he remembered his six-year-old son for the first time that night. He found himself looking down into the cupped hand which the bearded boy extended to him: a proffered joint.

He looked up and around. "Here?" he said.

The girl in the tank top stood up and slipped two long, slim fingers into her jeans' tight pocket and extracted a stick. "It's our town," she said, tapping and straightening it.

Legs stretched, feet touched. Seth took the joint and held it a moment as if he might sign his name with it. Each time there was this tiny moment of fright. Away from his parents, away from Mathilde. You drown in much too little water. After all, joints never had any effect on him.

"We do that, wow, and it'll start a whole movement," said the boy with the headband. He smiled at Seth and held out a hand to his friends near him. A joint was placed in it and the boy brought it to his mouth and pulled at it. He half closed his eyes and murmured, "Oh man."

If they looked at him, Seth knew it was to hear what else he had to say, not to watch him draw on the joint. He felt the sharp pain in one eye that preceded a headache, and thought of Mathilde dissolving two aspirins in sugared water, her hand on his forehead. He sucked on the cigarette, clamped his jaws, and held the smoke in his lungs. His eyes teared a little. He closed them, leaned back, and felt the girl who held his bus ticket carefully extract the joint from his fingers. When he exhaled, he saw no smoke, just felt the release.

"Groovy," said the bearded boy, and he reached across Seth to get the joint back. He drew on it and handed it to Seth again. Someone giggled; more in recollection of previous experiences, Seth thought, than what the present one could have yet produced. Maybe they had already been stoned at his lecture. He pulled on the joint and passed it to the girl. She leaned her head on his arm by way of thanks.

The bearded boy put a hand on Seth's thigh. "If we were at our pad . . ." he said. "It's on the second stick that you get the ideas." His hand squeezed Seth's leg. "Right, Seth?"

The barefoot girl crawled the short space between them, and kneeling before him rested her elbows on his knees and looked up at his face. "Three buildings in a semicircle like guard the approaches to the campus and at the other end is the river and the administration building is the fort there. We could hold it, baby, nobody could get in."

The bearded boy leaned forward giggling, put his left hand on her arm and his right on Seth's neck. "Right," he said, and drew them into a huddle. The girl on Seth's right kept her head on his arm. "Beautiful," she said, and passed the joint. The boy's fingers curled under Seth's collar. "How about it, Seth?" he said. Seth felt the boy's breath and the delicate pressure of the girl's.

The whoosh of the bus's brakes released him and the pop of the pneumatic door brought him to his feet. "Christ, it's here," someone said. "Fifteen minutes early." There were hands all over him. Seth laughed nervously and looked toward the street where the bus was parked. "Free, free," the bearded boy said like an exhalation, not in a roar as in the auditorium. "Free to touch, free to love, brother." A door he had never crossed was held open to Seth, and he froze.

The bus driver in a blue uniform jumped to the sidewalk. He was alone, and when he saw the group of students, he clasped his hands to his head. His cap fell off and uncovered his bright blond hair. "Oh no!" he said. "I was counting on a quiet run tonight."

The students preceding Seth to the sidewalk hid him from the bus driver. A girl took the driver's cap and tried it on. "We came to say hello," she said, and held out a hand with a half-consumed joint. "And to give you a drag."

There were two arms around Seth's waist; he didn't check whose. He took the briefcase and the envelope with the bus ticket. He nodded when the girl in the tank top said, "Next time, during the insurrection." She looked at the bearded boy and added, "We've got to let him off this time."

The bus driver glanced back at the bus quickly. "I better not," he said to the girl and then saw Seth emerging from the station door. "All right, fellas," he said sternly, "don't get in the passenger's way."

"Man, we're with him," the boy with the headband called.

The bus driver retrieved his cap from the girl's head. "OK, professor, I'm sorry," he said, with pro-tem respect.

Seth got up on the steps of the bus and looked down at the students. "Thanks," he said. "Thanks for everything." He felt as if he were running away.

Some of them raised their fists. Thank God the bus driver was removing the stub from his ticket and did not see them. "He's no professor, man," the bearded boy said, and the driver looked up at him and replied, "OK, OK."

From the dark interior of the bus, Seth took a last look at the sidewalk; the scene was like a photograph accompanying one of his articles. Some leaned on one another; their smiles reached for him over the driver's head; some appeared like stragglers passing by. Unlike French students, they exuded relaxation. That sharpness of the French was the legacy of Descartes; ideas carried to the pitch of excitement. OK, the concept wasn't his, but the comparison was: he'd use it—why not? He turned into the passageway when the driver stepped onto the bus. The green-tinted windows muted the light flowing from the small room of the station and dulled the sound of the kids' voices. From his seat two-thirds of the way back, they looked almost spectral. The students could not see him. *Clop* went the door, and the swing of the bus away from the curb broke the last connection.

The smell of sleep in the half-empty bus comforted him. So un-American, this mustiness. He pulled up the foot rest at the base of the seat in front of him. Good to be small, he thought, and raised his feet. Now would be the time, in this position, this relaxed, to talk to the shrink. Funny he had thought of Amelie, his French nanny, whom he had not seen in twenty-five years. The bus achieved the steady rumble of even speed, and he knew he'd sleep: no headaches, no breathlessness, no pain running up and down his arm, no stabs in his eyes. He always forgot that to take a bus, a plane, to drive away, miraculously uncoupled him, brought him the gift of this floating feeling. Like those divers in Jacques Cousteau films languidly moving in an unresisting world. The girl leaning her elbows on his knees and he looking down at the two dear bumps her nipples raised on her tank top He opened his eyes—a lost opportunity? Why had he run? He turned slightly on his right side, bringing his knees together, and slipped his clasped hands between his thighs, and closed his eyes. Oh no, it's only Bloom and me and dirty thoughts.

He is sitting in the reading room of the New York Public Library, ten books on the Spanish civil war piled in front of him. His father is in all of them. In Ehrenburg: the blond American from sunny California, son of frontiersmen. Wrong, he was from Ohio but his roots were in New England—dour, Puritan roots. In Vincent Shean: he was to *belles lettres* what Scott Fitzgerald and Hemingway were to fiction; he gladly became a propagandist for the Loyalists and fought at University City until the Spaniards pulled him out for better work. Seth knew he was not at the library; he is in the bus sleeping. On Amelie's lap. "But you know where your mother is, *cheri,*" she croons. "In Madrid fighting the fascists too." Too, too, too.

The bus had stopped. The door was open. Out the window he looked at the sign over the shingled diner: Truck Stop. Two windows, fluorescent lights, the bluish back of the driver hunched over the counter. No one else had left the bus. He was wide awake now and he sat forward and rubbed his face with his hands. Sitting alone there reminded him of his father closing the door behind him when he entered the study each morning in the house in Connecticut, or retreating to the grounds where the wall of cedars turned and made a green cove far from the house. What did he do there? In twenty-five years he had produced a small book on Sarah Orne Jewett. Nothing else. He did not bring papers home from Calvin, the school where he and mother taught. No obituaries at his death. Seth got out of his seat to put an end to these thoughts.

The drop from the bus door to the ground was no more than a missed step on a staircase, but it cost him an effort to make the leap.

Thr-rr-rr, pause, thr-rr-rr, thr-rr-rr. That heart flutter was an old friend. Two aspirins might quiet it. Or one Librium. Sometimes more. He opened the screen door of the diner, and the waitress who had been bent over the counter facing the driver looked up and said, "Here's a friend of yours."

The bus driver half turned and ran a hand through the blond hair, which the lights bleached white, and said, "Oh hi, professor." He tapped the stool next to his and Seth got on it and thought, They're both younger than I am and they look old, old.

"What can I give you?" the waitress said.

"Hey, honey," the driver said. "Watch your language."

Seth tried to grin. "Two aspirins to start with," he said, and looked at his watch. Three forty-five. He swung the stool half round and without getting off it searched for the men's room in the unlighted end of the diner, where there were tables and chairs. A row of doors. He peered at them.

"The last one," the driver said, and winked mysteriously. "The others are showers."

"What?" Seth said.

"The one you're looking for is the last one," he replied. "The others got showers. It's a truck stop."

Seth walked beyond the counter and the driver called, "Hey, professor?"

He turned and saw the waitress through the open end of the counter leaning down to get aspirins. Her white nylon uniform was tight over her buttocks. The bus driver said, "Everybody asleep?" The waitress's motions stopped; she waited for his answer too. The driver nodded his head toward the front door. "In the bus," he added.

Seth nodded. "I'm the only customer."

When he returned, there was a glass of water and saucer with two aspirins in front of his stool.

"What you need is a shower," the driver said.

"Something, anyway," Seth replied, and took the aspirins.

The waitress watched them with her arms folded under her breasts. "Not a body stopped by in two hours," she said.

"Some nights when my whole load is in the arms of Morpheus like tonight I take a shower myself," the driver said. "Breaks the routine."

Seth wondered what Gary would say about Bolivia. He'd see when he got to New York. He would call him and feel him out. First, a shower, then the shrink, then Gary and the committee. He thought: I'll take an amphetamine in the morning. I shall tell the shrink I'm through, and then Mathilde. He shuddered. I'll certainly need an amphetamine.

"What the sleeping customers don't know won't hurt them," the driver said, and nudged Seth with his shoulder. "Right?" He looked at Seth for a long moment, then at the waitress without speaking, and again at Seth.

Seth shivered and yawned. "Excuse me," he said. "I think I'll have coffee."

The waitress moved and the driver exhaled loudly, as if by speaking Seth had broken a spell. "OK, honey," the driver said. "I'll have the pie then. Make it a fresh one."

"I always give you a fresh one," she said, and walked to the far end of the counter and leaned down to open the bottom aluminum drawer. She kept her left arm up, the hand just above her buttocks, to hold down her tight uniform. The back of the skirt peaked like an open tepee. Her legs were fat but firm above the knees.

The driver nudged Seth. "How do you like that?" he asked quietly.

"I like it a lot," Seth said, but he did not mean it and he grinned quickly to keep his indifference from showing. There was something motherly and wrong there.

The driver moved his elbow along the counter to get closer. "You can have her in the showers," he said and winked. "Take it from me, I know."

Seth looked her way again and saw her straighten and the dress slide down her strong thighs. She rested her hands on her hips and studied the pie she had placed on the counter. Seth's chest contracted with a spasm of unexpected pleasure: he knew that sturdiness, that good, coarse nature. He'd butted his head against that groin—Amelie. He turned to the driver, smiling.

"I'll fix it," the driver said. "The two of us and her."

His vision of Amelie standing in the kitchen of the cottage in France was blotted by the insistent face of the driver, his bright hair like a demon's. "You're kidding," Seth said weakly.

"No, no," the driver said, and looked at his watch. "There's time—hey, baby!"

"Coming," she called.

"Soap and water," the driver whispered. "Then cold, cold as you can stand it for—"

"Here it is," the waitress called, and walked toward them holding the pie high and ahead of her.

Seth's head turned sharply toward her. There she was again, so full of life she was like a magnet. "I love you," he said, and she turned her head slightly in his direction. He readied himself for the pleasure of her gaze but she shifted to look beyond him. The screen door slammed and a young woman from the bus entered, carrying a baby.

"Look at you, look at you," the waitress said to the baby, and put down the pie with no more thought for the men. "Come over here, honey, sit at the table."

The bus driver cursed. "Professor, you wasted too much time."

"Oh," Seth said. He drank the coffee without a stop. He thought: so that's what they were planning when I came in. He put his cup down and said, "I'm sorry."

"Naw, that's all right," the driver replied. "You can't win them all, you know."

Seth placed a dollar on the counter. "I think I'll go back," he said.

The driver nodded and swung his stool around toward the tables. "No hurry, lady, you take care of the baby," he said.

From the steps of the bus, Seth could hear them laughing and talking. He looked toward the diner and wondered if the waitress would think of him when she picked up the dollar. A man in a front seat stirred. Seth found his again, and this time the smell of the bus repelled him. He thought: I'll never break away. He turned on his side, clasped his hands, and closed his eyes. It didn't work. Without looking, he felt for the pills in his pocket. He could tell by touch which he wanted, and he placed two Seconals in the hollow he made of his tongue. He had learned to swallow them without water, and that was some comfort.

Chapter 2

Seth slept through the morning and awoke dry mouthed and rumpled when the bus parked in the New York terminal. He wished, more intensely than other mornings, that he could remain there and think about his life. It was dark in the underground of the terminal, and the noise of the other buses would be cut off when the door of his was shut. He tightened his closed eyes to quicken himself into sleep, and thought, as if he had reached a profound conclusion, that sleep was better than analysis. That's what they do in the Soviet Union: put you to sleep and let your problems dissolve. But for a radical the Soviet Union must be a nightmare all the time.

He opened an eye and looked at his watch. Nine-thirty. His appointment with the shrink was for eleven. He was instantly pierced by guilt that he had not told the students his real reason for leaving last night. That girl who rested her elbows on his knees. He sat up and saw the bus driver enter the bus to take a last look. "Hey, professor," the man called. "You slept as good as if you got laid!"

Seth grinned and pulled at his clothes to get them into shape, and then yanked out his briefcase from under the seat. As he passed the driver, the man said, "You still look too young to be a professor—you ain't even got a morning's growth." He rubbed his chin to show what he meant and tapped Seth on the shoulder.

"That's my problem," Seth said, smelled the grease mixed with exhaust and stale cigarette smoke wafting in the door, and shivered involuntarily. He jumped down without looking back.

"That's OK," the driver replied. He called after Seth, "Take it easy now."

He thought: they all worry about me because I'm small. I haven't reached my full growth, I break their hearts, like those Arab boys shining shoes and pimping when you expect them to be in kindergarten being attended to. Gratitude made him turn to wave at the bus driver, but the man no longer looked his way. On the other side of the doors, in the underground, fetid passages of the terminal, a junkie fixed his eyes on him. He was all dead skin and wild hair proliferating. "No!" Seth said and sped by him to the escalator, telling himself that he was as tough, after all, as those Arab boys.

"You're uptight, man," the junkie called, and waved his arms and pointed at Seth, immobile on the escalator. "Did I say anything? Shit, all I want is the time—what time is it?"

"Nine-thirty," Seth called down, knowing the escalator carried him safely away.

"Shit," the junkie said, and looked about for someone else.

Seth rewarded himself for the morning's dreariness with a cigarette before breakfast, picked up a *Times* from a stand on the upper level of the terminal, and headed for the luncheonette. If coffee didn't work, he'd take an amphetamine. He sat at an inside booth; he did not want to look at Eighth Avenue yet. The waiter was Puerto Rican, and Seth spoke to him in Spanish and felt a slight rush of energy at being on stage again. The waiter's surprise was a reminder of his own uniqueness. He opened the *Times,* saw a photograph of Nixon, and closed it again. I'm not interested in politics, he thought; it's politics that's interested in me.

This was a secret with him. He was not sure that he believed it, but he teased himself with the thought. He once told Mathilde that his heart was no longer in his articles or lectures or the committees on whose letterheads his name appeared. She had contemplated him skeptically, as she had begun doing lately about everything he said. "It's true, true," he had protested. "I'm always having to live up to their image of what the son of the highest-ranking officer in the International Brigades should be—they never leave me alone about it. But the truth is, that goddamn civil war robbed me. Father and mother left me for months on end and I have been looking for those missing months of warmth."

"Put that line in your journal, don't forget it," she had said with newfound cruelty. "You look pleased with it."

He suspected that Mathilde too had been seduced by the glamour of his family history. She was born in Rochester, the daughter of a corporation executive, and time was when both automatically smiled when they said Rochester. Lately, he thought, Mathilde said it with nostalgia. She probably would like to live in a town like that, a member of an afternoon bridge club like her mother. No, a hospital volunteer like her classmates at Smith, who had gone on to be good wives. The little woman, she and he used to say about such girls. The little woman, he said to himself, and lit a cigarette. He finally looked across the luncheonette at Eighth Avenue. Great. He preferred filth, porno shops, sooty air. God, yes.

Things to do. He took out his notebook and his good pen; he turned to a clean leaf and wrote *I prefer soot and porno* and underneath the date and *Things to do*. First, the shrink. Second, Gary Epstein. Good boy, Gary. The thought of him made him smile. It gave him energy to call Mathilde. He crossed the luncheonette to the phone booth and kept the door of it open to watch his things on the table. That's New York, he thought, and told himself to make a note about it when he returned to the table. You had to keep your eye on your things at all times.

Mathilde didn't answer. She must have walked Pablo to the crosstown bus. It felt like a reprieve. He could say he had called. He opened his notebook again at the table, lit another cigarette, and paused. He could not recall what he wanted to write in it; the thought had evaporated. In a moment, he remembered it had to do with New Yorkers always being on the alert. So what? A cheap generalization. It wasn't even true. There was no place in the world where people wasted more time. Like himself. I waste time, I waste time, he told himself. I must schedule my days or I'll get nothing done.

Gary. He feared the committee was losing interest in Seth's proposal that a delegation visit Debray in prison. He had thought of it as a perfect way to break with Mathilde. He looked for the Puerto Rican waiter but a waitress came over. "More coffee?" she said, and he nodded and went to the phone again. Gary's voice sounded muffled. "I'm sorry, Gary," Seth said. "I didn't mean to wake you."

There was a long pause. "Who is this?" Gary said.

"Seth, man," he replied, trying to sound lighthearted. It pained him that Gary did not recognize his voice. "Go back to sleep, I'll call you later."

"Seth, I've been up all night—"

"I'll call you at the committee." He chuckled. "I was just reporting for duty."

"No more committee for me!" Gary's voice broke. "Seth, buddy, I've been cuckolded!" At Gary's end there was yelling. Seth could not make it out. "Trudy has been sleeping with Mackey and I can't take it. That old man!"

"Hey . . ." Seth said. What was one supposed to say? "You want to talk? I'll call off—I don't have to go home."

Gary yelled, "Get away—it's true!" Then silence. Gary must have covered the mouthpiece. "OK, let's act as if everything is normal," Gary finally said, his voice under control, "and meet at the office. But make sure, because I have to see you, buddy."

"Can I help?" Seth asked, but he hesitated and the phone clicked as he spoke. He sat in the booth a moment. He thought: what makes me think I can help? Who can help with Mathilde and me? He involuntarily giggled. He was graduating from patient to shrink in one day. Funny, funny, funny. He hurried out of the booth: he had forgotten to watch his table.

The gold pen from Tiffany's was not there. The one Sara and Gerald Murphy had given his father before he became political and went off to Spain. He was sure he'd left it on his notebook. He searched his pockets, then bent down to look at the floor and discovered it lying by the iron leg of the table. He reached for it and saw, from under the table top, the waitress's legs approaching. He quickly studied her. Her belly was slack and from his angle her nipples seemed to push at her uniform. "Well, lover, did you find it?" she asked.

"Yes." He had to swallow to reply; he always felt he had been caught in some mischief when he looked closely at a woman's body. "Thanks very much."

She pressed her thighs against the table. There was no resistance to her flesh; it appeared but for the uniform ready to spill onto the table. She waited, smiling resentfully. "It was a pen," he explained, and began to put away his things.

"I'm off in a half hour," she replied.

He thought: My God! He reached into his pocket for change. He wondered if he should put down a tip while she stood there.

"You're not too young, are you?" she said, and squinted.

He got up and placed a quarter next to his cup.

"That's all right." She shrugged. "I'm no good in the morning anyway. All locked up."

He had to brush past her to get out of the booth. He tried to smile. "See you," he said.

"So long, lover," she said. To his back she added, "For Christ's sakes."

The air outside was like stale breath in his face. When he was a child, friends of his parents at parties exhaled a smell like that. It was agony if they caught and held him close. With them he wriggled and got away and everyone laughed, but there was no turning away from Eighth Avenue. If I were tall, he thought, if I were tall, I'd get my nose into fresh air. He remembered his resolution not to take taxis, to live more like ordinary people, and walked across town, wondering if he should walk into a porno shop—why not?—and decided against it. Not just before going to the shrink, he said to himself.

He did not take the couch; he sat in the easy chair and faced Dr. Wainright. He smiled. Dr. Wainright did not return his smile, but his eyes appeared to enjoy Seth's dare. "Aren't your sideburns getting longer?" Seth asked. The room was cool; Seth wished he had showered and shaved. "What would you do, doc, if I got on your lap?" He giggled and stretched, holding his arms over his head and planting his feet firmly on the rug. "In a study like this I could write. I could write something better than . . ."

Dr. Wainright waited.

"Sometimes I think about you screwing," Seth said, looking at the bridge of Dr. Wainright's nose; an actress told him once that she did this when her partner in a scene did not respond correctly and she needed to keep her concentration. "How big your cock is, whether you go down on her before you mount her." He meant to laugh but instead began to cry.

"Would you like to lie down?" Dr. Wainright said.

"It's no use, doc," Seth said, smiling and letting the tears run down his cheeks. "I know what you're doing all the time. You're going to say this is a breakthrough, this is transference. I should lie down and let it all out because were really getting down to business at last. And then you're going to get me to say it's not a woman I see in bed with you but me with your cock coming at me. Hey, how big *is* your cock?" He laughed and brought up an arm and wiped his tears with his sleeve.

"It's no use," he repeated soberly, feeling better.

"Then you don't want to lie down," Dr. Wainright said and Seth thought: he's at a loss.

Seth said, "You know, I'm very charming when I'm with company, except when I'm with Mathilde, my wife, and except when I'm alone. In my head when I'm alone, I'm a big bore, I'm anxious." He leaned forward. "This *is* a breakthrough—what a dreary fool I've been with you for two months. Come on, you take it out and I'll take it out and we'll see who can shoot farthest. That's better than confession. I mean, it would be more fun than sitting around and talking about guilt and whether politics is aggression and all that."

Dr. Wainright finally smiled, but Seth thought he saw him hesitate a moment before he did so. A victory to catch him off guard, like discomfiting Mathilde at a party without the rest of the company knowing. He brought a hand down to his crotch but Dr. Wainright's eyes did not follow his gesture.

"Get set—ready! We'd get something out of it," Seth said, shaking his shoulders to simulate laughter. "You could write a paper on 'Some Aspects of Male Masturbation,' and I'm sure I could work up something for *Esquire.* They'd love it—'Shooting Off with Your Shrink'! What a gas, Seth Evergood not writing about politics."

After a moment, Dr. Wainright said, "Why did you say this was a breakthrough?"

He had so many things to do. What was he doing here still? Home and Mathilde, then Gary and the committee. My God, he had to phone the publisher who asked him to call. Two thousand dollars in the bank and the next royalty statement three months away. He sighed to ward off a wave of depression. "I said that?" He shook his head. "It is more like a breakdown. I really came today to tell you I have to break it off, OK?"

Dr. Wainright waited.

"Oh God, you see, you're acting like it's another subject for discussion." He put up a hand, as if stopping traffic. "I can't afford you.

It's a nice relationship—it's my safety-valve relationship. I come to this nice study, I cry a little, try out a few ideas, and I feel like I've had a brisk shower or been laid. Sometimes. But I wasn't home last night—I was out of town lecturing—and I've got to tell my wife it's all over. She's got to get a job, I can't support them both and myself—I have to get away."

He began to cry again.

"When did you decide this?" Dr. Wainright asked. "That it's all over, that is. You felt different during our last session."

He made an effort to remember. He looked at Dr Wainright. He had never asked him if he was married.

"You felt . . ." Dr. Wainright began.

"That I could get her to blow me." Seth got up. "She'd blow me and everything would be all right! My God!" He looked around for his briefcase. "I've got to go, I'm turning into a sickie."

Dr. Wainright remained seated. They looked at one another a moment. Seth thought: no one has ever walked out on him. He headed for the wrong door, the one leading to the reception room where the next patient waited. "I'm sorry," he said, and crossed to the street door.

"I am too," Dr. Wainright said, and Seth knew that was an extraordinary concession. "You have twenty minutes. Why don't you lie down here quietly and . . ."

Seth put out his hand. They had never shaken hands. Dr. Wainright's hand was slim and well defined and gripped his coolly. He must play tennis, Seth thought. What does he know about the real world? "Thanks, but I'll have a cup of coffee somewhere and think about what I'm going to do."

The air had cleared, the sun was out, and he pulled his jacket away from his body slightly to let the breeze in. Things are always nicer on the East Side, he thought; even the weather. He needed a shave. Fuck them, let them see how the anxious half lives. "Fraud, fraud," he said aloud about himself, and walked to the corner of Madison, bought the *Times* again, and went into a coffee shop. He sat in a booth, opened the *Times* to the book page, and said, "Coffee," to the figure that came to his table. An ad from the top of the page to the bottom, four columns wide, for the book on the Vietnamese village that had first appeared in *The New Yorker*. He remembered meeting the author at a party. He must've signed a contract that stipulated how much was to be spent on advertising and where. And he must have got a hefty advance. No, his father was a corporation lawyer; he could sign those gentlemanly contracts publishers love: no advance, no agent to hassle them, all the foreign rights left to the publishers. That's how he got these great ads, damn.

He took a sip of the coffee, put the paper down, and lit a cigarette. No, that wasn't the answer. The boy was a liberal, he agonized about the moral dilemma of Americans, his criticisms of American policy were confined to Vietnam—Vietnam was a tragic mistake. He was a luxury *The New Yorker* and all the liberal publications could afford. He didn't rock the boat. Gary had pointed out to Seth that a whole section of the American capitalist class had begun to suffer with the war and there were bound to be a lot of phonies appearing radical these days. Right. Whereas he (Seth) made clear that he thought the enemy was American imperialism; he had talked to the NLF in Paris, visited the defectors in Stockholm, spoken at Panther rallies, and consequently more and more of his articles were ending up at *Ramparts*. He was too strong for all the other magazines. Having set the record straight, he looked at the book ad again. One blurb from a famous critic praised the author for his spare, clean style. Why did I leave the AP, he asked himself, how will I make living? I'll never make *The New Yorker*: I simply don't write well enough.

But he hadn't come here to think about that. No, about Mathilde. He put a dollar down on the table, and thought as he walked away that he must start being careful with his money. He must call his agent, find out about lecture bureaus and foundations with clean money to give away, and as soon as he got home, he must return the publisher's call. Perhaps there was a contract and an advance in it. Of course he'd be all right, and he decided to take a taxi. As soon as he got inside it he saw the crosstown bus rumbling alongside and regretted he had not waited for it. The taxi was taking him home too fast. Mathilde. What would he say to her?

When he stepped out of the taxi, Chuck Rubin held the lobby door open for him. Rubin was a television writer, once blacklisted, now busy again. Seth had met him and his wife at a tenants' meeting and a month later at a New Year's party. At midnight, when everyone exchanged pecks, Rubin's wife opened her lips and tongued him. Since then Seth always felt constrained when he ran into Rubin in the elevator.

Rubin said, "Coming from somewhere glamorous, I bet."

"A lecture at a Pennsylvania college," Seth replied. "Nothing special."

"Now me, all I go out for is cigarettes," Rubin said, but he was dressed as if he had been out deer hunting. Seth thought: his generation's hang-up. "And now back to the typewriter."

In the elevator, Rubin added, "You guys!"

Seth grinned his little-boy grin. Maybe Mathilde wasn't home. That would solve things for now.

"You journalists have your story all laid out for you," Rubin explained. "Creative writers have to make it all up. We grind it out of our guts and then people think you just copied it out of a newspaper."

Seth waited for the elevator to close on Rubin before he put his key in the door. He would tell this to Gary later, he told himself, and add, Just the humiliation I needed at the moment. He opened the top lock, then the door, and stepped into the foyer quietly. As always, everything was so orderly that he could not tell whether Mathilde was in or out. He put the briefcase down, removed his jacket, and saw her stick her head out the kitchen door down the hall. "Seth sweetie!" she said, and skipped to him soundlessly in the ballet slippers she wore to be closer to his height. She put her cheek to his face and said, "Nice beard."

He held his arm around her and felt the familiar unfleshed ribs. Unprotected. A mistake to touch her; she would think it was a promise. "I need a bath," he said, and took his arm away.

She placed a hand on her mouth, opened her eyes wide, and once more skipped, this time toward the bathroom. He thought: why is she acting like a little girl? She raised a hand. "Go into your study first. There's two days' mail all waiting for you. Even a letter from mother. Your mother." She looked down with mock modesty, like a dutiful servant. "The bathroom is full of my things all drying. I'll whisk them away!"

She backed into the bathroom, and he was alone in his home. It seemed to him that he breathed for the first time that day without making an effort. It was a good apartment: Mathilde's plants were like a green curtain in the living room; his books started in the hall and surrounded his study at the end of it. The place drew him in. Looking at it, his problems seemed solvable. None of this would have to be broken up: his records, his file drawers, the political cartoons he had collected and framed, the ceramic pitchers he had bought for Mathilde in various countries that he felt were his. All this could remain together, a monument. If she was going to be like their first year together: that American girl in Paris for whom everything was a game and a delight, especially he.

He placed his briefcase next to the desk and sat on the swivel chair. He had bought the desk chair for himself, but Mathilde had given him the Eames chair in the corner; and his mother, when his father died, the chaise his father had used. On the desk his letters were laid out in a row, not simply dumped there the way Mathilde had done for more than a year now. No bills. He had left her the checkbook to pay any that might come in. She had taken it reluctantly. Indeed, she had only said, "Just leave it in your drawer. You're going to be gone two days—no need for me to worry." A reminder that he had taken that job away from her.

Marriage is a terrible arrangement, he thought, and looked at the center drawer without opening it. Something goes wrong and his using her bath towel can set off a wounding quarrel. If the checkbook is in the drawer, then she was still in her corner waiting for the bell to come out fighting. If not, she was sharing in his anxiety about money. But did he want that? He'd never break away. He drew the drawer out; the checkbook was not there. Oh God. He closed it again. He opened the stationery drawer. She'd taken envelopes, but the checkbook was not there either. What had made her change?

"The coast is clear, you can take your bath," she announced from the doorway, and he turned to her as if a gun had gone off. "You haven't read mother's letter? I'm anxious to know what she says. I forgot to write her about the money she sent for Pablo's birthday and I hope she's not hurt."

"Oh." He looked at the letters, and while picking out his mother's, he got the courage to ask, "Do you have the checkbook?"

"Yes." She drew out the syllable in order to control her nervousness. Then quickly, "I've decided that from now on you worry about politics and I worry about money. Division of labor, as you Marxists say."

"OK," he replied, not looking at her. He resisted the slight catch in her voice that told him this was a significant scene. It did not feel like a reconciliation: she did not rush into his arms, no music swelled. He tore the letter open. "I *am* going to continue to worry about politics," he said, his voice thin as during a quarrel. "If the trip to Bolivia is on, I'm going."

His mother's round, clear script did not form words in his mind. He waited for Mathilde's answer. But did there need to be an answer? A quick shooting pain traversed his head, from back to front. A punishment: he knew the Bolivia trip was unlikely. In a voice that was all assent, Mathilde said, "What does mother say?"

He made an effort to comprehend the letter. "She wants me to come up to see her." After he said it, his mother's request surprised him. "Alone," he added. He read the last sentence to himself again; the *you* might just as well be plural, and he heard Mathilde's voice in an old quarrel accusing him of never thinking as a family. "I, I, I, I!" she once yelled until she lost her breath like a little girl. He glanced up at her when she did not reply, and her face looked as if it might crumple. "Well, that's what she says. It's something about father. His papers, she says. She's so fucking formal, it may be just an invitation to tea."

But it was an appeal and it made him feel good. Particularly at this moment. With Mathilde standing by to see that there were people in this world thinking of him.

"You know, Seth, I've always thought you should write a book about him," she said.

He waved a hand irritably and then looked up at her when he heard her move. She had left. He had meant to hurt her, but it surprised him that just a wave of the hand had done it. He covered his face with his hands. Why hadn't he made her sit down and told her that he had to go his own way, that they must separate, for a while at least? He had to—he stopped, embarrassed by the phrase *to find himself* that was forming itself. He gripped his head with both hands to ward off the headache.

"Seth!" She was in his study again. "What's the matter, Seth?" She put a hand on the back of his neck, and when he uncovered his face, another on his forehead. He closed his eyes and the tears came down the corners of his eyes. She leaned down and kissed his forehead lightly, the way Amelie used to check, when he was boy, whether he had a temperature. "You're getting a headache, that's what it is," she said softly. "I'll get you some aspirins and then you take a warm bath—"

"I can't go on this way," he said desperately. "I can't go on this way—I'm suffocating!" He threw his head down, deliberately banging it on the desk. "I have to get away."

"I'll get you the aspirins," she said, and ran from the room.

He had frightened her. She knows, she knows. He sat up. The tears had stopped: how funny the way it all came and went, came and went, like blinking lights. The result of having been shunted between dear Amelie and a cold WASP mother. The thought braced him, and he picked up the publisher's letter and opened it. A graceful note reminding Seth of his desire to see him and asking him to call as soon as it was convenient. It could mean a job; he had told Tony Ybarra at the party that he was freelancing. He picked up the phone and dialed. Maybe a book. A fine, prestigious house, but that could mean a small advance. He gave the secretary his name and asked for Ybarra.

The moment he stopped talking Mathilde came into the study. "Oh Seth, dear, I didn't hear it ring," she said. "Let me take it."

He shook his head and held up a hand to keep her from giving him the aspirins. She was dissolving them in sugared water; he had taught her to do it like Amelie. The teaspoon clinked against the sides of the glass. He smiled as reflex and it made her happy.

"This is very kind of you to call, Mr. Evergood," Ybarra began on the phone. Any other publisher would have called him by his first name. "When can we meet?" He suggested his office the next day, and when Seth said he would have to be up in Connecticut—without looking at Mathilde to see how she took it—they settled on drinks that afternoon.

"I don't want you to comment now," Ybarra added as a postscript, "but I do want to tell you what I'm thinking about. Your father. A remarkable man from the little I know. I feel he would make the subject of a fine book—by you. Let's talk about it when we meet, shall we?"

"Very well," Seth said, and stood up when Ybarra said good-bye. "What a coincidence!" he said to Mathilde. "He's interested in a book on father—the very day mother wrote." He stared at her, forgetting it was she who had suggested it.

"Oh Seth, what did you say?"

"The way he put it, it wasn't even a matter of saying yes or no." He sat down again, amazed at the wonderful turn the day had taken. "But I hardly know my father—I can't do it."

"Oh Seth—"

"What do you know!" He picked up his mother's letter. "And he ended up apolitical, hardly an inspiration to anyone these days. I mean, he was a casualty."

"A casualty?" she said.

"A casualty of history," Seth replied. "There are lots of them—why write a book about one?"

"Seth, he was an important—"

"No, wait—maybe there's an angle there, a lesson for revolutionaries." He got up and walked to the window and addressed her across the room. "An interesting comparison with Che. Che goes from Cuba to the Congo and then Bolivia—unvanquished. Father from Spain to teaching and cultivating his garden in Connecticut." He held a hand up, as when he asked his audiences to stop applauding. "It's *the* American story—the inability to grow, to mature, writers who peter out after promising beginnings, political thinkers who end up mute quietists. Do you know what Thoreau spent most of the Civil War doing—tramping around in the Minnesota woods! You'd think he would have joined Frederick Douglass. Between them they could have been the great conscience of America, black and white. Only Douglass was undeterred, because he was—essentially—African, not Anglo-Saxon. The Panthers, the Panthers, they're our only hope."

He hugged himself, crossing his arms at the waist, and felt a stirring in his groin. He looked at her and saw she was not elated. "What's the matter? You don't agree?"

"No, no." She shook her head quickly. "I think it's wonderful!"

"What's wonderful? The point I'm making or Ybarra's offer?" He put a hand on a file drawer and lowered his head, looking at her from under his brows.

"Everything," she said, clasping her hands: a sign she was nervous. "Seth, do it exactly the way you want. It'll be a wonderful book."

"But it's not the way you want, right?"

"The way I want?"

"Too political, you don't want me to be political." He tossed his head, as if he had been dared. "Sure, you want me to be political—mushy liberal, the kind of thing that sets you apart in Rochester but is respectable in New York." He pulled out the file drawer and slammed it closed. "God damn it, just like my mother and her New England liberalism. Keep all your connections, don't burn any bridges. You're not going to do that to me!"

"Seth, I was wrong—I want you to be what you want to be!" She hurried across the room toward him, but stopped when he stayed by the file drawers. "I simply didn't understand for a while and I get scared. It's all right if I get scared, isn't it?"

"Existential anguish," he said.

His voice was neutral. She started him thinking about the choices his father had made, as charged with existential uncertainty as those of Sartre's heroes—God, father had been a friend of Sartre's! "God!" he said aloud, excited again.

The absence of anger in his voice meant acceptance. She began to cry, almost happily. "I guess it's because I'm a mother," she said, wiping the tears on her cheeks as she would water spilled on the dining table. "If I worry, it's because of Pablo. To be left alone. But I can live with that and you must not think about it. No."

He said, "I'm going to have to do a lot of research."

"I can help, as with the Paris book," she said. "Pablo is at school all day now."

"A list of all the men he knew—Malraux, André Marty, Pablo Neruda, Jean Cocteau, Ilya Ehrenburg." He threw himself on the Eames chair. He was seven: his father sat him on his shoulders and walked into the water until he began to scream; then his father put him down near his mother on the beach—relief. Saint-Tropez before it became Saint-Tropez. His father retreating from her sharp, deep voice, taking the gardening book to the nook the cedars made far from the house. The house in Connecticut. His voice was always laconic, skeptical, chilling; hers contained, maddening. They were harmonious to him now, as orderly and measured as in a piece by Bach, for they were playing themselves out in the book, his book, the book he would write. He pulled up his legs on the chair, as if he squatted on the ground, and straightened his back. Mathilde sat on the ottoman and waited for him to speak. "But first I must see what Ybarra has in mind. I don't know what he expects."

Elbows on her knees, she propped her chin on her cupped hands, like Katharine Hepburn. "All he wants is for you to say yes," she said. "Oh, how wonderful. I'm going to the library this afternoon and get everything on the Spanish civil war. And that secondhand bookstore, the one on Fourth Avenue."

He pointed a finger at her. "I want everything on the anarchists. Orwell too. Cesar Vallejo dying in Paris on a rainy Thursday. This is going to be a thorough, well-researched book. I don't want academicians punching holes in it. Bastards, now that the civil war and Orwell are respectable. They won't go out in the streets for Bobby Seale and Fred Hampton. The sons of bitches, I'll show them what real revolutionaries are."

"No one but you can write this book," she said.

"I'll have to talk to a lot of people. There are still many survivors. I'll tell my agent to negotiate an advance to cover expenses, not to be charged against royalties."

"Seth, did I meet Ybarra?" She drew the ottoman closer to his chair. "Was he at the Overseas Press party?"

He shook his head. "I met him a long time ago." He decided not to lie. "And then recently at a publication party. I had to go—it was for a book on Cuba. He has a Spanish Basque name, so he must be interested in Latin subjects. He told me then to call him up."

Mathilde continued nodding after he stopped, hoping that by keeping her face in motion she would not show any hurt that he went to parties without her. She had to clear her throat to say, "I won't be so dumb on this book. I was a modern history major, remember. I did a lot of reading on the Spanish civil war." She tossed her head to one side. "Of course, I forgot it all. But what if I immediately start a card file on the major figures?"

He nodded quickly and got up. "I've got to take a bath and be out of here," he said. Then he felt ungrateful. There'll be a real credit in the acknowledgments, Matty," he added. "Not just that stuff about thanks to my wife who typed the manuscript. The Paris book was journalism—it would've been pretentious to have a foreword."

He left her in the study sitting on the ottoman. Poor girl, he thought, I'm going to be better to her. He took an amphetamine, and hung his pants on the hook of the bathroom door, and threw his shirt and underwear in the hamper. He shaved while running the water for his bath, feeling good, somehow, that he was really dirty and needed a bath. His body was covered with layers of perspiration that had dried on him again and again for two days and when he lifted his arms to shave he smelled complacently the odor his armpits released. The cool edge of the washbasin supported his scrotum when he leaned forward to see himself in the mirror. Short man, tall basin: the enamel jockstrap. He remembered the jokes about that in the freshman dorm and felt the beginnings of an erection. He looked down to watch, for the first time in years, the unsheathing that had been, as he used to say, his first lesson in biology. He smiled into the mirror.

In the bathtub, his genitals broke the soapy surface of the water. Good to be short, you can stretch out. Keats was five feet and three-quarters of an inch tall. He hadn't thought of that in many years: the great discovery of his sophomore year in the course on the Romantic poets. He brought both hands to his crotch and cupped his genitals. Tall man, big cock, they used to say; small man, all cock! He heard the phone ring in the apartment, and relaxed when it was cut off during the second ring. He could not hear Mathilde's voice. Yesterday he would have jumped out of the tub and stuck his head out the door and given Mathilde instructions. No more. He must think about the book, about magazines that might be interested in chapters from it.

His eyes were half closed when he heard the knock on the door, and he'd only opened them when Mathilde walked in. "Hey!" she said. She had not walked in on him for years, not since Pablo was born. In those days she sometimes touched him. He closed his eyes to let her watch him unembarrassed. Is she getting her kicks with Pablo? he thought, and immediately sat up.

"That was Gary Epstein on the phone. He wanted to make sure that you would meet him at the committee office in an hour." She kneeled by the bathtub. "Do I know him? What committee?"

He began to throw water on his chest to rinse off the soap. "The Mackey Committee—he's the secretary."

"Oh."

He saw her come to a decision. She plunged her right hand into the water, moved her fingers around his penis, and squeezed. Later he remembered that he had looked at her and seen only her eyes, as in a movie close-up, frozen to a still shot, wide and expressionless. The next recollection: water dripping from her hand into his eyes. She had let go, got up and left the room, so quickly he did not see it. Just the water in his face. And then a pain in his crotch. He kneeled in the tub to look at himself, and felt his penis. It had almost retracted into his body. Frightening. He pulled at it; it was a small knot, numb and yet hurting.

"Oh God, God," he moaned. He lowered himself in the water and slowly massaged it. It grew and tingled and he stretched out in the water and glanced at the door. It was closed. He held on to himself but did not watch as he began the motions that comforted him in his adolescence.

Chapter 3

He saw Mathilde next when he came out of their bedroom dressed. Again she stuck her head out the kitchen door, a happy look on her face. "You're not wearing a tie to meet Mr. Ybarra?" she said.

"Nobody wears ties anymore," he replied. "Only publishers, and they understand." He had folded a conservative wool challis in his jacket pocket to put on later. "I don't know how long I'll be."

"Then wear a turtleneck," she pleaded. "The one Pablo gave you and you've never worn. The *Times* said the stuffiest restaurants allow them now, even with evening clothes."

"What's come over you?" he said. It was a good idea. "They make me look short," he added, and turned sideways, the first move toward the bedroom, and followed her when she went past him.

"You have perfect pectorals and a flat stomach," she said, and ducked into the bedroom. She opened his shirt drawer, and he watched from the doorway, really wondering this time what had come over her. "See, you've never taken it out of its wrapping and I got it for you at Brooks Brothers."

He removed his jacket and unbuttoned his shirt. He said, "Everyone gets their stuff at army and navy outlet stores."

She pulled it out of its plastic envelope and began to unpin it. "Off with your undershirt too," she ordered, "or it will show."

He felt self-conscious when he drew it over his head as if he had never been naked in bed with her. He smoothed down the hair on his chest involuntarily, and his nipples tightened. A smile formed on her face as she crossed toward him, but it was never completed, for her eyes half closed and one hand reached for his chest. She kissed him on

31

the neck. She used to do that on the beach when the sun made her feel good. Her free hand stroked his left biceps and he automatically brought up the forearm to make the bicep bulge. "Matty, you never want to fuck in the daytime," he said. He had meant to murmur but his voice sounded strained and complaining.

She left the shirt hanging on his shoulder and skipped away, as if she had been only teasing, but when she turned at the doorway, he saw she was blushing. "Put it on and make a grand entrance," she said, and disappeared.

She was smoking a cigarette in the living room when he came out. "Hey, it looks good," he said. "Great color."

"The wine-red sea," she said.

He checked his pockets and let her inspect him.

She crossed her arms and feigned a judicious expression, and he smiled, knowing what she was about to say. "Who is that intriguing fellow at that café on the Boule Miche?"

"I do believe," he replied, "that it's that charming journalist Seth Evergood."

"Not Seth Evergood! The only American Sartre trusts and whom la Princesse des Guermantes has allowed in her little circle!"

"He converses with Picasso in Catalan."

"He moves with ease from the Left Bank to the Right Bank to the Red Belt."

"A man with an extraordinary social range."

"Terribly handsome," she said.

"Brilliant," he concluded.

He took the tie out of his jacket pocket and shrugged as if he had just discovered it. He placed it on the table in the foyer and said, "Listen, you know Gary Epstein. He was here once, mostly in my study. You didn't like him."

"A red-haired fellow?" She held both hands over her head without touching it, to show his hair stood out like an Afro. "Jewish?"

"Epstein—how did you guess?" he said mockingly.

"Seth! I'm *not* anti-Semitic and I did like him. Or, rather, I didn't not like him."

He laughed.

"I think I had my period that day."

"Well, anyway, I'm going to be with him all afternoon at the committee and then I'll meet Ybarra. But I may bring Gary back here for dinner, OK?"

"I've got—no, bring him. Maybe I can invite a girl—"

"No, no, no, don't go making it social." He was suddenly irritated. "We have many things to discuss. We plan to go to Bolivia and try to see Debray in jail. And tomorrow I go to Connecticut."

"Bolivia," she repeated quietly, her eyes widening. "That's dangerous. Oh, Seth." She shook her head slowly, unaware she was doing it. "That's jungle country, not Paris or New York. Oh, Seth."

"OK, there are plenty of places where Gary and I can have dinner," he said. "Don't expect me." He picked up the tie and threw it down on the floor. "God damn it, don't put on that Smith-girl act again!"

She waved her arms, unable to speak, then rushed past him and leaned her back against the front door. "Wait, wait," she gasped, and took a deep breath. "Bring him here, please, I want you to. It's just that I get scared about politics. You must do what you have to do, I don't disapprove—you have to help me."

They looked at one another for a moment. He was astonished: she never surrendered like this. There had been a certain dignity in her anger this last year; she'd grown up, she was an adversary, and he suddenly did not want this victory. She used to wait upon his decisions with such breathless suspense during their days in France; days when she proposed a trip to a two-star restaurant in the countryside and hoped that he would agree. Now there was no play in their stances, and he waited not because it was fun to drag it out, but to allow them both to calm down.

"Gary has had a lot of trouble these days," he said finally, "and it would be good to have him here quietly."

"I'll make something nice," she promised. "Pablo will be in bed early and I want to meet him too."

After he had opened the door, he turned back again and said, "Will you call mother and tell her that I'll drive up tomorrow and be there sometime around noon? Don't leak anything about Ybarra and the book—I don't want any trouble about that."

He walked to Broadway meaning to take the subway, but he thought of some notes he wanted to make and hailed a taxi. He gave the driver the lower Fifth Avenue address, one of those unreconstructed buildings from the beginning of the century where newly formed committees for good causes rent temporary headquarters. *Or where mail-order houses with bad bargains and one secretary and one office boy start on the road, they think, to permanence,* he wrote in his notebook. He smiled; he knew that he would find that note much less witty when he read it again. But it was good practice, and he looked out at the lunch crowd and felt good.

"OK if I go through the park?" the driver asked.

Seth nodded. The radio was on and he did not want to talk. The driver's name, he noticed on the license, was Myron Weinstein. He was bound to be talkative—Irish and Jewish cabbies were very opinionated—and Seth held the pen to one cheek and stared at his notebook to head him off. One chapter, he thought, could be on the veterans of the Abraham Lincoln Brigade, which had fought in Spain. It could sell separately as an article. What reformists they were—to name their outfit after Lincoln. He looked up when he heard the radio announcer mention the Black Panthers. *The black militants came out with their hands on their heads during a lull in the firing. One policeman was shot in the leg and two blacks were found dead of wounds inside the headquarters, both presumably members of the Black Panther Party.* No more.

The driver cursed. "Those black bastards!" he said.

"I'm black," Seth said.

The driver laughed. "And you and I are paying for them. They're all on relief but that's not good enough, now they got the gun. First thing you know . . ." He shook his head; he could not think of something bad enough.

"What have you got against them?" Seth said.

"Don't get me wrong, I got nothing against nobody," the driver said, settling down to a good talk. "They should go to work. Like you and me. You want to work, you can find a job, right?"

"Wrong," Seth said, warming up. "You and I are living off the blacks. We live better because they live worse." He paused, waiting for the audience to respond. "All of us are living off them—because we're white."

"Naw, mister, you got it the wrong way round," the driver said, turning his head quickly to make his point. "They working this discrimination bit into a big racket—they're just lazy bastards. But everybody's letting them get away with it, so why not?"

"You own this taxi?" Seth began.

The driver replied sooner than Seth expected. "You know what one of them medallions cost? I'm just a poor schnook, but I don't go on relief and I don't go around with no gun killing people."

"Maybe you should," Seth said. "If you knew oppression like the blacks, you might talk differently."

"Take another look at my license—the name's Weinstein. Nobody ever did us a favor, mister." He held up a hand without looking back. "What the shit we arguing for? I know, you're one of those nice kids, you got a good heart, you want to help the other guy out. Believe me, it don't work, not with them."

Seth did not know what to answer first. He began to yell. "I'm no kid and you *are* a dumb schnook. You work for the taxi company and you talk like a big capitalist. Take a look at me. I'll tell you who I am—I'm an important journalist. I live off you, buddy, but I don't tell myself any stories. You are a dumb schnook."

"What's all the excitement?" the driver said.

"Pull over to the corner," Seth replied. "Stop right here."

"Suit yourself," the driver said.

Seth searched for the right change. "Black bastards, eh? Ever heard of the expression Jew bastard? You ought to know better."

"Hey, don't take it out on my tip," the driver said, and attempted a smile.

"You're such a fucking capitalist, you don't need it." Seth got out and left the door open to keep him from driving away before he had finished. The driver held both hands to his head. "All power to the people!" Seth yelled, and swung the door so hard that it resounded like a shot. The taxi drove off as if making a getaway, and Seth remained on the corner, panting and stunned by the noise he had caused.

He was afraid that people on the street were watching him. He forced himself to smile and look around. Don't let there be a cop, he prayed swiftly. He was on Columbus Avenue, a depressed area he never walked at night and avoided during the day. A black woman headed for him unsteadily. Her blouse was open, her skirt askew, the heels of her shoes uneven. He automatically shook his head, but she kept coming and he thought: she must not touch me. She moved her lips trying to speak and a trickle of saliva oozed out the corner of her mouth. She was close when another taxi came. He jumped in and did not look back. The driver said, "Man, the hookers are out early today." He was a young man with long hair, but Seth took no chances; he gave him the address and then leaned back and closed his eyes. He reached in his pocket for a Librium, but remembered he had taken an amphetamine at home. He thought: I'm fighting the wrong battles.

Gary opened the door for him at the committee's office, exclaimed "Buddy!" and explained that his secretary was out to lunch. He led Seth to his office, the only other room in the suite. On the walls were framed, signed photographs of Ben Bella, Raul Castro, Nkrumah, and Chou En-lai. Also, a slightly larger one of Ellsworth Mackey. Gary wore, as always, a dark suit, a white shirt, and a string tie. It was his red Afro, his moustache and his clipped beard that drew attention, but Seth knew they were not inspired by the new lifestyle but by Gary's trip to Cuba after the Bay of Pigs invasion when, at age twenty-one, he had undertaken his first mission for Mackey.

Gary looked as if he might burst into laughter; his green, unreflective eyes peered at Seth and shifted to his own hands and then back at Seth again. He grinned as if they shared a joke. "Seth, how old are you?" he finally asked.

"Thirty-six," Seth replied.

Gary nodded commiseratingly. "I'm twenty-eight," he volunteered. "You know what that means?"

Seth shook his head. "That we're friends?" he said mockingly. "Why the Socratic manner?"

Gary clapped his hands. "See! I've been ruined by this shitty committee. Trudy says that I always talk as if I were addressing a round table of prominent intellectuals." He pulled at his tie and loosened it. "Trudy!"

Seth said, "What happened?"

"No, wait," Gary replied, leaning forward to tap Seth on the shoulder to deter him. "You're thirty-eight—"

"Thirty-six," Seth interrupted.

"Thirty-six and I'm twenty-eight. We're old, we're ancient, as far as the young radicals are concerned. I don't know that *they're* concerned—they take everyone at face value but I'm conscious of it. Aren't you?"

"And too young for the Old Lefties," Seth said.

Gary shrugged his shoulders. "They don't matter. I'm talking about radicals. About revolutionaries. We went through college without protest. What a grind I was! I got my Ph.D. at twenty-one and made my folks very happy. And nobody else. All my intellectual reflexes are wrong—indeed, the problem is that my responses are intellectual. Curious, I read Nietzsche and listened to all of Wagner, even read the librettos of the operas but only to demonstrate that both represented a feverish, decadent—even apocalyptic—expression of the bourgeois sensibility at a time when the ruling classes of the West were at their most confident. And I was right, I do believe."

Seth looked at him blankly. He thought: He's going mad.

"Where was I? Oh yes, I didn't take from Wagner— but what does all that matter!" He propped a hand on each knee. "I guess I mean I don't have a gut reaction to anything." He laughed. "Gut reaction—I use the phrase with shame. I've stolen it from the kids, like the TV commentators."

"I speak to a lot of students these days, you know," Seth said. "I think we manage to communicate."

"Yes, yes, yes," Gary agreed. "Don't listen to me." He leaned forward as if he might whisper a confidence, and then looked up and past Seth to the outer office. Seth half turned. They were still alone. "Maybe there's hope for me," Gary said in a normal voice, as if he had changed his mind. "You know what I did to Trudy? I gave her a thorough gynecological examination! I got down on my hands and knees and took a good look at her cunt, I don't know why. Yes, I know why—I wanted to see if there was anything different, now that Mackey's cock has been in it."

Seth shook his head to keep from blushing. "What did you hope to find?"

"Nothing—what could I hope to find!" Gary pushed his shoulders up and down and threw one hand up and away from himself, willfully gesturing like a child. "And after all, Trudy and I aren't married. We weren't going to play that bourgeois game. She reminded me of that this morning when I happened to read her letter to Mackey."

"You read her mail?" Seth said, trying to imagine Mathilde and himself in that situation. Examine Mathilde! "Not nice," he said with a smile.

"It was lying on her desk, a letter to him, and I thought I'd add a note about the conversation that he and I had had yesterday on the phone about Debray—"

"What about Debray?" Seth asked involuntarily.

Gary frowned. "That's off, definitely. Mackey is in touch with his wife and his family. Maybe even with de Gaulle, for all I know." He stopped and again looked to the outer office, but shook his head and leaned back in his chair. He added, "No, I'd know, of course."

Seth shrugged. "Good, I'm glad it's off. Various things have come up with me and I'd have had to beg off. Anyway, chum, that's not what I came down here for. I was worried about you—you all right now?"

Gary leaned forward, placed his elbows on his knees, and looked straight into Seth's face. "I don't know, buddy, I'm still a little groggy. I said all sorts of wild things to her this morning—I was quitting the committee, getting away from her for a while, no for good, fuck the Movement, I was going to find a teaching job. . . ." He grimaced at Seth. "Pretty foolish, huh? Maybe I need a shrink. What do you think of that?"

Seth nodded. "Nothing to be ashamed of."

"Have you ever been to one?" He bit his lips and waited.

It took Seth a moment to nod again.

"Isn't that something!" Gary said. "I don't know why I asked, because I would never have thought so. It's because I'm Jewish. I tend to think you WASPs have it made. You never have trouble with your wives, you don't think about money, you don't move your bowels."

They laughed. Seth said, "But Trudy is . . ."

"A WASP," Gary said. "New England yet." He reached up and grabbed his Afro. "The flowering of New England I call her."

"You don't want a shrink," Seth said. "They don't know any more than you do. I was in a transition period. No trouble with Mathilde, though of course I've been hard to live with. I was out of the AP, I was getting my feet wet on this free-lancing, so I thought I needed a little advice, even guidance. But it's all over now."

Gary leaned toward him again. "So now you can devote yourself to my troubles and tell me what to do, like Marx with Engels, Lenin with Gorki, Bakunin with everybody—no, watch out for Bakunin." He laughed. "You know what I did?—I bit her clitoris and twisted it and the cunt loved it, she screamed but she loved it!"

It suddenly occurred to Seth they should not be talking this way; the office was surely bugged. He pointed up, then to the phone, and cupped a hand around one ear to warn Gary. "No, no," Gary said. "That's another thing about the kids, they don't care about the pigs, they don't give a fuck who's listening in or looking." He turned to his desk and wrote on a memo pad while continuing to talk. "In a crowded subway yesterday there were two of them practically fucking, their hands were below their waists and their bodies were swaying."

Gary handed him the piece of paper. It said, *I have to talk to you about something when we leave here.* Seth folded the paper and put it in his pocket. The hairs on his neck felt as if they stood out separately. He nodded.

Gary continued, "That's the trouble with organizations like this committee. You get to think you're a government power and that other organizations like the FBI are interested in you. Good, let them be." He took the top blank sheet from the memo pad, held it against the light, shook his head, folded it and put it in his pocket like Seth. "You know, maybe I'm really an anarchist. The kids are getting to me. I tell you what, let's go to the benefit for the Panthers at the Fillmore East tonight."

"Sure," Seth said, piqued that he had not heard about it.

"Just you and me," Gary added. He dug his hands in his hair, leaned back, and spread his legs. "Great to be on my own again. I don't have to call Trudy and make a thousand arrangements about meeting her. No more phoning home. But I'll do it anyway. Call, that is, not ask her. That's my Jewish sense of responsibility."

Seth brought a hand to the pocket where he had placed the note. Gary saw the gesture and winked. "Of course, it was Trudy who took me to the Café La Mama the other night," Gary said, to be fair. "A wild play, with Karl Marx played by a black with a huge Afro. That was a shock. And then there were some street kids from Bedford Stuyvesant in the audience and they badmouthed him. One of them yelled, 'Get down on the street and deal with the pigs, fink,' and the others, 'Right on.' The actor began to plead with them as if it were an open-corridor school—'I gotta write this book *Das Kapital,* brothers,' the actor said, 'I gotta save myself.' Pandemonium. As the kids say, it blew my mind." He stopped abruptly. "I'm kind of high, aren't I? I'm breaking out, breaking up, breaking down."

Seth said, "You're OK by me, chum," and he stretched out an arm and patted him on the knee. For a second he was embarrassed to have acted so paternally, but when he looked up and saw the expression of gratitude on Gary's face, he felt he would become a stronger, better, finer person if only he could make a gesture as generous as that each day. If this is what it does for you, he thought, why weren't others this reassuring with him, even when they got paid for it like the shrink?

"Thanks, Seth," Gary said. He took out a pack of cigarettes and passed him one and then lit it for him.

They were silent a moment. Seth thought: if I don't get away to Bolivia, I'll never break away. Then he remembered Ybarra and the book he was going to write. He nodded to himself; everything was all right. I'm such a fool, he said to himself, that I forget that I'm happy.

Gary broke the silence. "Nice to sit like this. Like the kids. They commune. Let it flow back and forth. But for that you need pot."

Seth pointed up and then to the phone.

Gary grinned. "OK, time to eat," he said, and brought his feet to the floor with a bang. "Let's be off." He pulled off his tie and stuffed it in his pocket. "Good-bye to all that."

There were people in the elevator. Seth waited until they were out in the street. "Shouldn't you be more cautious about what you say in the office?" he said.

"No, but I could see that you thought I should," Gary replied. "So they find out that Mackey has screwed around with Trudy and we had a fight. What can they I do with that—release it to the press?" Gary threw an arm around Seth's shoulders. "These are new times. My father used to say, *You have to go and do it in Macy's window?* Well, chum, if you do it in Macy's window these days, you'd be a culture hero."

"I'm glad you're feeling good," Seth said. He was free until he met Ybarra and it was a pleasure to be out on Fifth Avenue with Gary. He thought: happiness is all. He wished he could throw out his arms and take deep breaths or sprint down the block or even sing. We are estimable young men, he said to himself, we are living our times, we *are* heroes. Yes. He said, "I bet the weatherman is going to report that the air is satisfactory today." He stopped. "Hey, what was that note about?"

Gary's hand squeezed his shoulder. He looked around and said, "The street is the best place to talk."

Seth followed his eyes and found himself staring at the window of the Soviet bookstore.

"Well, maybe we should walk on a bit," Gary said. "Have you ever been in that place? One look and you know the Soviet Union is a reactionary society. Talk about bugging, have you ever been in Moscow? They scarcely make a pretense of hiding the bug in your hotel room. I once found it dangling inside the lamp on the telephone table."

Seth nodded. He had never been in Moscow but he knew it was a reactionary society. To have given Gary a precise reply—to have said, I don't know the Soviet Union—would have made a difference in their camaraderie. They would not have been equals. So he nodded again, but he decided suddenly that next time—indeed, from now on—he would be exact about everything he said. He would always tell the truth: soon he would begin writing the book about his father and he must not fake anything.

"Don't look so solemn," Gary said. "Say no if you don't think it's fun too—"

"Wait, wait," Seth said. "I didn't hear what you said."

"You didn't because I didn't say it." Gary crossed the side street and then waited for Seth to catch up. He spoke in a low voice and did not take his eyes off Seth's. "I need someone to drive me up to Vermont and come back. To pick up some stuff. You know what stuff. Or can guess. I only guess, I don't know. We'll only be couriers. What do you say?"

"Sure," Seth said. "Who are we doing it for?" Just as he was knocked down by the flics in Paris and he was not surprised to see stars, like any character in a comic strip, it seemed right that now Fifth Avenue should turn deathly still. Why did I say yes, he asked himself, why? His heart beat so insistently that he could feel the blood rushing throughout his body, closing his eardrums, blurring his vision, switching all distractions off to alert him to its message: danger, danger, danger. He could see Gary's lips moving, his beard rising and falling as he talked. A car horn honked and pierced the caul that held him inviolate, and all the noises of the street rushed in.

Gary concluded, "So it could be any of them. They're disorganized and anarchistic, thank God, but they're in touch. They need a leader." He stopped, then self-consciously added, "I mean leadership. So what do you say?"

"I said yes," Seth replied. He thought of an out: "It depends when, though. I have so many—"

"Tomorrow?"

Seth shook his head. "I have to drive up to Connecticut to see my mother tomorrow. I can't get out of it."

"No, no, that's perfect," Gary said. "Just perfect. We stop off there and then keep going. I'll find out tonight just where and all that, so long as we get there before the week is out. Tonight at the Fillmore East, that's why we're going there, not for theatricals." He stopped, pleased with himself. "I'll tell them you're my partner. They need to know whom I'm taking but I'm sure they'll trust you."

That was a surprise—that there should be any question of his reputation with the Movement. "Do you think they will?" he asked, suddenly wanting very much to be accepted. He thought: I must pay my dues. "They've no reason to—I'm just a writer."

"There's no question about what side you're on, Seth," Gary replied, so seriously that Seth felt this was a moment he must remember for his notebook. "Nor your loyalties. You haven't put in the years that Dave Dellinger has and you've come up a different route than Tom but—" He interrupted himself to grip Seth's arm. "You're Seth Evergood, buddy, my friend."

There they were again: in history. How right he had been to say yes. He believed he had done so instinctively. Gary turned down the side street to the Greek restaurant, once barely hanging on in the ware-houses that caught up with the district in the thirties and forties, now again coming into its own with the new high-rises. Seth thought: it will be famous in memoirs, *our* La Rotonde.

Gary turned toward him. "I'll cut off my beard this afternoon and tame down this bush," he said, one hand to his head. "But I'm keep-ing the moustache."

"And me?" Seth joked.

"You're perfect as you are," Gary replied.

Chapter 4

La Gravure: this year's literary restaurant, empty at five-thirty but soon to be filled for after-office chats. For dinner came quiet middle-aged ladies, sometimes with their husbands. The after-the-theater clientele was totally different too, nonliterary and nervously elegant, made up in the main of discreet aging homosexuals and unsure younger companions. Now it was all relaxed affability; the waiters approved of people like Seth. He stood at the bar waiting for Ybarra, letting the martini on the rocks cool his hand and occasionally bringing his hand to his forehead to temper his excitement with its moisture. He wished this were a Barcelona bar, the counter crowded with tapas and his drink a bitter Cinzano soda; he'd be certain to impress Ybarra then. He must go back there, stay at the Continental, follow the stations of Orwell's cross—a nice phrase. He took out his notebook and wrote it down. His father might have hated Orwell. A theme to take up in the book—Stalinism and Trotskyism versus anarchism—relevant now.

Ybarra tapped him on the shoulder. "Good afternoon, you're kind to have waited," he said, his smile showing that he had seen Seth put away his notebook.

"I've already started," Seth said, holding up his drink.

"But of course." Ybarra stepped back. Behind him a waiter also stepped back and extended a hand to guide them toward the far end of the restaurant. Ybarra did not look at the man, only at Seth, his head slightly inclined as if waiting to hear that Seth preferred some corner other than the one the restaurant reserved for him. But the waiter walked ahead and Seth followed, carrying his drink, reassured by the motions and gestures that told him he was playing his part right in the ritual.

When they sat down, Ybarra simply nodded to the waiter; the man knew what he wanted. "I'll confess what it is makes me different from other editors," he said to Seth. "I skip lunch and come here almost every afternoon for drinks. No chance then of being sat elbow to elbow in the dining room with another editor and his author."

"That's not right," Seth said. "You're depriving some poor young writer of a glamorous lunch."

"Oh, I admit it's a totally selfish policy of mine," he said, picking up his scotch and soda. Seth knew that Ybarra did not mistake him for a poor young writer. "I had a vision one day, when I was forced to join my guest in a third drink before lunch, of editors all over midtown falling asleep at their desks that afternoon, and that's when I stopped."

Seth smiled. With Ybarra he could be at ease; he was the kind of company he kept before he was politicized. "I'm glad you go to cocktail parties," he replied, "because that is how you met me and got the splendid idea that I should write this book."

Ybarra cocked his head.

"I've brought it up too soon," Seth said, his professional manner still with him. "My bad training as a newspaperman—we always rush things."

"No, no," Ybarra said. He placed both hands on the table, palms down. "There are several replies to what you've said. I must take them one at a time—that's my bad training as an editor: neatness."

"My turn to say no, no."

"First, then you want to do the book?" He held Seth with his gaze, and managed, Seth did not know how, to convey both the solemnity of the question and the pleasure that a yes from Seth would give him.

"Yes," Seth said; he could have added "sir" to his reply and it still would have been right: an easy acknowledgment that they belonged to the same world. "I have been thinking about such a book for a long time. Even while my father was alive. Someday, I told myself. When he died six years ago, I felt I was still too young and too close yet . . . you understand?"

"But now is the right time, isn't it?"

They had created, between them, a fruitful silence. The book was written, launched, reviewed, and had taken its place on permanent bookshelves, a credit to them both. It was unnecessary for Seth to say yes. After a moment, he nodded and Ybarra quickly nodded, too. Ybarra said, "I'm going to call you Seth."

Seth lifted his drink to that.

"My name is Tony," Ybarra said. "Who is your agent? I'll talk business with him and I expect there should be no trouble."

Seth told him and added, "I'm going to need two years." He stopped and continued when Ybarra nodded. "One year of research and one year to write. Maybe less. I warn you, I'm not going to write one of those biographies that begins with his mother in labor and proceeds day by day until he's dead." He stopped again and decided that Ybarra's smile was an approving one. "I'm going to do his Paris days, the fun days when he seemed to have time to do everything—to run down to Maxine Elliot's at Cap Ferrat or to Pamplona with Hemingway and still do his journalism. Do you know that he knew Winston Churchill quite well? And D'Annunzio and Berenson and Colette? God, whom didn't he know! And then Spain. Spain will be the climax."

The waiter brought him another drink. Seth shook his head. He said, "I didn't see you order this."

Ybarra smiled. "What about the last years at Calvin?"

"You know that he and mother taught at Calvin?"

"My son attended Calvin for five years," Ybarra replied. "I met your parents on a few occasions. On parents' weekends. I might even have met you but I'm not certain. You must have been away at college or already working."

"Or before that at the Lycee here in New York," Seth said. "Mother wanted me to know French as well as English." She wanted me away, he thought, and became silent. And then suddenly apprehensive. How much did Ybarra know about him? No, I must not go into a funk, he told himself, I must not fumble this.

"Those last years," Ybarra began.

"Oh yes, the last years," Seth interrupted. "I want to telescope them into the narrative of his life during the civil war." He paused to see what Ybarra thought of that; he had improvised, but he felt now, when he saw Ybarra smile once more with interest, that he had it in mind all along. "The seed of those quiet last years. . . ." He held a hand up to show that he was searching for the right phrase, but he hesitated because he had been about to show political disapproval of the old man's last years, a judgment Ybarra might not share. "Those withdrawn last years must have begun to take shape in the midst of war. Spiritually, at least," he concluded. No, that was too down a summation. "In any case, I plan to organize the book—his story—like a narrative, not your standard biography. Without fabricating anything—he won't look out a window and have an interior monologue—sticking to the facts all along. It will move like a story, with certain things simply indicated and the important periods dramatized. It will, like any good story, come to a climax and then end."

Seth sipped his drink, and since he did not hear Ybarra respond, he kept looking into it. He lifted the glass to his mouth again and looked at Ybarra.

"Will you be in it?" Ybarra asked.

Seth nodded. "No stickiness. I have to be in it, but I shall refer to myself in the third person."

"There is a certain drama in that," Ybarra said.

"Also a sign to the reader that this is a truthful work concerned with facts and with history." Seth nodded. "Yes, with history."

"Well, Seth, that sounds fine to me." Ybarra accepted another drink from the waiter, and with a glance indicated that Seth should get another. "Indeed, I think it should make a relevant biography."

"But not an academic, authorized one, remember," Seth said.

"Oh, I like that most of all," Ybarra replied. "I see myself now writing a note to the copy editor: No index, please, and no table of contents. What astonishment there will be in the office! It will be a first for us."

The third drink arrived for Seth. The waiter placed a plate of hot hors d'oeuvres on the table and handed them small cloth napkins. "Does this mean you agree?" Seth asked, pointing to the drink and the hors d'oeuvres; he kept his voice light to show he joked, but his mind kept asking, How much of an advance? Will part of it be for expenses not to be deducted from royalties?

"I've never had any doubt," Ybarra said. "Only uncertainty that you'd take time from your work to write it. You're so much in the center of the political maelstrom—"

"Nothing will interfere with this book," Seth said. "My political interests—"

"Are fine with me," Ybarra finished for him. "It's now more than ten years since the Hugh Thomas book was a best-seller. It is time for another on the civil war, not only a more personal one, such as you writing about your father, but one which how-you-say sees it all from the point of view, that very fresh point of view of the young radicals. However you bring it in. Though I prefer, of course, that it be implicit, not preachy."

"I am not a propagandist," was the first thing it occurred to Seth to say. Should I have said that I am not committed? he wondered.

"That was inept of me," Ybarra said. "Please forget it. I was wrong. Implicit or overt, your ideas and opinions must be in it or it will not be the book I want. I got the idea for it when I saw you at Columbia and the ambience that was there should show up in your book, that ferment, even danger, that sense of having to trust to your immediate feelings only about what is to be done. No time for reflection before you make a choice."

Seth did not quite understand but he nodded. The drinks made him hear only the tone of Ybarra's talk, and like this dim, muted bar, it comforted him, wooed him. He tried to look judicious, and he gazed at Ybarra and slowly nodded again.

"I'm terribly sorry," Ybarra said. "It came out a series of clichés. I suppose what I meant is that written history, with few exceptions, is never like that afternoon I spent on the Columbia campus when the young people had just taken the buildings and the leaders talked from the crosswalk above the Amsterdam Avenue to the thousands of us down on the street."

"You were there?" Seth asked.

Ybarra nodded. "The university guards had closed the gates. The student rebels were inside but the young people on the street, all eager supporters, could not get in. The question was: Should they rush the gates and let everyone in? Around the corner were the trucks of the tactical squad, police on horseback—would they be called into action?

One of the student speakers warned us. He said, 'Look around and you'll recognize the plainclothes pigs by the tiny blue-headed pin they wear on their lapels.' The man next to me quickly brought up his hand to cover his lapel, and smiled sheepishly at me. The way I was dressed, my age, made him think we were allies."

"You really were there!" Seth said. He looked at Ybarra as if for the first time. The same elegant, composed man returned his gaze. Seth hastened to explain. "*Life* magazine thought it would be a good idea if I flew to New York for thirty-six hours to be at Columbia— since I had been covering the Paris uprising." He stopped. Any more and he might not sound neutral; he might have told him he had brought posters and greetings from Cohn-Bendit and Geismar to the Columbia rebels.

"You were on the crosswalk, and at first I thought you were one of the students," Ybarra said. "I don't think I would make a good detective, but I remember every face up there at the microphones clearly. To this day. I had a good reason—my son was running the meeting. He introduced the speakers and spoke himself. At one point he gave a rundown of the situation—the police a block away, the closed gates, the balance of numerical forces. 'Shall we rush them?' he asked. Then he stepped back, raised a fist, and began yelling in a voice I thought him incapable of—'*Up against the wall, motherfuckers!*' And all the people in the street and all of you up on the crosswalk raised your fists and joined him. I thought the moment had come. What would I do? I saw the plainclothesman reach under his jacket. He kept his hand there and I watched. I watched until he brought his hand down."

Ybarra looked at Seth with a half smile; his eyes were moist with tears. He was not embarrassed. "Those wonderful children," Ybarra added. "I envy you your involvement with them, your closeness to them."

Seth's jaw had gone slack with surprise. He thought: why was I afraid to be myself with this man? "I remember that day well, too," he said, and looked away a moment to give Ybarra time to wipe his eyes. "It was my day with them and I was interviewing them all—of course! Your son is Bill Ybarra! Where is he now?"

"He calls himself Guillermo," Ybarra said. "Third World, though my family was Basque and his mother. . . . He speaks Spanish with an atrocious accent." He smiled and shook his head. "Maybe not anymore. He has gone underground, perhaps with a Puerto Rican group, and his Spanish may have improved. Could that be?" He looked at Seth, and there were tears in his eyes again. He seemed to make no effort to control them, like a person in mourning. "I am frightened for him."

"Was there a warrant out for him?" Seth asked. "Was he called by a grand jury for questioning?"

Ybarra shook his head. "I think not."

"Then he is all right," Seth said, squaring his shoulders and nodding firmly. "He can come back when he wants."

The waiter placed another platter on their table. He hovered a moment, and Ybarra looked questioningly at Seth. "Another?"

"I've had three," Seth said. "No, thanks."

"I never have more than three," Ybarra said, and the waiter left. He looked at the waiter as if ready to call him back. "Why is that? With a son like mine you'd think I wouldn't be tied to habits still. There *is* a Puerto Rican group, isn't there? You simply don't want to alarm me. We've made no effort to find him or get in touch with him. My antennas tell me I might endanger him. This talk we've had is confidential."

Seth held his drink in both his hands, hunched his shoulders, and nodded. "Agreed," he said. It suddenly occurred to him: he wants me to put him in touch with his son. "There is a Puerto Rican nationalist group, I don't really know them."

"MIRA," Ybarra replied. "A terrorist group. That much I know."

Under the table Seth's knees began to move uncontrollably. He brought them together and put both his hands there to keep them still. Vermont! Vermont! The comforting ambience of the restaurant had been dissipated. He could not help this man. Had he clinched the book? He looked at Ybarra to ask and saw him getting up.

"Excuse me," Ybarra said, and headed for two women being led to another table. Seth watched him walk without hesitation, without having to think of how to greet them. "Tony!" the younger of the two women exclaimed. There were simultaneous greetings and laughter.

Ybarra held the older one's hand a moment and bent slightly to talk to her. They were literary people; not journalists, Seth said to himself, out of my class. He added: the class I'm heading for. Why do I envy them so, he asked himself. I'm a fool, he replied, a terrible fool.

Ybarra returned looking as composed as when he had entered the restaurant. Seth stood. "Well, Seth," Ybarra said, "I feel as if I've come back to an old friend." He touched Seth's shoulder lightly. "I have told you, I hope, how happy I am that you want to write that book. I'll talk to your agent tomorrow and there should be no problem, none at all." He placed a large tip on the table and looked at Seth.

"I plan to go up to Calvin tomorrow and see mother," Seth said, following him out of the bar. "His files are all there and now I have an even better reason to be up there."

Ybarra held the door open for him. "Call me whenever you like. My secretary can help you find books you need. All sorts of things. I mean that."

Ybarra held out a hand, and when Seth shook it, he felt he had failed the man. "About your son Bill," he said.

Ybarra looked at him expectantly, gratefully. "Ah, my son," he said.

"I'm going to ask about him." Seth nodded to emphasize his determination. He wished immediately that he could recall all this; he was promising too much. He had not been exact and he was being untruthful.

"Thank you," Ybarra said, so gratefully that Seth felt compromised. Then Ybarra added, "May I ask you a favor? Do not inquire about him. Best not to alert anyone about him." He thought about what he had said. "I did not mean to burden you, and you have shared the burden by listening to me. It's best, I think, if we let him be the one to get in touch with us when he's ready."

Seth thought of a passage from his lecture. "They are the beautiful people, our warriors and our saviors, and when they call, we must all respond," he said. At that point he always made a fist and raised it high and yelled, *All power to the people!* He could not do this under the canopy of La Gravure; it would seem that he was hailing a taxi, and there was one there already, waiting for Ybarra. Instead, he added, "Your son does you honor."

He let Ybarra take the taxi alone; it seemed tactful not to accept his invitation to be dropped off at home. In any case, he wanted to be by himself, to go over their talk, to exult, to savor the good turn his affairs had taken. He went back to La Gravure to find a phone, and the waiter led him to a comfortable booth outside the rest rooms. He called home, hoping to God that Mathilde didn't have the line tied up, and told her about Ybarra in a rush, gratefully, when she answered on the first ring.

"Oh Seth, how super," she kept repeating. "And will there be a good advance? Is it really set?"

"He speaks to my agent tomorrow and there will be no problems," he said, mimicking Ybarra's tone. "Whatever I said, he thought was fine. He sees the book my way—what a pleasure to deal with a real editor! He's not the shlock vulgarian you meet in the newspaper world. I'm really eager to do it now."

"I'm putting a bottle of champagne in the fridge," she said, and he laughed. He heard her say to Pablo, "Yes, it's daddy, he's coming home."

"Listen, Matty, don't promise him too much. There may be a holdup," Seth said. He could hear Pablo speaking to her, and it made him anxious to get off. "Don't make him any promises," he said louder.

"But I've made dinner for you and your friend," Mathilde replied. "Aren't you coming?"

"Can't you hold it up and make it a late dinner for the three of us?" he said. "There's an important function—the Columbia students, the Living Theater, in defense of the Panthers—that I'm expected to look in on. The kind of thing I should be in touch with. I may have to speak, but the moment my part in it is over I'll be home with Gary. OK? It's a drag but I really have to do it."

"That sounds like you won't be home before ten," she said, as if to herself. "OK. Wait, Pablo wants to talk to you."

He closed his eyes in exasperation. His father used to say that it was a waste of time to talk to children and madmen, everything is lost on them. "Pablo?" he said and waited. He heard breathing. "Pablo, big boy, how are you? This is dad. Dad, remember?" He laughed a little, but there was no reply. "What did you do in school today? If you won't tell me, I'll tell you what I did. I was at a school in Pennsylvania and then I took a bus all the way back to New York, and when I got home, you were not there. You were at your own school. Right?" He listened for the breathing, but was not sure he heard it. "When I get home tonight, I'll look in on you. Maybe I'll wake you. Would you like that?" He waited and this time he heard the breathing. He wanted to yell but instead shook the phone. There was no breathing. A terrible bang in his ear. He pulled the phone away and quickly brought it back and heard a series of knockings. "Pablo!"

"Seth?" Mathilde said.

"What the hell is the matter with him?"

"Nothing, he listened with great interest," she said. "The phone fell off the table when I wasn't looking."

"OK, I'll see you later," he said, and added when she said yes, "I'll bring Gary."

He sat in the paneled booth and rubbed his face as if that might wake him from his sudden depression. Across the corridor a man came out of the men's room. He looked like Philip Roth. All the pleasure of his meeting with Ybarra returned to Seth. Was it Philip Roth? He left the booth and looked at the man as he turned into the bar. Yes. He went into the men's room, removed his jacket, rolled up his sleeves, tucked in the turtleneck of his shirt, and washed. When he finished, he reached into the jacket pocket and took an amphetamine; just one, he said to himself, and his heart would not race. He moistened his hands slightly and brushed his jacket with them to remove the lint. Now to meet Gary. He looked at himself in the mirror and stepped back to get a better view. Not bad. First he'd have a drink here at the bar. Just to think, to recall exactly the things Ybarra had said. There were also a couple of things he wanted to write in his notebook. When he turned into the bar there was no one standing at it, and he did not want to stare at the tables to check whether Philip Roth was there, so he walked straight to the door after nodding to the waiter, feeling that the waiter's recognition was acceptance into a new world.

"Fool!" he said to the empty sidewalk, laughed and hugged himself. He stretched out in the taxi as if it were a chaise, his head on the armrest, and smiled to himself when he saw the driver look back quickly to check on him. He had given him St. Mark's Church in the

Bowery as his destination, and the poor man must be confused. At the next red light the driver looked around again, and Seth said, "Just resting."

"You OK then?" the driver said.

"Fine," Seth replied.

The driver cleared his throat. "You a man of the cloth?"

Seth believed it must be the turtleneck. "What makes you think that?" he asked.

The driver shrugged. "Well, what with nuns going around in short dresses. You said St. Mark's, didn't you?" He shrugged again. "No offense."

Seth sat up. He thought of the Berrigans, the Catholic Left, the worker priests; he was not offended. The taxi stopped. "Here we are, Father," the driver announced. Seth kept his head down while looking in his wallet. Should he correct him? No, it would make too good a story. He gave him a large tip, and it was not until he was standing on the sidewalk that it occurred to him that the big tip was what the driver had in mind when he called him Father. New York: everyone was a con artist. That man with a valise coming toward him now grimacing to get his attention—what was he selling?

"Gary!" Seth exclaimed. "What did you do? Wait—don't tell me."

Gary faced him, smiling, his shoulders going up and down to keep from laughing aloud.

"No Afro, no beard, no hair—"

"But I kept the moustache," Gary said.

"I didn't recognize you," Seth said, and looked around. He lowered his voice. "I guess that's the idea."

"Right," Gary said. "But I kept the moustache. It's the MIR moustache."

Seth looked at it. It was a broad, thick moustache, and it turned down slightly at the corners of the mouth. "What MIR?"

"*El Movimiento de la Izquierda Revolucionaria,*" Gary explained. "In Chile all the kids, all the kids who can, wear one because Miguel Enriquez, the head of the MIR, has one like this."

Seth shook his head. "Not a red one like yours."

"Well, comrade, the conditions in all countries vary—you cannot apply any theory mechanically," Gary said, stroking his moustache.

"Red for us, black for them." He threw an arm about Seth. "God, I'm high, I can't wait to be off. Notice I have my bag all ready?"

Seth looked at passersby nervously. Also irritably; he was full of his own news and Gary had not asked. "Yes, but—"

"Nothing to worry about. Come, let's sit on the steps of the church." Gary led him down the cobbled walk to the church. He sat at one end of the portico and indicated to Seth that he should sit next to him. Under one of the columns, across the portico, lay a drunk. "Don't worry—he's out." He also waved dismissingly when Seth looked at the hippie couples in the churchyard.

"What a scene!" Seth said. "Second Avenue. I'll bet none of the old parishioners come to St. Mark's anymore. The East Village."

"Right!" Gary said. "I always forget you're a WASP. Too bad, you're being displaced everywhere."

"WASP, WASP," Seth replied. "It's you Jews who have been displaced on Second Avenue. We gave it up in Henry James's day. You're the new beleaguered establishment."

"You bum," Gary said and then leaned against him. "You can't have a conversation like this with any of the kids. They think Second Avenue was born yesterday. Nothing has any reverberations for them. They don't know about nostalgia. . . . Still, I love them, I love them." He stretched his legs forward stiffly, then his arms, and lifted his feet off the ground until he touched them with the tips of his fingers. "I'm still in good condition. God, I went home and had another big fight with Trudy and I fucked her again. A furious fuck. I'm enjoying sex like crazy all the time I'm fighting her. The moment I start yelling at her I get a hard-on. I'm such a bastard—what do I care that Mackey laid her?"

"Is that why you packed a bag?" Seth asked. "Have you got a place to stay?"

"Yes, your place!" Gary laughed aloud and slapped Seth on the shoulder. "Surprise."

"No, no," Seth replied quickly. "I meant just that, to come to my place tonight and then we can leave tomorrow from there."

"That's what I figured," Gary said. "I didn't pack because we fought and we didn't fight because I packed. I fought on general principles—ho-ho! All the time I gave it to her she was calling me a male chauvinist pig, but, buddy, she liked it. A new sensation." He grabbed his crotch. "For me too—I went into her dry. Anyway, she knew I was going away on a project. I told her I was going with you to Connecticut. What did you tell your wife?"

"Jesus, I hadn't thought of that," Seth said. "She knows I'm going to Connecticut to see my mother, but she won't expect that to be for more than a day. I have to think of something."

"I'm no good at plain outright lies," Gary said. "Trudy is a hip kid, she knew something political was up, so she didn't ask about that. She knows it's better not to know beforehand just in case. You can't slip up when they question you if you really don't know, right?"

Seth nodded, screwing his face into a judicious look. He thought: I really don't know.

"Hey, Trudy hasn't seen me without the beard and Afro," Gary said. "I'll bet it will give her a thrill. Like sleeping with a new man." He paused. "Since this morning all I think about is sex. I never did before. I mean, think about it. I just did it."

"Now you know what it is to be a sex maniac," Seth said. Then thought: that's what I am; Gary talks the way I feel inside. He looked at him appreciatively. "Buddy," he said. "*Copain.*"

Gary winked. He put out a hand and shook Seth's. "*Copain, copain, copain,* like in the Brel song. But *I* mean it." He gave Seth's hand a squeeze and let it go. "God, what am I going to do with the valise when we go to the Fillmore? I didn't think of that. What's the use of looking different if I'm going to attract attention with this thing?"

"I'll carry it," Seth said.

"So they'll look at *you.*" Gary shook his head. "The place is going to be full of pigs, it's bound to be." He stopped. "Maybe not. Nothing's coming off—it's just a benefit, not a demonstration. No pigs, just the agents living in the communes." He snapped his fingers. "I got it—I'll leave it at Rappaport's."

"The restaurant?" Seth said.

"A *Jewish* dairy restaurant. I'm a nice Jewish kid—they'll do anything for me even if they don't know me," Gary explained. "They get all the kids now because it's vegetarian." He jumped to his feet. "Come on, we'll have a bite there before we go to the Fillmore."

They ate an eggplant steak. They had meant to have only soup because Seth remembered Mathilde would be holding dinner, but the waiter shook his head at the soup. "You don't want it," he said. "Give another look at the menu." He did not think the eggplant steak was enough, but gave in when Gary told him this was just a snack until they got home. "Shame on you, you not home already," he said, then winked. "Out on the town, eh?"

"Listen, are you on all night?" Gary asked him, while Seth tried to look casual.

"You think this is a part-time job?" the waiter replied.

"We have to make a business call," Gary explained, "and I'd like to leave this bag with you for an hour or so. At most two hours."

"Some business," the waiter said. He looked at the bag. "What you got in it? A bomb, God forbid."

"You make me feel at home," Gary said.

Seth looked at the waiter and then at Gary. They've got this ethnic thing, he told himself.

"Or marijuana maybe?" the waiter continued. He winked at Seth. "Your friend a pusher?"

Seth flushed but said, "I stand behind him."

"Oy," the waiter said.

Gary pulled the valise up to the chair next to him. "Look in it, it's not locked. Just clothes for the weekend."

"The weekend?" the waiter said. "The weekend is three days away."

Gary leaned his head on both hands. "You're a regular Jewish waiter, you know."

"*Chaleria*, you so smart," the waiter said. "OK, I'll take it but you better come back when you said. We got some Porto Rican dishwashers in the kitchen and they don't turn up their noses at nothing, old clothes or marijuana. Pots or pot." He returned after taking a few steps with the valise. "Strike that. I was just kidding—them Porto Ricans are just like you and me." Then winked again. "Only worse."

"Puerto Ricans," Gary said.

"Oy, I got a feeling I got a couple of Arab sympathizers on my hands. Don't answer that, I don't want to know." When he came back, he placed the bill on the table and said, "The things I do for a tip."

Seth took the bill. He did want to give him a big tip for being so engaging. "You're OK," he said, wishing he had had the whole exchange with him.

"Pay no attention," Gary said. "It's just an act to make you part with your money. I bet he was on the Yiddish stage. Right?"

The waiter cocked his head. "Oy, Second Avenue. We're the last, Café Crown, everything, gone. Jacob Adler used to walk in here. Menasha Skulnik, Molly Picon, Paul Muni when he was Muni Weisenfeld." He poked Seth's shoulder. "Now a Jew walks down Second Avenue he gets mugged. Believe me. It started with them Ukrainians after the war. Now what haven't we got? Even the fancy *goyim* send us their castoffs. It's no melting pot, it's a boiling pot. You know how I get home to the Bronx each night? To be safe I go by pneumatic tube!" He walked away laughing but turned after a while to see if he still had their attention. He winked.

Seth smiled broadly and waved. Gary was reflective. "That's us Jews, all right," he said. "Always playing bit parts." He winked at Seth, imitating the waiter. "This is my day. I haven't thought so much about being Jewish since my bar mitzvah. Well, I'm not thinking about it anymore. Our generation, nobody's Jewish."

"Too bad," Seth said. "I like it here." He looked around the restaurant; everyone seemed to be eating with gusto, their heads bent eagerly over their plates. On every table the rolls, black bread, salt sticks were piled high in baskets. He thought of La Gravure. "It's nice."

"My father says the Jews are headed for one big fall," Gary said. "When he was young he was in the CP. Now he sounds like an Old Testament prophet." He made his voice deep and he held out an arm. "As a people we are more arrogant than the Germans. We are always tempting God to strike us down!"

"Because of Israel?" Seth said.

"Because of Israel, because of New York, because of Miami, because of Great Neck—you name it."

I must remember to make a note of that, Seth thought. "I'm glad we're going to be together the next few days, buddy," he said. "I want to talk to you about the proposal I got from that editor I told you I was meeting. He wants me to write a biography of my father."

"Your father?" Gary asked, puzzled.

Seth nodded.

Gary let his jaw drop. "Was he famous?" he said. He covered his face with one hand. "No, don't tell me." He peeked at Seth between two fingers. "Who was he?"

"He was a rather popular journalist during the twenties, spent a lot of time abroad—"

Gary snapped his fingers.

"But, more important, he fought in Spain in the International Brigades. He was the highest-ranking officer."

Gary snapped his fingers again. "A friend of Scott Fitzgerald. What was his name?"

Seth smiled. "Evergood. James."

"Right," Gary replied, unselfconsciously. "He wrote a book called *Something New*, ran around in the international set. Hemingway envied him his knowledge of the bullfights. Even Mencken liked him. Then he became serious, I mean political. Jesus."

Seth waited. He did not want to sound boastful.

"And you're going to write a book about him?" Gary asked. "God, I envy you."

"I said yes, I need the money," Seth replied. "Should I have? Aren't there more important things to do?"

"You're crazy!" Gary shook his head. "What's with you—some residual Puritan morality?"

"I think I would like to do it," Seth said. "One reason I'm going up to Connecticut."

Gary continued to shake his head, but he kept his eyes on Seth. They were full of admiration.

"You're embarrassing me," Seth said. "It feels like a put-down."

Gary raised a hand to interrupt him, then let it drop without speaking. Finally he said, "I'm sitting here feeling Jewish again. As my father says about himself, I'm just a schnook, a nobody, Mister Never Was."

"Are you kidding? Why, you've dealt with every important revolutionary in the world today! And as an equal. Everybody knows you—you're the head of the Mackey Foundation."

"Getting cuckolded knocks everything out of your head, you know," Gary said. "Tell me some more."

Seth laughed. "Remember when we all first heard of you? You came back from Cuba after meeting Fidel and it was said that you brought a message for Jack Kennedy. You were just a kid, but the exchange of the Bay of Pigs prisoners began because of that little mission of yours. I bet Debray is getting better meals in jail because of your press releases. OK, buddy?"

Gary clapped his hands. "OK. We're not bad chaps, eh? Our spiritual ancestors would approve, right?" He got up. "Come, let's go to the Fillmore. Let's look in on the troops. As soon as I make my contact we can split."

Seth got up, check in hand to pay the cashier on the way out, and thought, guiltily, that he should not be paying. He looked at the total and added the figures. Gary plucked the bill out of his hand. Gary explained, "Let Mackey pay, the fink." And Seth felt a twinge of shame at having thought he had been stuck with the bill.

Chapter 5

The crowd began on the sidewalk and continued in the lobby. Not as much a crowd as clusters, with emissaries and offshoots that wandered from one to the other. Seth could not tell whether these kids were entering the theater or leaving it or just visiting where they stood. It was not a theater crowd; there was no expectancy or tension in the air: you did not feel watched and you did not preen. Beards and hair and bright fabrics and army clothes. Babies in shoulder packs.

"The crazies are here," Gary said, leading him on. Seth nodded and looked around to learn who that might be. He saw only the same kind of young person that appeared up front at his lectures. Like last night, except that the girls seemed brighter and the boys sleepier. None of them, he told himself, virgins. Squeezing past two groups in the lobby, he heard a boy say "Clear thinking won't help" and no one laughed. He touched his jacket pocket to check he carried his notebook; he wanted to write that down. Then he thought of his wallet. Check that often, he thought; they're all rip-off artists.

"It's almost nine," Gary said. "Hasn't it begun?"

A boy wearing a headband, whose colored beads spelled out Make Love Not War, answered him. "It's a break, man, the Sour Balls just finished." A long red arrow crossed his blue tank top and jumped the belt of his jeans to end at his crotch. "The Living Theater is on next."

"Thanks," Gary said, and reached into a jacket pocket for his invitation. He held it out to a tall young man leaning against the open door of the theater. "Me and my friend here," he said to him.

The young man did not take the invitation. "We gave up trying to collect tickets an hour ago. It's against everybody's principles or something. I'm just supposed to see they don't take the seats out with them. They're all anarchists."

"Ho-ho," Gary said.

As they went by him, the young man said to Seth, "You're going to have a ball. I've been groped fifty times."

Seth did not have to be alerted. His chest was tight with excitement, and he walked on his toes to look, over Gary's shoulders, inside the theater. It was dark except for the stage. White lights made it appear like a window too bright with sunlight to see beyond. A man walked away with the mike and left it bare. Clouds of smoke hung between the stage and the back of the orchestra where Gary stopped to look around. Seth smelled the sweetish odor of marijuana. That's what those groups outside were doing: passing joints around. He was not shocked; he was disappointed no one recognized him and clustered round him. The New York scene was not Harvest College: everyone was his own Jerry Rubin.

"Listen, this is what I'm going to do," Gary said, taking Seth's arm. "I'm going to hang around here at the back and wait. Get it? You don't have to stay with me. In fact, better if you don't. But don't get lost, it's a big house." He gave Seth's arm a squeeze while looking dartingly at the young people. "Aren't they beautiful?"

"Sure, sure," Seth agreed. "Where's the men's room?"

Gary showed him the back wall with a movement of his head, and Seth headed for the lighted doorway. A wide marble staircase led down to the basement lounge, turning as it descended, a relic, no doubt, of the Yiddish theater's grand days. He stopped halfway down and leaned against the wall. He took out his pen and notebook and wrote, *It doesn't help to think clearly.* What was the other thing he wanted to note? Oh yes, *Jewish hubris, New York, Miami, Great Neck.* What was the Yiddish word for *hubris*? God, everybody used it, what was it? He held the pen over the notebook and half closed his eyes to make the word come. Climbing footsteps came to a halt in front of him, and he automatically smiled when he looked up. A tall young man with long blond hair; it hung past his shoulders, unevenly bleached by the sun.

"Man, you're really into words," the boy said, facing Seth. He wore a cape that covered him down to his ankles. He held his arms akimbo, as if demanding an answer, and the cape parted to show a black tank-top shirt. Two round holes hemmed with red thread high on his chest stared at Seth like unblinking eyes; the boy's pink nipples at the holes' centers making blank, happy pupils. "I used to write my poetry down. Now I just say it. Nobody has to listen—it makes good karma. It goes into the air, fights pollution, right?"

"I never thought about it that way," Seth said.

"That's no way to rap, man, makes you sound like you're over thirty like." He brought both hands up and stroked his blond hair. "I dig your shirt but you got to let the nippies breathe. You got a joint?"

"Sorry," Seth said and tried to smile sympathetically.

He let his arms drop and the cape covered him again. "I better get upstairs then," he said and jumped up two steps. "That's poetry, man. I better get upstairs, I better do my thing, I better do my fling, I better, I better, I better—upstairs!"

Seth wrote in his notebook, *Tall boy in cape, nippies sic showing, improvises poetry I'm better upstairs, doing my thing.* Gay? He shook his head. He wrote, *Not sexually oriented.*

The door to the men's room was wide and twice Seth's height. It was made of carved wood and looked heavy. There was no handle. He put his shoulder against it, feeling like Alice shrunken, and pushed. The moment it gave, he heard a woman shriek, "Up against the wall, motherfuckers!" He stopped just inside the door. He had not made a mistake. It was the men's room, long, tiled, high ceilinged, a row of old oversize urinals against one wall. A tall barefoot girl stood at one halfway down the line. She wore a *djellaba,* which she had pulled up to her waist, and she weaved trying to throw out her pelvis with legs outspread and yet keep her balance.

A young man hunkered beside her. "Throw out your cunt, Beatty. You can make it!"

At the washstand near Seth two young men were talking. A third in army fatigues held his head back in silent laughter. He said to Seth, "When Beatty finishes pissing we're going over to integrate the ladies' room. You know how?" He threw back his head again without laughing. "By pissing in the basins!" He threw his head back once more. "With our cocks, I mean."

Still holding her dress up to her waist the girl skipped back from the urinal bowleggedly. "For Christ's sakes, get me some paper, Chuck, I'm wet!" Her legs were unshaven, and when she turned sideways she showed a large tuft of black pubic hair. Seth stared. "Hey you, you don't belong here," she yelled at him. "You fucking sexist!" She tried to fan her legs with her dress, and then let it drop. "Shit," she said, chagrined. "Come on, Chuck, let's go over to the sisters' room."

She tapped the squatting boy with her foot and he sat back on the floor laughing, unable to get up. She leaned over him and began to laugh too. "What a trip, what a mother," he said, and held up a hand to her to be helped. She yanked with both her hands, and when he stood up they leaned against each other, arms clutching one another's waists. At the door she motioned to the boy in fatigues and at Seth too. "Come on over to the sisters' room, motherfuckers!"

Seth waited until they had left before moving to the urinals. Only the two boys talking at the washstands were still there. He admired their equanimity; they had never looked away. He kept an eye on the door, and the fear that any second another girl might walk in kept him from urinating. He had only begun when he heard a squeak from behind. He looked quickly over his shoulder. A wooden door of one of the toilets was wide open. A middle-aged man with long hair, an Indian headband, strings of beads stood naked inside. His clothes hung on the hook of the inner door. "That cunt left?" he asked. He held one hand around his erect penis.

Seth looked away and tried to stop urinating but could not.

"Turn around," the man said. "Let's see what you got."

Seth turned his head toward the washstands. One of the boys there smiled and shook his head and waved a hand dismissively at the toilet. "What do you think he's got?" he said. "A lollipop?" Seth heard the door bang closed and inwardly sighed.

On his way out, he nodded at the two and said, "Thanks." The tall, stooped boy winked and made a V sign and then said to his friend, "Let's go." Seth held the door for them and saw he nursed a joint cupped in his hand. They stopped outside at the bottom of the marble stairway. "Thanks for saving me from rape," Seth said.

"Man, the Movement is getting infiltrated with these middle-aged freaks," the tall one said. "Old bohemians looking to ball all the time. You never see them in action."

The other took the joint and said, "Pigs maybe." He drew on it and offered it to Seth.

Seth accepted to be friendly. He knew it would have no effect, and in any case, he did not hold the smoke in his lungs. The others did not notice. When the joint returned to Seth, the tall boy stooped toward him and said, "You're Evergood, right? I saw you at the meeting at Foley Square. For the Panther 21."

Seth nodded and looked serious, trying not to show his gratification. This time he held the smoke a while. He put out a hand and each slapped his palm lightly.

"I'm Mike," said the tall one who had recognized him. "This brother is Stanley."

An outburst of noise drifted down the stairs. "That must be the Living Theater," Seth said, and suddenly felt like laughing. It worked, Seth thought; no one's said anything funny. He shook his head and looked down. "Why did you think he's a pig?" he asked Stanley, to get back to normal.

"Mike and I were rapping about the problem of pigs in the Movement," Stanley said. He was short and stocky and when he talked moved his shoulders like a weightlifter. "The legal heads say we got to watch out for them—provocateurs."

Mike exhaled but no smoke escaped. "I mean, at SDS at Columbia we had a policy. We'd say at a meeting, if one of them got up to speak, we'd say, *The brother may be a pig.* We'd lay a rap on him right there. If he objected, we'd say, OK, brother, we're just saying what we've been told, that's all. Nobody's throwing you out, the brothers and sisters got to know." He giggled. "They usually left soon after."

Stanley weaved a little. "That's when everything was out in the open. No more."

"Columbia?" Seth said to Mike. "Did you know Bill Ybarra?"

"Sure," Mike replied. He dragged on the joint and kept his head down. Seth looked at Stanley. Stanley pulled his jaw to one side and then to the other, as if loosening his neck muscles. Seth turned to Mike again, and he looked back from under his brows and smiled thinly. "You know him?" Mike asked.

"Yes, and his father too," Seth said. "Everything OK with him?"

"I don't know," Mike replied. "Didn't he go under with the Weathermen?"

Seth shrugged his shoulders and felt he was growing taller than Mike's stooped shoulders. He held the joint in his hand and wondered if he should take another drag.

"Organization, organization, that's what those guys are into," Stanley said, and he stepped back, squaring off like a wrestler. "You can't protect yourself from the pigs if you're in an organization." He tapped Seth's shoulder. "The big question: don't you think everybody should be in small groups? Five or six, one into chemistry, another explosives, another, well, you know. A tight group and no group knows the other and every group decides for itself. Me, I know electricity, Mike has been building erector sets all his life, you're a writer. In fact, you're a celebrity—who would think you're into action? What do you say?" He held up both arms and then lowered them to the sides, elbows bent as if he were supporting a two-hundred-pound bar over his head. "Huh?" he grunted.

Seth made an effort not to respond. He kept his face blank, and he looked at Mike to see if all this was serious. Mike giggled. The joint in his hand was too small to puff, and he reached into a back pocket, stumbling forward into Seth as he did so, and took out another. He held it out to Seth for help. It was squashed and crooked, and Seth was glad to be distracted from Stanley's question; he took it and smoothed it and put it to his lips. Mike put the burning end of the old one to it, and Seth drew but did not inhale. Mike giggled again. Stanley whispered, "Our first job—we stink up Radio City Music Hall!"

The sudden noise from upstairs was like a reply to Mike's proposal. "I'd better get up there," Seth said, and handed the joint to Stanley. He took a couple of steps up the stairs and then nodded good-bye to them.

"All power," Mike said.

Seth knew the ritual. "Right on," he replied.

Stanley made a fist. "What I said, give it some head. Hey!"

Seth paused.

"It rhymes!" Stanley exclaimed, and threw out his arms as if grappling with an opponent. "What I said, give it some head!"

This time Seth only winked and went on up. Everyone had come back into the theater, except for some people who stood at the rail in the back of the orchestra. Gary was talking to a young man near a side aisle, and Seth headed for him. The lights were on in the orchestra and also on stage. Seth hurried. He could feel excitement in the air. Excitement without danger: theater. He put a hand on Gary's shoulder and got up on tiptoe to see into the orchestra.

Gary looked quickly at him. "In case you've never seen them before," he said, "those people in the aisles are actors."

In the center and side aisles and against the side walls of the theater, there were people who looked just like the audience. Some moved like dancers. Others were in a trance. A girl in the center aisle leaned forward and then threw the upper part of her body back. "I am not allowed to smoke marijuana!" she called. All the actors in the aisles moved and then abruptly stopped. From the center one of them whispered loudly, "I am not allowed to smoke marijuana!" In a chorus, several: "I am not allowed to smoke marijuana!" Seth looked at Gary, and both he and the young man on the other side of him turned to him and shrugged.

A tall thin man near the stage leaned down as if confiding in the member of the audience in front of him and said, "I am not allowed to smoke marijuana!"

A boy in the audience stood up. "Here, man, take a drag," he called to one of the actors. He held out a joint. The actor did not respond but repeated, with one actor in each of the aisles joining him, "I am not allowed to smoke marijuana!" All over the orchestra arms went up waving lit joints. The boy was still standing extending his. "Don't you want it?" he called. "Take it, take it, I got another." The actors moved away, their eyes blank, as if nothing had been said. Some people shushed. "Sit down," a girl yelled to the boy. "The brother wants some pot," the boy replied. All together the actors chanted, "I am not allowed to smoke marijuana!" This time the audience laughed.

"Oh, my God!" Gary said, and covered his face with one hand.

The young man with him threw back his head and laughed.

Seth said, "I guess it would go over better on Broadway." He looked at the young man again when he stopped laughing. He looked familiar. Was he the contact? "My name is Seth Evergood," he said to him, and put out his hand. The young man shook it and nodded but did not give his name. Instead, he looked into the orchestra and Seth, curious, did too.

The actors had managed to bring the audience under control again. By being quiet, Seth said to himself, by remaining calm. He thought: that's a lesson I must learn. The actors moved; some went up the aisles, others retreated; they seemed to respond to waves of fear. They would stop as if making a stand; then move again submissively. Finally, one moaned, "I am not allowed to travel without a passport!"

A black got up in the audience. "Man, listen to me," he called. "I'm under indictment—I can't even leave Manhattan!"

In the ensuing noise it took Seth a moment to feel the hand pulling at his elbow. The young man had reached over to get his attention and now motioned to him to step to the back wall several feet from the railing. The young man went ahead. Seth looked around. Everyone at the railing was looking into the orchestra. No one watched him or the young man. What am I getting into? he asked himself and abruptly walked over. He leaned against the wall next to the young man and faced the theater.

Out of the corner of one eye Seth looked at him. He thought: I am accepted; he trusts me.

In a casual tone the young man said, "Gary doesn't know what make of car you'll be driving."

Seth waited.

"What make?" the boy asked.

"A Chevy," Seth replied, then added, "Four-door sedan."

The young man nodded. "I was worried it was a Volks, you need a full-size trunk." He shifted a foot and looked at Seth and smiled. "These days everyone has a Volks."

"OK?" Seth said.

"Leave the trunk unlocked all the time," the boy replied. "Don't look in it. That way you'll look surprised at whatever is inside—if the occasion should arise. You can say you don't know who put the stuff there and it won't have your fingerprints."

Seth nodded; he did not trust his voice.

The young man chuckled but it rang false. "You and Gary keep your bags in the back seat. You're OK, you know, you're right on." He detached himself from the wall.

"Not at all," Seth said, moved by the tribute. "Not at all." He did not know whether to put out his hand. The boy kept his in his pockets. So he said, "Where are we going?"

The young man replied, "Gary knows that." He looked at Seth and his eyes were bright with excitement. "The less everyone knows all along the line, the better. See you." Without warning he spun around and walked to the exit.

Seth watched him; he did not look back. When he was gone, Seth remained leaning against the back wall of the theater. He closed his eyes and listened to the beating of his heart, but heard only the noises of the audience. I'm cool, I am, I'm cool, he said to himself. He opened his eyes and discovered they had watered. He looked about. Everyone was at the rail. He inspected all the sides of the back area carefully. No one. He noticed for the first time that at one end there was a stairway to the balcony, and did not remember if there had been people there when he and the young man had stood together.

He was still staring at it when a woman appeared on it. She was in a hurry and jumped the last two steps. It was the tall girl in the *djellaba* and her two companions followed her, unwilling to run with her across the back of the theater to the center aisle. She saw Seth and called, "They're taking their clothes off!" Seth stepped off the wall, and she turned back and came to him.

"You're the right size," she said to him. "I got an idea that'll blow your mind. You take your clothes off and I keep my *djellaba.* You get under it and I'll look pregnant. Then on stage—zip!—I pull it off, and there you are— sucking on one of my tits!"

"Beatty!" one of her companions called. He stood at the head of the center aisle removing his pants, skipping on one foot. "Beatty!"

She looked over her shoulder. "What do you say?" she asked Seth, and reached for his crotch.

He jumped back, and she laughed and ran off to the others.

"Jesus Christ!" he said aloud and then laughed and hurried to join Gary at the rail. This time Gary leaped up when Seth placed a hand on his shoulder.

"I don't know what to expect anymore," Gary explained. He was flushed and excited. "Look what's happening—Milton's Paradise, Walpurgis Night, ho-ho!"

The actors were all on stage. They had undressed down to dirty white bikinis, and some were lying down on the stage, abstractly touching and caressing one another. That was no surprise to Seth;

everyone in New York knew about the climax of the play. The call to the natural life. Whitman, Allen Ginsberg, the Movement. Reading a feature article about it in the Sunday *Times* he had reached an erection. He stood on tiptoe now and peered. Except for two girls, the actors had unappealing bodies, stringy, pale, worn. Everywhere in the orchestra the audience was undressing. Some stood in the aisles totally naked, the girls clambering onto the backs of the boys and slithering off with wild screams. Some simply jumped up and down and waved.

Gary nudged him and motioned to the left. At the head of the aisle Beatty was arranging herself on her two companions. They were crouched and she wrapped her arms around the neck of one; the other held her legs on his shoulders, his head peering above her buttocks. She was lying head down, and as the boys rose slowly, the people near them cheered. Her breasts hung full below her. The three moved slowly, wobbily, down the aisle. A naked boy crouched alongside the caravan and reached up and fondled Beatty's breasts. "Romulus and Remus!" Gary yelled, but he could not be heard above the noise.

When Seth next looked at the stage, there were more than two dozen nonactors standing about naked. One girl leaned down and tried to remove the bikini of one of the actresses on the floor. He could see the actress waving her arms about, trying to stop her. Then his vision was blocked by pink buttocks rising from the row of seats in front of him. A couple had undressed, and the girl was now climbing on the boy's back, emulating those in the aisles and riding to the stage and yelling, "Hi-ho, Silver, away!" To get out to the aisle the boy leaned forward and the girl's buttocks rose and parted. Seth looked directly into the pink, tight anus. He clasped his hands together to control his desire to reach out and squeeze the buttocks, and turned his face to Gary. Gary's eyes shifted from the girl to him, and they seemed to be starting out of his head. "I don't believe it!" Gary said.

The stage was almost totally filled. Facing the audience, a boy with hair hanging below his shoulders masturbated with one hand and waved with the other. Couples hugged, their long hair making the boys and girls indistinguishable while they remained locked. They weaved and pumped and yelled. One boy brought his girl as close to the footlights as he could and there tried to penetrate her without lying down. A layer of bodies had fallen on the actors, and the floor of the stage was in motion. An actress struggling with her bikini—"Venus! Venus!" Gary yelled—rose from them and tried to tie the bikini again. She looked angry, harassed, and stopped to slap a hand reaching up her thigh from the floor; then gave up and ran to the wings, stepping on the bodies as she went. The tall girl, Beatty, reached the stage, and she walked about in the little space now left, a hand under each breast displaying them proudly to the audience. They were large and perfect and did not need the support of her hands. Seth reached down and held himself.

He immediately felt wrong. In the midst of all that openness and laughter to be encouraging his secret arousal. In the audience those who had not undressed howled and laughed, and those who had undressed did the same. No one groped. They poked and screeched and clapped. Only on stage was there any activity, and that was more theater than sex. Seth thought: I am the only voyeur. A tall thin actor waved from the footlights. He looked up toward the balcony straight into the lights and again waved his arms as if trying to erase them.

"Is that Beck?" Seth asked.

"If they douse the lights," Gary yelled in Seth's ear, "there won't be an unplugged orifice on that stage!"

The actor seemed to realize this, for he stopped waving and covered his eyes to overcome the blindness caused by looking into the lights. A boy between his legs reached up and pulled at his bikini. It came away and revealed a tiny knobbin sunk into a black patch of hair. The actor did not try to retrieve the bikini. He shifted his attention to the steps leading to the stage from the orchestra pit, and waved back those trying to climb to the stage. His mouth opened and shut but no sound carried back to Seth and Gary.

Seth watched without blinking. All this must go in his notebook. But what drew him were the naked bodies. He tried to tell himself there was not much more nakedness than at Saint-Tropez, but those breasts, those winking mounds, assailed him, and his eyes went from one to the other. He glanced away from the erect penises but he went back to them guiltily, nervously. The masturbating boy seemed to be reaching a climax.

"Look at him," Gary cried.

Seth cleared his throat. "I think he's just acting it out," he said.

"Well, I wouldn't want to be sitting in that first row," Gary said, without turning his head to Seth. "This must the greatest circus since Roman days!"

"And the Living Theater thought it was bringing the revolution to the States," Seth said harshly; it helped relieve him of his desire to be closer, on stage but invisible. "The Movement has outstripped them."

Gary threw an arm around him. "That's a pun, buddy!" he said. He squeezed Seth's shoulders. "All that fucking I did today wasted—I could have been up there instead."

"Go on," Seth said, giving him a little push. "There's still time."

Gary looked around. "Where's our friend?" he asked.

"Gone," Seth said.

Gary looked away from the stage and whispered in Seth's ear. "Did he ask you about your car?"

Seth nodded. Beyond Gary's shoulder he could see a new couple at the head of the aisle. The boy stood close behind the girl, his arms wrapped around her, and each hand twirled her erect nipples.

Gary poked him to get his attention. "Then we can go now, I said," he said to Seth, and hunched a little to look into his eyes searchingly. "Ho-ho, you want to watch, don't you, you dirty old man!"

Seth shrugged. "You're the one with the glands."

Gary glanced around as if to check whether it was worth staying. A girl shrieked, "Yippee," and they saw her, naked, riding a naked boy down the center aisle. "What the hell, no one can recognize me in my disguise," Gary said. "And if there're any pigs around they're beating their meat in secret." He clapped his hands. "Watch me, I always wanted to do it."

"Go ahead," Seth said paternally. You're my surrogate, he added to himself.

Gary handed him his jacket and began to step back slowly to the head of the aisle. His eyes were brilliant and moved unseeingly like revolving lights. His hands were on his belt buckle as he turned ninety degrees to face the theater. He was suddenly standing in the light. He hesitated a moment and looked quickly at Seth. Seth knew Gary could not focus and would not see his encouraging gesture, so he called, "Do it!" In three motions, as if he were being timed, Gary opened the belt, pulled down the zipper, and with both hands helped his pants and shorts over his hips. He then held out both hands as if acknowledging the applause of an audience, and let his pants and drawers go down the rest of the way on their own.

"Good-bye Marxism!" he yelled, but no one turned toward him. "Farewell Friedrich Engels!"

Seth thought: I ought to join him; and he placed a hand on his belt buckle. Gary's shirttails still covered him front and back, but the look on his face was that of having dared all. I'll do it, Seth thought, and started to move. What have I got to be ashamed of? Small man, all cock! Gary looked down and saw the overhanging shirttails. With both hands he pulled them up to his chest, and there was something so funny about the bright red pubic hair glistening in the light, the delicate pallor of his long legs, the perky roundness of his buttocks—so charming to Seth that he began to laugh and the challenge was gone.

Just as quickly as he undressed, Gary drew up his pants, zippered, and buckled his belt. With one hand pulling at his crotch, he came to Seth. "Weird, it shrank." He pulled again. "I thought it was going to disappear right into my belly, I swear."

"I wasn't watching," Seth joked. "There were better sights around."

"Ho-ho, it was *you* my little old hairy Harry was afraid of," Gary said. He threw his arms exuberantly. "You rutting goat! God, I feel wonderful—"

"I know, I know," Seth said with a wise air.

"No, no, not sexy, just good," Gary said. He put on his jacket and looked toward the stage. "So this is what a happening is! I'm converted." He exhaled loudly.

"Well?" Seth said.

"Now it's your turn," Gary said. "I promise to watch."

Seth shook his head quickly. He looked at his watch. "Say, it's ten. Mathilde is holding dinner."

"And I've got to get my bag from Rappaport's." Gary took one last look at the stage. "I think that boy made it. Come on, let's go." He made an effort to look serious. "Can we do it in two days?"

Seth struggled to calculate. The transition was too rapid and he also had to fight the temptation to say it was impossible. "Depends where we're going," he replied.

"Vermont, Vermont," Gary said.

"Oh yes," Seth said, remembering. "I want to spend the night in Connecticut, and if we start early in the morning we can reach any part of Vermont the same day."

Gary slapped him on the back. "I've been too serious all my life," he said. "The Jewish curse." He leaned on Seth's shoulder and talked into his ear. "You take everything in your stride because you haven't always been on the political track only. I think I'll make you my father figure."

"Ho-ho!" Seth replied, imitating him.

"Don't look back," Gary said, heading for the exit. "We'll turn to salt." He held the door for Seth. "We ought to march out singing 'Three Principles of Discipline and Eight Points for Attention.' The first time I heard it, would you believe it, I was standing next to Chou!"

The young man who had stopped taking tickets sat on a stool in the outer lobby. "I'm taking a break," he said to them. "I'm all worn out."

Gary raised his eyebrows.

"Naw, not from that," the fellow replied. "Just from flicking it down every time it came up." He made a circle with forefinger and thumb and snapped the forefinger forward as if shooting a marble. "I had to flick it down so often it's sore."

Now that he was out of danger, Seth laughed expansively.

"I couldn't get a chick to take care of it for me," the fellow said. "They were only interested in getting up on stage. Shit."

Chapter 6

Mathilde was asleep on the living room couch. She wore her long tight green-velvet hostess gown, and the side slit revealed her leg and thigh. Seth knew she was wearing nothing underneath, and he wished he could wake her in time to keep Gary from seeing her. He remembered where they had been and instead chuckled like an indulgent husband.

"Look what you've come home to," Gary whispered, and he remained in the foyer while Seth ostentatiously tiptoed into the living room.

Seth kissed her lightly on the forehead and at the same time placed a hand on her bare thigh. She jumped. "Oh Seth," she said, opened her eyes slowly and then closed them fast. She let herself fall back again, this time hiding her face against the couch.

"Hey, I brought Gary with me," he said.

She sat up, covered her face with both hands and then straightened her hair and smiled toward Gary. "Welcome," she said, and Seth knew she was going to be all right. "Forgive me, I really was looking forward to your coming but I let myself take a little snooze first."

Gary stepped forward. "It's my fault. I held Seth up, what with getting my bag and all." He held out his hand, impressed with Mathilde, and she shook it.

Mathilde continued to smile, but Gary could see that she was puzzled. He looked at Seth.

"Gary is going to stay overnight," Seth explained. "He'll leave with me in the morning."

"Of course, of course," Mathilde said. She stood in the middle of the room, uncertain what to say next. "Now let's see. Dinner. Would you like to wash up first? Your bag?"

Seth put an arm around her and drew her to him. He nuzzled his face in her hair and she smiled and let him. Seth said, "I'll show Gary the bathroom. He can sleep here on the couch or in my study—"

"Your chaise is too short," Mathilde said. "But all that comes later. First, dinner."

"And I must look in on my son and heir," Seth said. The look of admiration on Gary's face was what he had hoped for. "I haven't seen the boy in two days."

Mathilde cocked her head perkily at him. He chuckled. "And you too, my dear, you too," he added. She held out a hand to him and he took it. He thought: with witnesses we're always fine.

Mathilde continued fine throughout dinner. "Ah, you knew, you knew I'd be late," Seth joked when he saw that after the consommé Madrilene the other dishes were also cold. She flirted with Gary, making him feel that only Seth could precede him in her interest. A compliment to Seth always. He crossed his legs and leaned back happily and saw that Gary was thoroughly tamed. "Coffee?" he said, and she nodded quickly and got up.

She stood a moment by Gary before he realized that she meant him to get up and offer her his arm. Seth almost laughed. Instead he waited paternally until Mathilde led Gary to the living room. By his chair was an ice bucket with a bottle of champagne; on the coffee table three hollow-stemmed glasses. Perfect.

"To celebrate the book," Mathilde said. She took Gary to the couch with her. "Did Seth tell you about it?" she asked.

Gary nodded. "And it's worth celebrating too," he replied lamely, and grinned as if that might give wit to his words.

Seth knew Gary was making comparisons with his own, and thought suddenly, I'm a bad friend. "It's not written, it's not written yet," he said, meaning to be modest but sounding grandly complacent. He picked up the champagne and was startled when water dripped from it. He looked for a towel and saw none and tried to reach for his pocket handkerchief. The water fell on his pants.

"Oh, my God, I forgot," Mathilde exclaimed, genuinely embarrassed, and ran to the kitchen. By the time she returned Seth and Gary were sitting laughing, the bottle back in the bucket. "I goofed, I goofed," Seth said, and asked Mathilde to wrap the bottle with the towel while he held it up. Removing the wire from the cork took a long time and Seth pricked a finger with it. He scratched his head ostentatiously. The cork, after much prodding, flew by Mathilde's head and she screamed. Gary beat the couch cushions as he laughed. There was no returning to being the perfect hosts.

"Ordinarily I let the butler do it," Seth said, and poured.

"I should have had strawberries," Mathilde said.

"To the book, to the book," Gary said. They held their glasses up, and Seth sucked on his scratched forefinger. "Take your finger out of your mouth," Gary said. "You don't look like the famous author that way."

They sipped. They looked at one another and sipped again. This time Mathilde looked at Gary for his comment, and he said, "I ask you, is it as good as Pepsi-Cola?" He beat a cushion with his free hand. "God, I feel good. Who'd have thought I'd be having such a good time when the day started so lousy."

"Me too," Seth said. "I was in the dumps this morning, right, Matty?"

"You were fine," she said.

"No, I wasn't fine," Seth insisted. "I apologize."

Mathilde puckered her lips and blew him a kiss. Seth shook his head. He did not want to play that role any more. "It's my fault," he said, and saw that Mathilde did not understand he was serious. "I mean it, I apologize."

Mathilde looked embarrassed. "I accept," she said finally.

"Aren't you both nice!" Gary said. He turned to Mathilde. "You don't know Trudy, do you?"

"Your wife?" she said.

"The woman I live with." He picked up his glass and drank it down. "I found out this morning she's been sleeping with another guy." He suddenly laughed and waved a hand at her to keep her from replying. "That's all, you don't have to say anything. I just wanted you to know."

Mathilde picked up her glass and sipped from it and looked at Seth.

"I didn't say anything when you told me," Seth said, getting up. He filled Gary's glass again, and added, "I think it's rotten."

Gary shrugged. They were silent. Finally, he said to Mathilde, "You're on her side, I bet."

"I don't know her," Mathilde said. She straightened and placed an elbow on the back of the couch and looked again at Seth for help.

"Why doesn't somebody argue with me!" Gary said. "In novels, in movies, your best friends always say, *Give her up,* or, *Do you love her?* or, *Do you think you can forgive her?* Or something, for Christ's sakes."

Mathilde smiled. "You're all right so long as you can talk about it. Go ahead, talk about it."

"That's good, that's a good response," Gary said, and clapped his hands. He stopped when he saw Mathilde blush. She started to get up and he pulled her arm. "Pay no attention to me. Let's change the subject. The truth is there's nothing to say. I guess I'm not in love and I'd a hell lot rather be here with you two than home." He made a funny face at her. "OK?"

Mathilde laughed. "I thought you were a serious politico."

"He is, he is," Seth said. He winked at Gary. "Well, you're going away for a few days. You can think the whole thing over."

"I am?" Gary said. Then started. "My God, I forgot. We'll both be gone a few days."

"A few days?" Mathilde said.

"Didn't I tell you?" Seth said. "Oh no, it all happened after I saw Ybarra. Gary is coming with me to Connecticut and then go on to Vermont." He stopped and looked quickly at Gary. Gary closed his eyes as if saying, It's OK, was only a slip. "He'll pick me up on the way back. I can use the time in Connecticut to dig up father's files and talk to mother and . . ."

"Fine, fine," Mathilde said. She drew her legs up under her. "I've got an idea. Friday afternoon, as soon as Pablo's out of school, I'll take the train up and we'll all come back together. How's that?"

"It won't do," Gary said. "We've got two chicks lined up and there won't be room in the car."

Thank God, Gary made Mathilde laugh. She leaned over and tapped him on the knee and he made a grab for her hand. It gave Seth time. He said, "Let me call you from Connecticut, Matty, and tell you if the coast is clear. I don't know what mother wants to talk to me about and I want to interview her as much as possible. Remind me to take the tape recorder tomorrow morning. I want to get her to reminisce for the book."

"The book," Mathilde said, and turned to Gary. "Don't you think it's the perfect thing for Seth to write? I'm so excited!" But there was a residue of disappointment in her voice.

"Yes, it's a great thing," Gary said. He shook his head, looked up to say something and instead shook his head again and remained silent.

"But shouldn't I be writing about the struggle now?" Seth said. "I've been thinking—thanks to you, Gary—that someone should be taking a serious look at the revolutionary movement in Latin America and writing about that. Am I not copping out? It's going to take two years out of my life."

"Division of labor, remember," Gary said. "Even in revolution there's got to be a division of labor."

"I was telling Matty," Seth replied, "that father's story could have political relevance for today."

"Yes, yes, somebody has to do the Spanish anarchists justice," Gary said. "Especially now. I think the kids are into anarchism and you've got to show them who their forefathers are."

Mathilde was happy to be included in this talk. She unthinkingly interjected, "Yes, Seth. That's your job. There are activists and observers—two sides of the same coin."

"I hate that! I hate that!" Seth got up and looked down at Mathilde on the couch. "I live here in Manhattan, go to parties, write about the Movement, while a few blocks away—in the ghetto—they're doing, *doing* and getting killed."

"Oh Seth, Seth, I didn't mean that!" Mathilde said, and appealed to Gary. "I don't want Seth to be a chic radical."

"You *are* doing something, buddy," Gary said.

Seth's eyes darted to Mathilde, but she was too worried to catch the significance of what Gary said. He sat down, feeling both vindicated and deflated, and suddenly tears welled up in his eyes. He stretched his neck and rested his head on the back of the chair to control them and to avoid seeing that look in Mathilde's face that made him feel like a fake.

Anonymous martyrdom, he had written in his notebook a week ago. "I am haunted by the anonymous martyrs of history," he said, and Mathilde's and Gary's compassionate attention gave him confidence. "In Paris a year ago, when we needed money, I got the idea of writing something about my father. A profile for *The New Yorker,* maybe. Something light. Father in Madrid at the Hotel Florida with all those famous names. So I picked up a story of the civil war and came across a passage that stopped me. You know what it was? You couldn't guess. Just a couple of sentences about the outbreak of the war in Galicia. In that remote province when the peasants heard there was danger to the republic they walked to the cities or came in their slow ox carts to see what they could do to help. They arrived too late, the fascists were in control, and the peasants were all shot."

"And?" Gary said.

Seth thought that he had not written the profile because he decided he could not write well enough. A profile would have to be shaped by him; it could not be like his book on the May uprising, which by recounting the events as they happened formed itself. He sighed. "Well, would my father have done that? More to the point, would I? Would I make the effort if my sacrifice did not cause a splash?"

He stood up, pleased that the others were silent. He picked up the champagne bottle and divided what was left evenly. "Is there more?" he asked with an ironic smile.

Mathilde nodded eagerly. "I put a second one in the fridge," she said.

"You're a good girl," Seth said, and left the room to get it. In the hall he imagined Gary and Mathilde turning to one another and sharing with a quiet look their admiration for him. He had expressed himself well, he thought. Doc, he said to his analyst, I think my marriage is going to be OK. I made the leap; I jumped the barrier.

He did not switch on the light in the kitchen but went straight to the refrigerator. He opened the door and the lit interior reminded him of the theater. He crouched in front of it and something—was it the top of Pablo's orange soda lying on its side?—stared at him like the dark pink anus of the girl. He put a hand around the top of the champagne bottle and withdrew it quickly. He stumbled when he straightened. Dizzy. Again the anus stared at him. He slammed the door closed and held the bottle to his chest. If he spread Mathilde's buttocks, would her anus glare at him? "I don't know," he said angrily, "I've never seen it."

He was outraged by the loathing the world focused on him and was surprised to see the gladness on Mathilde's and Gary's faces. He waved the bottle at them as proof, he told himself, that he deserved their trust. I'm not bad, he urged on them, I'm not bad.

Gary got up. "I've been thinking about what you said," he announced, "and it applies to me. It's just like you to be berating yourself about not doing things when the perfect example is me. I mean it, I've just been operating like the worst elitist. Fuck the committee. I'm through with it. I've been listening to you and for me it's been a struggle session."

"Keep talking," Seth said, turning the bottle and easing out the cork. "I want this to pop as the climax to your self-criticism."

"I mean it, I mean it, I should have known that old lech Mackey had more than a paternal interest in us—see, I told myself it was in *us!*" He looked at Mathilde. "I was too busy visiting new socialist countries and heading delegations of important intellectuals. Who the hell was I but a young schnook with another Ph.D. on Heidegger, for Christ's sakes." The cork popped. "Hurrah, hurrah, fill it up!"

"To Heidegger!" said Seth.

"To the masses," Mathilde said quietly.

"Good girl," Seth said.

"To being cuckolded!" Gary yelled. "The greatest prick to one's self-esteem. To the greatest prick, period—me!"

"Now wait a minute there, buddy," Seth said, still holding out his glass. "I'll not be the subject of invidious comparisons."

"Then drop your pants," Gary said, and slapped himself with one hand and slopped some champagne on the coffee table. "I did. You saw the evidence. They're putting up a plaque at the Fillmore this very moment."

"Drink up," Seth said, to distract him.

Gary recited, "On this spot Comrade Epstein unveiled—"

"I thought you two were going to give speeches there," Mathilde said. "What is this all about?"

"Ho-ho! Ho-ho! Seth buddy, is that what you told Matty? Ho-ho!" He carefully finished his glass, placed it on the coffee table, and fell on the couch. He crouched on it and looked directly into Mathilde's eyes. "Let me tell you about it—God, it was funny!"

Mathilde giggled but did not know why.

"It's very simple," Seth said, but could not get their attention. He raised his voice. "The Living Theater put on that thing that got them into trouble in New Haven, and Gary took off his pants."

"No," Mathilde replied.

Still crouched by her, Gary nodded and nodded like a pet dog.

Mathilde looked at Seth. "And you?"

Gary shook his head in the same rhythm as he had nodded. "Oh no, oh no, he's my patriarch," he said. "Do not look upon thy father's nakedness or something."

Seth saw Mathilde's relief, and looked away as she turned to him. When he looked at her again, she began to giggle. She tried covering her face so as not to see Gary's grimaces, but she could not control her giggling.

"And me, I'd never even been skinny dipping before," Gary said. He pulled a hand away from her face so she would see him. "Not even with the fellas. Come on, let's take our clothes off. I guarantee it, it's great, it's liberating, it's the revolution!" Shrugging and wiggling he got one sleeve of his jacket off.

Seth leaned forward to stop him but instead stood up.

"I don't need help," Gary said, and pulled off the other sleeve. He raised his jacket above his head with both hands and threw it across the room. He turned to Mathilde. "Now you take something off."

Mathilde crossed her legs and sat forward. "I'd catch cold," she said.

Gary looked at Seth to appeal to him. Seth sat down and reached for the bottle. Without looking up he filled the glasses again. Gary's suggestion was dead. Mathilde had helped him handle it right; he wanted to let her know without hurting Gary's feelings, so he picked up her glass and handed it to her. "Thank you, Seth," she said.

"What a day," Seth said, building a bridge to a new subject. "Last night I was in Pennsylvania."

"Last night I was my old self—the big politico," Gary said. "I fucked up, didn't I? I have to learn to act natural. I've been so used to formal warmth. Receptions, handshakes, and speeches. I don't know how to be with friends."

"Oh no, Gary, you're fine," Mathilde protested. She placed a hand on his shoulder and cocked her head to one side to look at him. Seth knew how she must appear to Gary. Full of concern. The way she had looked at him that morning. It was not fake, after all, he knew now. He stared at her hand on Gary's shoulder. He saw her hand move back and forth, feeling Gary's flesh, comforting him. Gary turned to her and smiled like a little boy and then he just as naturally looked at Seth and smiled again.

"Buddies," Gary said. Seth winked at him for reply.

The image of her hand on Gary's shoulder, with only a thin shirt between it and his flesh, returned to him later. He lay in bed on his back thinking, his way of falling sleep—as to an illuminated lecture, he once told his analyst—and decided that, of course, Gary did not know that there must be more than friendliness in the movement of her hand. Nor she either. I never give her any outlet for her warmth any- more, he thought. He moved his own hand on his belly and felt the intervening fabric of his pajamas become a loving abrasive. He had last seen her heading for the bathroom, her nightgown and robe on her arm. Gary sat on the john. His shirt was off. This time her hand on his shoulder touched bare flesh. The other hand reached down and point- ed him up and she lowered herself on his lap. He braced himself with his hands on the seat and raised himself into her. He was not tall but he made up for it with the length of his spear. He awoke with an erec- tion and removed the hand that had been on his chest amplifying his heartbeat. He looked at Mathilde's bed and it took him a moment, dur- ing which he thought of them in the bathroom, to make out the outline of her body hunched on her side asleep. It felt late. What if he rolled her on her back and entered her dry? He had never done that. The door to the hall was open. He made a circle of his forefinger and thumb and snapped the forefinger against his erection. It worked. He turned on his side and recalled that the naked body on which she had lowered herself in his dream was his own. He blinked but saw only that it was light. He kept his eyes shut; he wanted to sleep. He felt watched. Why didn't she go away? Or say something. She insisted on martyrdom. Martyrdom. He opened his eyes. It was Pablo, standing in the doorway. He was about to say something but instead closed his mouth and continued staring. I must have looked angry, Seth thought. He sat up. "Hello, buster," he said.

"He's in the bathroom," Pablo said.

"He?" He closed his eyes: Connecticut, Vermont. He looked at his watch.

"Mom is taking me to the bus later," Pablo said quickly. "I'm going to have breakfast with you and him. She wants me to wake you. She's making a super breakfast."

"That's OK with me," Seth said. He got out the side of the bed away from Pablo and put on his bathrobe. He kept his back to him; Pablo was no longer a baby.

When he turned around, Pablo was still there. "He's a funny guy," Pablo said. "He scratched me with his chin."

"His name is Gary," Seth said.

"Yeah, he wants me to call him Uncle Gary."

Seth thought: he must have got into her last night. He was loath to walk out of the bedroom. He would know the moment he saw either of them. He sat on the edge of the bed to think things over. "Don't you think you ought to get dressed for school now?" he said to Pablo. He stared at him for a while. Pablo stood his ground. "Do that," he added, but Pablo did not leave. "What do you want?" he asked. "Don't bother me now."

"Dad, I want to stay home and help," he said, ready to cry. "To pack and all that."

"Help? We're leaving right after breakfast," Seth replied. He looked at Pablo again and shook his head. "I don't care, I've nothing to do with it. I'm not going to be home."

Pablo ran away before he finished. He could hear him calling, "Mom, dad doesn't care if I stay home! Did you hear?"

He was still waiting for Gary to leave the bathroom when Mathilde came in. He looked up at her when she handed him a glass of orange juice. She smiled. "It's the champagne," she said, and put out her hand. There was a vitamin pill in it. "Therapeutic potency. I took one myself."

"You look pretty good to me," he said.

She curtseyed. "Why, thank you, sir."

He sat on the bed and watched her. "How's Gary?"

"I haven't seen him to speak to," she said, "but Pablo was in there playing with him. He's nice, I like him." She looked toward the hall and leaned down to whisper. "What's his wife—that girl like? I feel so sorry for him and yet he makes me laugh. He *is* nice."

He put out his arms from his sitting position and drew her to him and snuggled his head in her belly. He could feel her caution, her surprise at his gesture, and then she relaxed and his face sank lightly into her flesh. She laughed and he knew he had not been the cause. From the hall, looking in on them, Gary called, "Hey, none of that! I want breakfast." She pushed at Seth's shoulders to break away, and before he turned his head to Gary he saw the flushed, excited look on her face that once had been incentive and signal for pursuit. He smiled at Gary and stuck his tongue out at him. Gary said, "Coitus interruptus is the name of the game," and they all laughed and went their separate ways until breakfast.

Grapefruit and honey, strips of bacon, eggs scrambled with chervil, muffins. Pablo stood by Mathilde and passed the plates she served. He was quiet but wished to be noticed, and so he got up again for the coffee and then ran to the door and brought back the *Times* and the *Wall Street Journal.* He looked at his father and when he nodded offered them to Gary first. "You don't wait to pick it up at the newsstand?" Gary said, and frowned at the front page of the *Times.*

Seth lit his first cigarette. "What happened?" he asked, when Gary turned the pages for the continuation of the story.

Gary glanced quickly at the rest of the story. "They've arrested some kids who were supposed to have bombed the draft offices and the police headquarters," he said. "They say they caught them when they were about to place another bomb." He held out the paper to Seth, and they looked at one another for a moment. "They're going to charge them with everything in the book."

"Are they Weathermen?" Mathilde asked.

"Weathermen!" Pablo said. "That's funny."

"It doesn't say," Gary replied. "If they—"

"I forgot the jam!" She got up. "I'm sorry, tell me when I get back."

Seth smiled to show Gary that Mathilde was innocent, and hoped his smile covered his own fear. He whispered, "Do you know any of them?" Then looked at Pablo with caution.

Gary shook his head.

Mathilde placed three crystal servers on the table. "Strawberries, damson, and apple jelly," she said, pointing to each in turn. She sat down and put some apple jelly on a muffin and handed it to Pablo. "Tell me, Gary, couldn't all that be a frame-up?"

Gary looked up from his paper. "So imperturbable the *Wall Street Journal*, they've got nothing about it," he said. He replied to Mathilde, "Oh, I don't know. Maybe there was a pig involved and that's how they caught them."

"Pig!" Pablo giggled. Gary poked him and he giggled some more. "That's funny," he said, and tried to hit back. "You know what a pig is at the Lycee?"

Gary nodded exaggeratedly.

"I bet you don't," Pablo said.

"Pablo," Mathilde said.

Pablo became quiet.

Gary said, "You tell me."

Pablo opened and closed his mouth. He could not remember.

Seth looked up to tell Gary that the *Times* said the bombs were homemade. Pipes with dynamite and clocks. Then decided against it. If they were on to this group, he thought, why shouldn't they know where the supplies were coming from? It took an effort not to say it aloud. "I'd better pack," he said. Mathilde pushed back her chair. "No, no, I don't need any help," he said.

He was halfway to his room when he heard her say to Gary, "Let Seth drive—he seems none the worse for the champagne." He stopped. Gary replied, "He'll have to. I don't know how to drive." Seth waited and, thank God, Pablo exclaimed, *"Cochon!* Pigs are *les cochons,* see!" Gary replied, "Ho-ho!" and Seth sighed and went on to his bedroom.

He said to himself, I'm not going through with it. I'll think of a reason on the way. Let Gary find another driver. No, he could not let them use his car either; the excuse must include using the car for . . . He held a pair of dungarees in his hand and hesitated: dungarees meant Vermont. He put them in, also a sweater. He could feel his heart beat faster. The pills—

Mathilde stood in the doorway. She must have figured it out. "Take a good shirt and tie," she said, "in case your mother has guests one evening."

"You put it in," he said, and started toward his study to get away.

She stopped him halfway. "Seth," she said in a low voice. "Gary said he can't drive."

"Sure he can," he replied but could not get past her.

Her fingers on his arm were tense. "Seth, you're going Vermont." Her voice broke and she tried to put both arms around him. "Please don't leave me, Seth, please. I love you."

"For Christ's sake," he said. He held his arms to his sides. She was so dumb, she did not know what anything was about. He thought: there's no real worth in our quarrels. Finally, he said, hoping to head off her tears, "He's going to Vermont to lecture at a college and he's going alone."

He waited for her to let go of him. He brought up a hand and touched her shoulder. "You don't love me anymore," she said. "If you were just sleeping with someone else, I could stand that. If you loved me."

It had been a mistake to touch her. He stepped back and her arms fell away from him. "I'm not sleeping with anyone," he said, "and I'm not going to discuss love at this moment."

She covered her face with both hands and held her head down. He heard the sharp intake of breath that meant she was going to sob. He leaned forward trying to look into her face. "Matty, I said good-bye to the shrink yesterday," he said. "I'm OK, for God's sake."

There were still tears in her eyes when she removed her hands from her face, but they made her look even happier. She put an arm around his neck and said, "Then give me a kiss." She pressed against him and he lowered his mouth to hers. Her tongue darted out and then withdrew and she held her head back and smiled at him. He thought: I shall never be through with her or rid of her. As if she knew what he was thinking, she said lightly, "If you want to fuck some girl when you're away, go ahead. But you have to come back to me."

He smiled. He knew that someday he would literally count on this approval she gave him. But he must make her grow up. "Look, I'm going to tell you the truth about Vermont, but you must not let on that you know," he said. She nodded and put on a serious look, and he saw that she expected some slightly scandalous story about Gary. "The truth is that Gary can't drive. I'm going to go up with him. He's going to lecture but after that . . ." He paused. "After that we're going to pick up a deserter and drive him over the border into Canada."

She sat down on the bed and held on to one of his hands.

"Now finish packing for me," he said and squeezed her hand. "I've got to get some other things."

In the study he picked up the Christofle silver pillbox she had bought him in Paris. He kept it in the middle drawer of the desk and never used it; he carried pills loose in his jacket pocket, since he did not, he believed, depend on them. This trip was different; he hoped Mathilde would notice the pillbox's absence, he did not quite know why. It would give him stature with her; also show her he was human. In the bathroom he filled it with Libriums, Seconals, and amphetamines. He did not know whether to take a Librium now or an amphetamine. He thought it over and decided on a Librium.

When he returned to the bedroom, she looked purposeful and contained, as on their wedding day. She had finished packing and was waiting for him. "You mustn't worry," he said. "It's nothing."

"I'm glad you told me," she said in a level voice. "Next time I want to help." Then grinned. "You forget I've always been very good with customs officials. They take one look at me and think, Rochester—she's fine."

"There's always a chance and I don't want you to take it," he said, then shook his head. "But not really, it goes on all the time."

She drew an arm through his when he picked up the bag. She leaned her head on his shoulder and pressed his arm against her body. "You're such a good person, Seth," she said.

Chapter 7

"I had to make up some story about driving you to Vermont," Seth told Gary once they were on the West Side Highway. "She noticed you said you didn't drive. I said you were lecturing at some college there and only last night told me you'd promised them you would bring me along."

"She believed that?" Gary said. "It doesn't quite make sense. I mean, it was only last night she learned I was coming along and all that. Why couldn't you have told her everything at once?"

"I guess she didn't think of that," Seth said.

After a moment Gary asked, "What college?"

"I didn't say," Seth replied.

"What if she'd asked?" Gary said, and sat up. "Are there *any* colleges in Vermont?"

Seth thought a moment. "Bennington and Goddard. Just the kind of places that would ask us."

Gary slumped again. "That's one web I would have tangled." He closed his eyes and then opened them a moment. "What snobs we are—Bennington and Goddard! There must be a University of Vermont."

"Go back to sleep, you've got two hours," Seth said. He wanted Gary to talk about the group that had been arrested, but he was not going to bring it up. He hoped Gary would decide that their capture should at least delay their own trip to Vermont. When he told Mathilde that he was spending those days in Connecticut, it had suddenly struck him as the right thing to do. Now was the time to ransack his father's study and to talk to his mother. He could then return to New York feeling that he had really begun and with enough material to sketch out his research. He looked over at Gary and saw he was attempting to sleep. Maybe mother would help him find a way to call off the trip.

On the Cross Bronx Expressway Gary opened his eyes and said, "You and Matty are really a thing. A good thing."

"Oh, we have our troubles like everybody else," he said.

"Come on, she's not screwing around with anyone but you," Gary said. "I like Matty." He started to lean back again to sleep but laughed before he closed his eyes. "I laugh because I heard my mother reply to what I just said. She said, You don't have to tell me she's a *shiksa*, right? She thinks I have this thing about gentile girls." He made a grimace. "And I have. I've never laid a Jewish girl. Not that I have ever turned any down. You could say that mainly I've been politically active. From now on—ho-ho!"

When Seth stopped at the first tollbooth of the Connecticut Turnpike, Gary opened his eyes again. "What will your mother say?" he asked.

"She'll be pleased to see you," Seth replied. "She doesn't get much of a chance to meet new people during the school year."

"I should have meant that but I didn't," Gary said. "All this representing the committee makes me think I'm being awaited everywhere by delegations. Some dope I am, I never think I may be an inconvenience."

"Well, you're not," Seth said, and noted that this formal reassurance carried the sense that if Gary were an inconvenience he would not be with him. Was that ungenerous? Was that what Gary would call a WASP response? He started to add that inconvenience be damned, but thought better of it. "There's a guest room for Mathilde and me and another for Pablo. Anyway, Mathilde will have called and told her we're on our way."

Gary nodded and nodded. They were not arriving unexpectedly. Not the way he did at his parents' apartment. He stopped nodding and looked depressed. After a while he shrugged and said, "No, what I meant was, how will your mother feel about your writing the book about James Evergood? It means writing about her, too."

"I never thought about it," Seth said before he could stop himself, and then forgot about Gary. His mother was not Mathilde. He could see her suppress her first response, straighten her back, and take a puff of her cigarette. Have you really thought it over? she asked. He was yelling at her; it was a din in his ears. He yelled because he could not control himself. Sometimes he yelled to frighten her into thinking he could not control himself. At seven, the first time he came home from the Lycee on holiday, he struck her. What an ill-bred child, she had said. He had lost then, and the shrink had made him believe that each subsequent battle was an attempt to overcome that defeat.

He finally heard Gary talking. "The way you're speeding," Gary said, "I must have hit a nerve."

Seth eased his foot off the accelerator. "I'll have to work hard to bring her around," he said, "but I'll do it." He thought of something that would please Gary. "With her I'm not a Wasp, you know."

It did please Gary. He laughed and clapped his hands. "I don't suppose you can fool her like my mother," Gary said. "My mother! I don't even have to fool her about such a thing. I could say, mom, I'm writing a book about pop and how he kidnapped the Lindbergh baby and, believe me, she'd turn it into one swell piece of news to tell the relatives and neighbors. She's the mother in the old joke—That's nice, don't fight."

Seth's eyes filled with tears. He didn't care. He turned to look at Gary; let him think it was the wind that caused the tears. "God, how I envy you. A shrink would think it's Freudian, the old Oedipus and all that. But it's not, it's cultural. My first years with a French peasant girl taking care of me and then away from home going to the Lycee. No, school was very strict, very middle-class French. But I stayed with a couple in New York, friends of my parents, and since I wasn't their son they were more permissive."

"I'm listening to you," Gary said, adopting a Jewish intonation, "and all I can feel is envy. So what is it you envy me?"

Seth smiled. Gary was right: his was a rather special background. "It's not a question of envy, I guess," he explained. "I simply prefer a way of acting, like the French peasant woman and the Jews—"

Gary interrupted. "Watch your step there, you goy."

Seth continued. "I mean like all non-Protestants and the working class."

"Ah, the working class," Gary said.

Seth persevered. "Having known a bit of that as a boy in France, I prefer it to the way my parents and their friends are. Reserved. You keep troubles to yourself and you don't boast of good news, so you finally end up not knowing how to show your emotions at all."

"Well, Jews hide *some* things," Gary said. "Good news, for example. You don't spread it outside the family or you may jinx it. Troubles, that's another matter. I've figured out that the folk song of the Jews should be 'Everybody Knows the Troubles I Seen—and Nobody Gives a Fuck.'" He chuckled contentedly. "God, I haven't talked about Jews this much since I was thirteen and refused to be bar mitzvahed. Oy, did I give them a trauma!"

"What happened?" Seth asked, and felt a small thrill that he worried might be due to anti-Semitism.

"The whole family went into mourning," Gary said with pleasure. "It shook the Jewish community of Ridgewood, New Jersey, to its foundation. It was the beginning of my meteoric rise to fame. I loved it all. I've been a crummy elitist ever since."

Seth looked over at him. "As you say, ho-ho."

"Never mind, I haven't been among people like your mother since I was in college with the tweed-and-pipe set," Gary said, "and I'm a little scared. I don't know how to meet people who aren't the head of a political movement. You know, one of those question-and-answer confrontations with interpreters and photographers around. I'm great at that."

"She'll like you," Seth said; then added as self-criticism, "She likes young people with gumption."

Gary sat up straight, as if mentally preparing himself for the meeting. "I'll call her Mrs. Evergood," he said, "but what's her name?"

"Eleanor Morgan," Seth replied, "but you'll be calling her Trick. Her grandmother's nickname for her. Southern girls got given the wildest nicknames in the nineteenth century and her grandmother was born in 1849 and lived until 1930, Southern to the end. And Trick was Grandmother Morgan's name for her."

"Roots, roots," Gary moaned. "But I thought your folks were New Englanders."

"Middle westerners," Seth said.

"Middle westerners!"

"Not Nixon middle westerners," Seth explained. "Not Polish or Irish or Scandinavians. Not even southern, except for Grandmother Morgan." He paused and looked over at Gary; he was still attentive. "They were mostly New Englanders who had for theological reasons"—he shook his head with amusement—"and economic reasons moved west. My father's great-grandfather was in Lane Theological Seminary with Lyman Beecher and Harriet and Calvin Stowe." He stopped because Gary moaned again.

"Go on," Gary said; he slumped in his seat. "We've got three-quarters of an hour. Give me the whole thing. Christ, Ridgewood, New Jersey, the Lower East Side and then total darkness—that's my background."

Grandmother Morgan came from Louisiana on the Mississippi, halfway up from New Orleans to the Arkansas border. A commercial family, though of course their friends were plantation owners, especially on the Mississippi side of the river.

Gary interrupted. "My head's whirling already. If you told me the Fiji Islands are in the middle of the Mississippi, I wouldn't dispute it."

Papa—"That's very Southern, that 'Papa,'" Seth said parenthetically about Grandmother Morgan's father—Papa was in river traffic and imports and exports, and he dealt with more than just plantation owners; he knew commercial men from abroad and from the North. He was a businessman and his mind was open to things other than the plantation way of life. They were townspeople and there were good books at home. Still, one son fought for the Confederacy, the other for the Union. The Confederate one was an officer in the cavalry and he died in a Northern hospital near Washington. Papa got a letter from a man who used to visit the hospital regularly, bringing the wounded books and food. A beautiful letter signed by Walt Whitman.

Gary moaned again. "As long as you're making it up," he said, "you might as well tell me they were lovers."

Indeed, Grandmother Morgan sold the letter late in life to a collector for a tidy sum. It is now at the Smithsonian.

"You sure you want to hear more of this?" Seth asked.

"In my family we can't even boast of an illegitimate child sired by Jacob Adler," Gary said. "I want to hear the whole thing. Just don't rub it in too hard."

Grandmother Morgan was fourteen or fifteen when the war began to get close and she was already known as someone with very unorthodox opinions about the conduct of the Yankees. She didn't think they were devils. What's more, Papa had already freed their few house slaves. The family stayed in their mansion when everyone else fled to the woods as the Union army took the town. It didn't help. The house was looted, the furniture demolished, the gowns shredded, and the whole thing escaped being burned to the ground because Grandmother Morgan appealed to a Yankee officer, who stopped the men. For one reason or the other that young Yankee officer came through town several times in the next year, and at the end of the war they were married.

"Ho-ho," Gary murmured.

He settled down there and tried to restore Papa's business. Papa died of a broken heart at the devastation of the war and the bitterness of Reconstruction. At least, that is what Grandmother Morgan said. As Reconstruction faded they drifted up the Mississippi and got into one business or the other until they were involved in Indian land grabs. The real estate of the day. So were my father's people. His great-grandfather was one of those young Presbyterian ministers in trouble with his people because in church matters he was anti-Calvinist and in politics abolitionist. That's why he went west. He knew Lovejoy, he knew John Brown. But his children and grandchildren also looted the Indians, and they all ended up with huge Victorian houses in the suburbs of Chicago. They sent their children east to school and summers to Europe. That's how my father and mother met. On a tour.

Gary sat up. "I think my father and mother met at the corner delicatessen buying potato salad and coleslaw. Or maybe at Loew's Paradise."

"Think of Grandmother Morgan though," Seth said. "She was around for both the Civil War and the Wall Street crash."

"And wiped out by both, I bet," Gary said. "Still, that was a rich, full life, as they say."

Seth looked over at him quickly and then back again at the road. "Not exactly, I think the old lady hung on to real estate here and there. And Trick—my mother—was her only female descendant." He stopped. "Anyway, I don't think she was broke when she died. She didn't believe in stocks, she'd seen too many panics in her lifetime."

"So she left your folks a pile," Gary said.

"I don't really know," Seth said. "I've never asked."

"You never asked!" Gary said. "Oy, you goys."

Seth did not reply immediately. He turned off the interstate, and he could never remember until he reached the light at the first intersection whether he must turn right or left on the county road. Finally, and it seemed the appropriate moment, he said, "Well, I'll be asking a lot of questions now. I want the book to have all that."

"OK, OK," Gary said. "But while you're at it find out about the money. It's a nice thing to know."

There was some money in nontaxable Chicago and Minneapolis bonds and rents from Evanston real estate and a summer place on Lake Michigan and the house here. How much it came to he did not know, but some arrangement should be made before his mother's death to avoid inheritance taxes and the complications of probate. He and his mother had yet to discuss it. So he simply smiled at Gary and said nothing.

"I mean it," Gary persisted. "You might need some of it to keep you going and not be at the mercy of assignments. To write this book, for example."

Seth turned to him a moment. "I'll tell you something, buddy. If I make a long distance call from mother's phone she sends me the itemized section of the bill at the end of the month. She even calculates the part of the tax that applies to my call and she asks me to pay promptly whether I'm in New York or Paris or wherever."

"Not my folks," Gary said. "They'd just get that self-commiserating look and talk about how they're supporting AT&T the next time I'm around. So then I tell them I want to pay and we have a big fight and they offer me more advice than I can put to use in a century. I end up accepting as a gift a box of shirts they bought from a friend in the building—*Wholesale, darling, what's the big deal?*—and which I would not be caught dead wearing."

On the outskirts of the town, they passed a wall of cedars that continued until the street became country road again. "That's Calvin," Seth said. "One more mile."

"It's not country and it's not suburbs," Gary said. "None of these trees look like they've grown here by chance. Not that I know. I can tell you about agrarian reform in the Third World but I don't know the name of any trees."

Seth turned into a circular driveway almost hidden by tall thick lilacs lining the road. "Too bad they've already bloomed," he said. "They're white and the scent puts you to sleep marvelously."

Gary saw the white clapboard Georgian house. A wide front door, black shutters, and two square chimneys. "Christ, I forgot to put on my tie," he said. "I've got it in my pocket."

"It's midday," Seth said. "You should be wearing an ascot and anyway mother doesn't care."

"Well, fuck it then," Gary said.

Seth threw him his bag from the back seat, and wondered just what his mother would think of Gary. She'd treat him like a Calvin alumnus, he thought, and that is better treatment than I ever got. He went ahead and opened the door for Gary, and decided from the look on Gary's face that his mother must be in the entrance hall. He ducked his head in and saw she was coming down the stairs. She looked in good humor, thank God.

She waited until both were inside to speak. "Mathilde called and told me you were on the way. And you're Gary Epstein. I've spent the morning wondering whether you'd be the publisher or that dangerous young man." She paused and Seth knew he was expected to peck her on the cheek and then she would shake hands with Gary. All the while she was turned toward Gary to let him get a good look at her brilliant blue eyes and her fair, lined face. She spoke in her deep voice, and each word emerged separate and equally weighted. "You must be the dangerous young man," she added.

Gary instinctively bowed. "I am," he said. "I hope you've counted the silver."

"Later," she said, and chuckled. Seth recognized himself in the sound of her laughter, the times when he wanted to appear judiciously appreciative. She looked at the bags they had placed inside the door. "Seth, I've a great deal to discuss with you," she said. "But why don't you take Gary—I'm going to call you Gary—upstairs first. I shall be down here. I've already had lunch but I've got some waiting for you and I'll have coffee with you. There are towels on your beds."

"Mother, we're using both rooms," Seth said. "We're staying overnight."

Only Seth knew that her raised eyebrows meant she thought he was gauche. "Of course you're staying," she said. "A couple of days at least. I said we have much to discuss."

At the bottom of the stairs Seth decided he should make it clear immediately. "No, only overnight," he said. We have to be off in the morning."

She turned and walked past the stairs toward the door to the kitchen. She seemed not to have heard.

"What a sweet house," Gary said in the small corridor at the top of the stairs.

"There's going to be a tug of war about when we leave," Seth said grimly, then realized that could be his excuse for not going on to Vermont. "But don't worry."

Gary looked surprised. "She didn't say anything. She did not object."

"She never acknowledges opposition," Seth said. "Anyway, she likes you." He pointed out their rooms to the right of the stairs, over the kitchen and dining room. On the left were his mother's. "Your room is to the back and there's a connecting bathroom with mine." He led Gary to his and when he saw the towels on the bed, said, "Oh, oh, mother is out to be nice. Those are the best towels."

"It's a boy's room, all right," Gary said.

Seth thought: it was never mine. "She keeps my children's books here for Pablo," he said.

He went to the rear window and looked down at the patio on which the back door and his father's downstairs study opened. He studied the cedars, several yards beyond the patio, for the first time in years. Once he had stood here often, waiting to see movement on the other side of them that would mean he could join his father. His father had kept an outdoor chaise there and a metal table for his ashtray and the tall glass of water flavored with bourbon. Away from the shade of the cedars he cultivated a small vegetable plot. He sometimes wrote in a notebook. Seth never saw it open; it lay on the table, a cheap composition notebook, with the gold pen Seth had inherited placed on top of it like a seal. Those notebooks must have been his journal, for after the civil war he published only that short book about Sarah Orne Jewett, which Seth once started but did not finish. Seth had not walked behind the cedars since the funeral, six years earlier. He had died there quietly, of a second heart attack that must have come suddenly. At sundown his mother, who never went to "the retreat," as she called it, had gone looking for him. He lay on the chaise, his left arm dangling, the hand just missing the grass.

She waited for them in the kitchen, at the old, laquered harvest table. Not the dining room; further evidence that she had accepted Gary. At one end, for Seth and Gary, she had set it for lunch. A large salad, a cheese board, bread and crackers; also wineglasses and a bottle of Beaujolais. At her end, a cup of coffee, already half finished, and a small pewter ashtray for the cigarette she had lit.

She said, "Something light now, because we'll have a real dinner tonight. There'll be a couple of people dropping in."

"Not for the whole evening, I hope," Seth said. "We have to leave in the morning and I too have something talk to you about."

"Seth, dear, you open the bottle," she said. "I wasn't sure you wanted some. There's also coffee. But wine is always nice after a drive."

Gary volunteered to open the bottle, and Seth allowed him because he could see that his mother took it as a compliment. A proper young man, her smile said. Seth served the salad. "Bibb lettuce!" he said. It was his father's favorite.

"I've been keeping up the garden," she said. "These are the first this year and they're wonderfully sweet."

"Oh God, it's not coming out," Gary said. "I've never used an opener like this."

She looked at the bottle in his hands and said, "Just one more turn, Gary, and it will be out." She waited. "Perfect," she said as the cork rose out of the bottle. "It's the kind that French waiters use."

Seth knew she was capable of another hour of small talk. He said abruptly, commandingly, "What's this about interest in father's papers? Who's interested? Are they willing to pay? Or do they think you're going to feel honored to turn them over for nothing?"

She smiled, then looked at Gary. "I see that Seth doesn't startle you any more than he does me—"

Gary interrupted. "He's my buddy."

"Good, good," she said. She looked at Seth and puffed at her cigarette, and he saw her calculate that Gary's presence would help her keep the conversation under control.

"Well?" he said. "Who wants father's papers?"

"Yale," she replied. She turned to Gary. "His alma mater."

"That's not the only reason surely," Seth said quickly. "Father was very well known at one time. Important, too. He knew many important people and they must've written to him."

"Yes, dear, no question about it," she replied. She drew on the cigarette again. "They're also interested in me. I also knew all those important people. Sometimes I think I got the better of Jimmy with our friends. Did you show Gary my sitting room?"

"What?" Seth said. What was she up to?

Gary shook his head.

"Jimmy liked to go in the afternoon to Miss Stein," she said, and Seth knew he had to wait for the end of the story to get the point. She would not be hurried. "He sat at her feet and asked about Picasso and she of course told him. She loved telling, whatever the subject. But I sat with Miss Toklas and paid her court. She taught me needlepoint. She was most meticulous. Her moustache would quiver at some of the stitches."

Gary threw back his head and laughed.

"You didn't expect father to learn needlepoint," Seth said impatiently.

His mother chuckled. "The chair in my sitting room is upholstered with one I did under her supervision. A copy of one which was designed for her by Matisse. I had already done half of it when Miss Toklas took fright, and we had to seek Miss Stein's approval. Miss Stein insisted on changing one of the colors. Matisse had selected a gorgeous pink. I had to settle for mauve. Still, it's a valuable piece."

"I should say," Gary agreed.

"But it's not an original Matisse," Seth said.

"Well, when the ladies died, I didn't read anywhere that Miss Toklas's needlework survived," she said. "It doesn't matter, of course. I'm not about to put it up for sale at Sotheby's."

There was a moment of quiet. Seth felt bested. Then realized how far she had taken the conversation from the question he had asked. He picked it up again, like a fallen weapon. "What have you said to Yale about father's papers?" he asked. "Have they mentioned money? You can't just give them away."

"Money?" she said, and he stared at her to see if she had not thought of that earlier. "I suppose they'll pay something for them. They have yet to see them and there are boxes of letters written to us by all sorts of people—important people, as you say. Some of that is also correspondence with me and I don't know that I shall want to give them up just yet."

"Why not?" Seth said. "They simply included you in their letters because of father."

His mother shook her head reprovingly, as if he were little boy, and took up a new cigarette. She looked at Gary, but he did not gather he was to light it. "Seth, my, dear," she said. "I do believe you're being rude."

"Male chauvinist pig," Gary said, and then noticed she still held the cigarette unlit. "Christ, let me give you a light."

Seth made an effort not to raise his voice. He wanted to hear her out before he sprang his own news. "I'm sorry," he said. "I didn't mean it that way."

"I'm afraid it's all coming out in fits and starts and so you are confused," she replied, mollified. "The correspondence includes letters addressed to me and your father but also I have bunches of his letters to me. Especially letters he wrote me during the time in Spain."

"Seth, your book!" Gary exclaimed. "Perfect for your book."

"Yes, I want them," Seth said quickly. "About Yale—"

"What book?" his mother asked.

Seth grimaced irritably.

"Oh, it *is* all fits and starts," she said. "Are you going to write about your father?"

"Tell me about Yale now," Seth insisted.

She drew on her cigarette and exhaled slowly. "A member of the library board will be here to dinner," she said. "I take it you want them to have his papers."

"What makes you think that?" Seth said.

His mother shrugged her shoulders and appealed to Gary. "Wouldn't you have thought that?" she said, and then turned to Seth. "You didn't want me to withhold any of them."

Seth thought: I'll wait, I won't say anything for a moment. Instead, he said, "Is this what you wrote that you wanted to discuss with me? Did you want my opinion?"

"Not just your opinion, Seth," she said, and looked down. "I won't do anything without your approval. I can't."

He was ashamed. He looked away and saw that Gary admired his mother. Gary winked at him and nodded. His mother carefully flicked the ashes of her cigarette. Seth said, "That's all right, mother. I'm sure whatever you do will be fine."

"That's sweet of you, dear," she said, and finally looked up. When she smiled her lined face became young and her blue eyes shone. Seth remembered how playful she could be. "We'll go over everything together."

"I want to, I want to," Seth said. "Gary let the news out of the bag—"

"Oh, Christ," Gary said. "Sorry." He looked at Seth's mother. "I don't mean to curse so much."

She was amused. "The crowd we went with in our youth was a plainspoken one."

"Mother," Seth said, and waited for her to turn to him. "They want me to write a book about father. His biography. A very fine editor proposed it yesterday."

Her eyes stayed on him but her thoughts were elsewhere.

"Isn't it wonderful?" he said.

Her nod was almost imperceptible. She put her elbows on the table, and leaned her face into her hands. When was it, he thought, he had seen her take this stance? It was important. Then he heard her sob. When he was a boy. The last tantrum he threw. His stomach constricted. He leaned forward a little over the table. "Mother," he said quietly.

She tried to get up without pushing the chair back and it clattered to the floor. She brought her hands down to pick it up but did not manage it. Her eyes had reddened and her face was wet. Her jaw trembled. "Oh, Jimmy, Jimmy!" she exclaimed. She leaned on the table with one hand and tried to control her chin. Seth put out a hand for her but she did not see it. He tried to guess whether she was moved to happiness or fear.

"Forgive me," she said. "Oh, I'm so happy for Jimmy."

Seth bit his lips and immediately felt tears. Good tears, they flowed easily.

Under her brows she looked toward Gary. "I'm sorry, young man. I didn't mean to make a scene."

"Oh no," Gary protested. "It's beautiful."

She turned abruptly to the sink and threw cold water on her face. She tore off a paper towel from a gadget above her and roughly wiped her face. "The good times have come back," she said, "but Jimmy isn't here for them." She shook herself and went to Seth. He did not hide his tears. She placed a hand on his head and he felt it like a blessing, a thrill that went through him to his knees. They began to tremble under the table. He reached up an arm and hugged her waist.

"I'm going to write a good book for him," he said. Her hand came down and covered his mouth, and he looked up at her, feeling wonderfully like a child. When she took her hand away, he added, "I swear."

"I'm sure you will," she said, her voice clear again. "But let's not say anything more for now or we'll jinx it."

"Ho-ho!" Gary exclaimed. "Just like my mother."

Chapter 8

They sat at the kitchen table until they finished the tall pot of coffee. They reminisced, sometimes prodded by Gary, sometimes encouraged by his exclamations. When they touched on the subject of the biography or the papers, it was only in a glancing way. Seth knew that soon he and his mother would go into the downstairs study and begin to look at the papers. He was not in a hurry. It seemed to him that from now on everything would be right between them. This new face they presented to Gary (Seth wished Mathilde were there to see them) and Gary's delight and groans were an augury of what was to come: the book was written and it was a success.

"And Hemingway?" Gary asked, for there had been a pause and he was afraid their talk was done. "You must have known him."

Seth stopped himself from replying. He must let his mother speak from now on. Everything she had to say had value for him; it was material for the book.

She nodded, smiled, and flicked ashes into the ashtray judiciously before she replied. "He was a friend, he really was. We were younger than he, he was already famous when we met, and Jimmy did not compete with him in any way. So he could, indeed, be Papa to us."

"Did you read about yourself in his biography?" Seth asked, unable to hold back any longer. She shook her head slowly. Seth had not read the book, only looked up his father in the index and found, to his surprise, a listing for his mother as well. "It said you—you, mother—were the only person who could stand up to Hemingway and get away with it when he was in a bullying mood. Down in Key West this was and you were described as *Little Trick Evergood!*"

103

"He was an indefatigable man, that biographer," she replied, "but I managed to avoid him."

"Why?" Seth asked. "Why didn't you talk to him? Will I have that kind of trouble with people who knew father?"

"Oh no, dear," she answered, but the words were no sooner said than her face belied them. She compressed her lips and then took a long puff of her cigarette. "Those last twenty years weren't happy ones," she said, and shook her head slightly in Seth's direction to tell him he must not take that to heart. "After we took jobs at Calvin we did not see anyone or travel anywhere. That was the way Jimmy wanted it, and I've become used to it. Jimmy had just died when Papa's biographer first got in touch with me. I don't know how he tracked me down. I did not feel like talking about the past." She got up with a sigh, put a hand on Seth's shoulder, and smiled. "But it's been awfully good to talk today."

Seth thought: I must make a note of that. "I'm going upstairs to get my notebook," he said to her, "and then I'll meet you in father's study."

"I'm going out to the garden," Gary said.

She called to Seth as he walked out of the kitchen, but she also meant Gary to hear. "Seth, do you have to leave tomorrow morning?" she asked. "There are so many things to go over. You *are* your father's literary executor, don't forget."

"I am!" he exclaimed. He stood in the doorway to the hall and leaned against the door. "Oh my, oh my," he added. "I did not know. You didn't tell me."

"Of course, Seth," she said. "It was in his will."

He had not read it; he could not remember why. "Father did that?" he said; the fact crowded everything out. "He never discussed it with me, he never told me." He felt weak with happiness. "He gave me his gold pen, that must have meant—did he tell you he was going to make me his literary executor?"

She shook her head. "He left me everything. Well, the little there was and he specified that all the income from his work was mine. But what is to happen with it is for you to decide. So, must you leave tomorrow morning?" Seth had forgotten Gary was there until now. This was his chance, and he looked at him quickly, appraisingly.

"We'll see," he said, for Gary's face was in profile and he could not tell what he thought.

"You could come directly back from Vermont," his mother urged. She turned to Gary. "I'd love to see more of Gary, too."

Seth saw that Gary's grin was solely for her. Gary kept his eyes averted. "We'll see," Seth repeated, and felt cowardly that he did not say yes. Going up the stairs he muttered, Damn, damn, damn. Gary should have let him off—he should have volunteered it. Why had he allowed himself be drawn into this? Why didn't he think of himself first? Why were they doing it, anyway? He and Gary had never discussed it in a tough-minded, political way.

He picked up his sober brown-tweed jacket from the flowered chintz bedspread and removed the notebook pen from the inner pocket. His father's pen. Since he was unobserved, he gripped it with his whole hand and brought it to his heart. He tried to remember if he had actually ever seen him writing with it. No. Only lying on top of the composition notebook out in his corner of the grounds behind the cedars. He could not recall how his father looked. He closed his eyes, but his memory would not yield the image. He wished he had called him dad, not father. It was his mother's fault: that southern training Grandmother Morgan had passed on to her. Mother, not mom, not mommy; nor *maman* as Amelie would say.

Mother. How could she not have reminded him earlier that he was father's literary executor? It was almost seven years since he had died. Hadn't she given thought to his work? He immediately thought: did I? He had never read his journalism, and only the opening pages of the book on Sarah Orne Jewett. Father deprecated his work and I believed him, but she should not have. For the first time he suspected that she preferred it that way. A kind of revenge. For what? For having made her live out the rest of her life here, teaching at Calvin. She had just said, That was the way Jimmy wanted it. Which meant that it was not her way. She was Grandmother Morgan's heir, after all. Could he blame her? He thought: my political beliefs are just a kind of jumpiness. Flightiness, Grandmother Morgan would have said. The old bitch, I wish I could have known her.

Money. That was it. Yale's money must have aroused her interest once more. And she *had* to confer with him. He chuckled and the sound startled him—it was just like hers. There must be agreements to sign and she did not dare pretend to them that she was literary executor. Yale must've asked for proof of her authority. How do I know that is all I get under his will? I never read it. What else has she been holding back? And all that hesitation about whether to turn over the papers because some of the correspondence is hers as well. She is bargaining for something. He made a turn around the room. She is bargaining for something. What?

He went down the stairs slowly, numb with thinking about all this, and was forced to return to his room because he had forgotten the notebook. The second time he descended the stairs, he thought: nonsense, she's my mother and she loved him. She was so happy when she heard my news that she cried. You are a fool, Seth Evergood, he told himself, and jumped down the last two steps, as he once always did.

In the study was confirmation of his good sense. She sat to one side of the files, leaving her father's swivel chair at the desk for him, and she held out a sheaf of papers in one hand. "I thought you would like to read a copy of your father's will," she said in greeting. "The original is at our lawyer's, with mine."

He sat in the swivel chair, and his feet barely touched the floor. "Oh, that's all right," he said.

She made him take it. "It's all in legal language, except the paragraph about you. It's obvious that your father wrote that."

He skimmed the first two pages. His house, his pension, his life insurance. At the top of the third page: *To my good son, Seth Morgan Evergood, nothing but an onerous task: to act as Literary Executor of the mess of marginal notes and tentative essays and journals that I have penned during my retirement from the Fourth Estate. They are but reflex twitchings and only merit consignment to the burning pyre of my remains, but since the passing moments devoted to them were robbed from the parental time that had been better spent with him, they are truly, truly his their fate to decide. My legal amanuensis urges clarity about this: my son is Literary Executor of both my published and unpublished work, including correspondence and journals. I urge upon my son one of the meanings of the verb from which his new title derives: to put them out of their misery. He can be certain that whatsoever he decides my love for him remains untouched.*

He read it twice. The second time to calm his feelings. He needed another Librium. But when he came again to the phrase "my love for him" he shuddered with the need to cry. He suddenly saw his father's face: the elegant nose, the watchful eyes with one eyebrow arched receptively, and the thin lips turned down at the corners. When he smiled, only half of his mouth curled up, apologetically as if it were the best he could do. Seth looked at his mother and smiled at her in the same way.

He said, "He believed I should burn his manuscripts. I can't do that!"

"Of course, dear." She clasped her hands like a young girl. "There was a diffident, modest side to his nature and it gained on him in later years. He did not believe in his talent."

"Well, I believe in it," he said fiercely, and saw that his mother looked at him eagerly. He thought: I am going to read every line he has written. "Did you think that I didn't?"

"What do you mean?" she said, straightening her back.

All the anger he had felt upstairs returned to him. "That I would burn his manuscripts. Did you think I would do what he says?"

She half closed her eyes. "I have been waiting all these years for you to show some interest," she said, enunciating each word carefully. She pressed her lips together to keep from saying more.

"You kept me from knowing," he said. "You knew I hadn't read his will. I didn't know I was his literary executor—you didn't want me to know. I thought it was all in your hands. You didn't involve me. Why?"

"Seth," she began and then held her hands up as if to ward him off and evenly spaced each word that followed. "You never said a word that showed the slightest interest in your father's work." She got up and smoothed her dress. "Not a word."

He came to the decision that had been forming in his mind since lunch. "Yale may not release a single paper until my book is published. Even if it means you do not get your money now."

"Money!" Her deep voice became guttural. "You are going to have to decide whether it's money that interests me or—" She waved a hand at the files and desk. "Suppressing his work." She sat down. "Why do you think I've kept it all, every scrap?"

He stared at her, his thoughts at a dead end. "I want all the corre-spondence," he said finally, "whether addressed to you or not."

She placed one hand on the other and both on top of her crossed legs, and tapped her foot. "I shall have to think about that," she said lightly, as if she had found him out and were now daring him. "I don't know that you can be trusted. If you act like a child, I shall have to treat you as one."

He slapped the desk. "That won't be new! Ever since I grew up you have treated me like a child. But not before. Not before, when I did need to be treated like a child. Then I was shunted off, abandoned to anyone that came along. Yes, abandoned!"

"And your father?" she said. "Did he abandon you?"

"Father had his work to do," he said quickly, to erase the thought she tried to insinuate in his mind. "It was your duty—you were my mother." But the thought reached him and he added, "OK, Father abandoned me too but it is not abandonment to fight the good fight. Father fought for everyone, including me. He can't be judged that way."

She studied her hands for a while, and when she looked up, said, "Seth, I'm beginning to think you're not the best person to write about him. He wasn't heroic."

"You've always cut me down," he replied. Now he knew where the disheartenment had come from, that mood that came upon him at home and made him finally eager to go back to school. "And now Father too."

"Oh Seth," she said. "Neither of us means this."

But he had thought of an answer and he could not suppress it. "Whatever you think, I *am* going to be writing about him," he said. "And about you too."

"How disgusting!" she said. Her mouth hung open and she gasped and closed it and then her jaw slowly dropped. Her face had gone pale and now it flushed so red that her eyes disappeared. She moaned with a long exhalation and brought a hand to her breast.

"Mother," he whispered, and leaned toward her as he had done earlier. "Mother!" He thought: it does not help to be sorry. He reached for her hand but did not manage it. She leaned back in her chair and threw her head back. She breathed deeply and looked at the ceiling.

"You're right, Mother," he said desperately. "I didn't mean it." And waited.

Her hands relaxed their grip on the arms of the chair. She slowly sat up. She did not look at him and after a while he gave up trying to catch her eye. He thought: I must sit here quietly and everything will be all right. They heard Gary whistling in the garden, short, breathless whistles, as if he were trying to get an animal's attention. Seth half rose from his chair and looked through the French windows. Gary was down at the bottom of the lawn, his back to the house, looking up at one of the cedars. Seth sat down again.

She sighed. "This Jewish boy has more sense of what's due me than you do," she said.

He smiled with relief. She would not have allowed herself to describe Gary thus if she had not forgiven him. I am her son, that's what she's saying.

"I want you to tell me what to do," he said eagerly.

She got up. "No, Seth," she said resignedly. "I'm going up to my room now." She was calm, and there was no edge to her voice. "Everything is here. In the center drawers are the keys to the files. It's all for you to decide. His letters to me are also there. Everything. You may have them. I had better stay out of it from now on."

He swiveled toward her as she walked to the hall. "I don't want it that way, mother," he said. "I want you to work closely with me."

She shook her head. "No, Seth," she repeated. "You're probably right that I treat you like a child. I can't help it, you *are* my child. So it's best I stay out of temptation's way." She smiled and half turned to leave. "In the future I'll treat you like a child about other matters, minor matters. Agreed?"

He tried to nod like a little boy, to please her.

"Russell Sargent of the Yale Library Board will be here tonight," she said. "You make whatever arrangements with him that you think best." She hesitated. "Yes, you handle it."

"But I need you in all this," Seth said, trying to hold her in the room. She waited. He added quickly, "It would be good if I could work here, rather than at the apartment."

She pressed her lips together, thinking his proposal over. "I really don't know why Mathilde didn't give me the news on the phone," she said. "It would have given me a chance to think things over before you arrived."

"You see why it would be better for me to come here, don't you?" he said. He got up and took a step toward her. "It's home for me. It's where this book should take shape."

"You really feel that, dear?" She stood straight, her shoulders squared, and she half closed her eyes as if she feared his reply would be in the negative. He hunched his shoulders and swayed a little, like a small boy, and nodded with fast motions, happily. She clasped her hands at her waist and returned his nod. He thought: I have won her back; and looked up at her and smiled. She added, "I must speak to Mathilde," and he knew that the blame for their quarrel had been shifted.

He stepped back and appealed to her, with a wave of one hand, to come back and sit down. She shook her head flirtatiously. She said, "You see why you should stay more than one day? Russell Sargent had mentioned something about sending over a graduate student to start cataloging the papers before they're moved."

"I'd like to," he said, and suddenly decided to tell her why. It might frighten her, but she would believe him. He motioned her toward him and walked to her at the same time. "Don't let Gary know that I've told you," he whispered. "We're taking someone across the border to Canada. A deserter. I've done it before. There's no real danger, don't worry."

She was so pleased that her eyes almost closed completely. When she opened them, her smile remained. "You forget that you come from a family that practically had a monopoly on the Underground Railroad in northwestern Connecticut," she said. She took his hand to hold him by her. "Now it's my turn to confess. I put up a young man in your old bedroom last February." She let go of him and made a face at him.

He thought of another story. He said, "It may not be a deserter this time. It may be Jean Genet. Yes. You know he's been here making speeches for the Panthers. Well, he entered illegally through Canada—they must know but they haven't bothered him—and now he has to go back the same way."

"I don't know that I like the Black Panthers—they've caused Yale so much trouble," she said, but she shook her head dismissing the thought. "I don't care. It's like the good times again. It makes you *feel* again, feel alive."

He wished Gary were there to hear her. "You're Grandmother Morgan's heir, all right," he said.

Her face became serious. "Seth, I hope you've not told Mathilde," she said. "She's not up to such things, poor dear."

He shook his head. "Poor Matty," he said. "I've wanted to talk to you about her."

"You should not talk to me about her, Seth," she said generously, as if forgiving her faults. "She's a good person. I'm sure you will work things out."

She clasped her hands against her flat belly and waited. They were silent a moment. He went to the desk and sat down. He leaned his head on his hand and his elbow on the desk, and he looked pensively at the files. "I can't wait to get started," he said.

It was right to go on to Vermont with Gary. It was in the mood of the book. He thought of his father's last years. "Mother, one of the things I'll want to talk to you about is why father stopped being political."

She nodded slowly but did not reply.

He opened the center drawer and took the ring with two keys.

"There's one for each set of files," she said quickly.

He got up. "Don't go until I check," he said. "I want to see the journals first. Are they here?"

She pointed to the file closest to the desk. There was a solemn look on her face. He felt like telling her that he understood. When he turned back to the file, she said, "The double drawer at the bottom."

The first key he selected worked. He grabbed the handle of the drawer and pulled. The metal groaned, but the drawer rolled back. There they were. Four neat piles of identical composition notebooks reaching to the top of drawer. He thought: if he had lived longer, there would have been no more room. Then he asked, "Are they all here?"

"Seth," she began, and the sound of her voice made him turn round from his squatting position. "I *was* holding something back. You suspected that a while ago—I'm so transparent—but it was not what you thought."

He stared at her but did not see her.

"One of his notebooks," she said, and she quickly brought a hand to her hair and smoothed it back. "So foolish of me. You would notice the break."

"You destroyed it!" he said, and he heard his voice sound as guttural as hers. "Oh mother—"

"No, no, I only removed it," she replied. "It's upstairs in my room. I'll get it." She moved jerkily, her body stiff with anxiety. She turned to him. "It is the one thing I want to talk to you about. You should not use it, you really should not."

"It's always best to tell the truth," he said. He sat down on the floor and pointed a hand toward the ceiling to urge her to get the notebook. "We'll talk about it."

As soon as she left the study, he knew what it was. A love affair. During the war or after? Or maybe frequently. They must have both been passionate people. He leaned an arm on the open drawer and said to himself, Women, women, she's a woman after all. She wants their life together to be what it appeared on the surface. They were always together—wasn't that enough? Except during the civil war. That must have been when. The countess who had worked for the Republic? Some militia girl?

Or perhaps it was she who had the affair? She had been busy with the press section, she had arranged for tours of the front by famous personages, had set up press and newsreel interviews of them. Paul Robeson? Pablo Neruda? Archibald MacLeish? So many possibilities. Even young Jack Kennedy had paid a visit. But it was more likely an affair of father's, he thought and picked up the notebook his hand had been caressing. His father had written his name in the rectangular window on the cover, and on the line for subject the dates the entries covered: *Jan.-June 1945*. Roosevelt's death. Seth smiled: I still think only of political matters. "Now there is romantic interest," he whispered to himself. Ten years ago, it might have been a shock, as when at fourteen he had walked into the beach shower and seen his father naked. But this was perfect for the book. He heard his mother's steps on the stairs, and turned toward the open door with an understanding smile.

She held a composition notebook, identical with the others, to her breast. She did not see his smile until she held it out to him. "Oh no, Seth," she said. "It's not that."

"Not what!" he said, laughing.

"You'll see," she said, and looked at the notebook in his hand as if she might take it back. She glanced toward the windows on the patio. "He was visited by the FBI. In 1949."

"Those were the days," Seth said. Still holding the notebook, he got up and sat at the desk. "Everyone was."

"You think it's understandable?" she said, her voice beginning to regain its natural tone. "But he seems ashamed of it." She opened the notebook for him to the third entry. He saw her hand tremble a little. She added, "He refers to himself as 'we,' sometimes he calls himself James Evergood, but only when they come to visit, not at other times."

"But what's wrong with that?" Seth said. "Why do you want to . . .?"

She nodded inconsequentially. "They tormented him about me," she said. "That's why he cooperated." She straightened her shoulders. "Oh, this is all foolishness. you can leave it out. It was just those years. . . . I'm going upstairs to lie down. You read it. You don't have to discuss it."

She was gone before he could call her back. He did not want to; it was his father he wanted to call back to the vision he had of him until a moment ago: a man who fought the good fight and retreated to the private life when there was no longer anything pure to fight for. He had begun to love him yesterday and he now feared the notebook lying open before him. He thought: maybe it was the book about him that I loved. I'll tell it all, he decided; it will be an even better story. But what a down ending to a book that he had hoped would inspire the Movement! Should he leave it out? he asked himself, and agreed, as if with an immanent observer, that he could find the answer only in the notebook written with the pen he had inherited.

20 April 1949. We were setting the poles, once young larches oozing sap but now stripped and dry and smooth after four years of use, at three-foot intervals along the rows of peas. The peas had pushed their way but one inch above ground and James Evergood was thinking he need not begin the embroidery of string from pole to pole for a few days yet. Trick was at school for the afternoon. After the poles were set, we planned to write in our journal about Ramon

Sender, but that had to be postponed and we have only now, while she prepares dinner, taken up the notebook. Not to pen some thoughts about that doppelganger of ours, a man whom the Civil War also displaced and desolated, but to recount the visit of the Feds. Not recount, for we have not, and will not, tell this story, even to Trick. Especially to Trick. We sit at our desk now, perhaps more with the intent of hiding from her the physical vestiges of the disturbance their visit has caused than with the desire to write about it.

The Feds did not come to the house but around it. Two young men in business suits, one with an expression of greeting on his face and a hand reaching into his inner jacket pocket and the other staring with the bullishness of a football tackle. Our immediate thought was that they had lost their way and needed advice. We may have even begun a statement to aid them when the younger one (we do not know that he was younger; he was simply pleasanter in appearance) said, "James Evergood?" and as we nodded, withdrew his hand from his jacket pocket. It travelled an arc in front of us and stopped only long enough to reveal, cupped within it, a badge bound in leather. "We are from the Federal Bureau of Investigation," he said, and the badge disappeared before the sentence was done.

It is small comfort that after the first moments of stunned silence from us that we began to recognize the technique of their performance. We had read about this; indeed, the two men at our embassy in Paris who had interviewed us about our request for a passport, on our way back—ah, the way back!—from Spain, had a similar intent. One appeals, the other denounces; one cajoles, the other threatens. It did not work in Paris, but it is no longer 1938. It may be that they are better trained, but it is more likely that we know our role better. We do not need their questions nor their accusations: we know we are guilty.

We were seated on the patio before James Evergood became himself again. (We shall never be ourselves again.) Rather, it was because we were James Evergood and not the Lieutenant Colonel at command headquarters that we had not known how to make short shrift of them. "The Bureau knows that you were idealistic," the pleasant one said. "You thought you were fighting for democracy, right?"

Before we could reply the Tackle growled. "He was working for the Reds," he said. "That makes him a Red."

The pleasant one directed a look at me which I was to interpret as apologetic. "That is what we would like know," he said. "I hope you will tell us."

There seemed something for us to say at last. "Surely, sir, you must know that I was not a Communist."

"Communist!" the Tackle interjected. "Only Commies say Communist." He cleared his throat preparatory to expectorating but never spat. "We say Commies or Reds."

"Let's not get into that," the pleasant one argued, and the Tackle subsided. "We are interested in whether you worked with them. Did you know Ercole Ercoli?"

We knew who that was but waited. The pleasant one also waited and the Tackle moved in his seat. "Perhaps you knew him under another name?" the pleasant one asked.

"I think that was Togliatti," we said, "but I never met him. At least, I don't think I met him."

"Did you or didn't you?" the Tackle said.

The pleasant one shook his head. "Think about it, we can talk again," he said. "What about Josip Broz?"

This was all book stuff, easy enough to discuss, nothing which could land us or Togliatti or Tito in danger. "It has never been proven," we said, "that Marshal Tito ever visited Spain."

"Perhaps you can prove it," the pleasant one urged.

There was no reply we could make to that.

"Come on, we're wasting our time," the Tackle said. "He's a dyed-in-the-wool Commie. Let's talk to Trick—she was the one who was running around with all the international agents."

"We don't want to do that, do we, Mr. Evergood?" said the pleasant one. "You both teach at Calvin?"

We nodded. The Tackle did not let us speak. "For that kind of small-time stuff, you can turn him over to the committee," he said to his colleague. "I for one am willing to let him get away with their little smarty-farty spying if—but only if—he helps us with the big stuff."

"Are you willing?" the pleasant one asked us. "That seems like a good bargain to me."

Transparent, any reader will say, though we are not to have any readers. Trick, my son Seth? Will they know someday? There will be time for that, as my interlocutors say, time to decide. Trick goes about the business of making dinner innocently, and innocent she shall remain. We will it. They promised to leave before she returned home, and they did. Whom to discuss this with? Our family lawyers? All upright New Englanders, they will, undoubtedly, say that we should clear ourselves. They will take for granted that we did no spying. We shall have to say, But I did not spy for anyone, I simply served as a soldier. All the more reason to clear yourself. They will cough discreetly and add, Keep Calvin's headmaster informed. They'll stand by you. So long as it stays out of the newspapers. They have the parents to consider.

Everything is lost before the defense begins. All honor, that is. The wolves must be given a carcass to rend and flaunt. Who is the toughest? They can yowl at the internationals but they cannot claw them. What case can they make for Togliatti and Tito and Malraux and Sartre and Ehrenburg and del Vayo that they have not made for themselves? It is not with them that they need our help. Whom in the list that they ticked off? The Eislers, Kantorovich, Brecht? The Hollywood crowd and the Group Theater? "That Joan Crawford sent you an ambulance, right?" said the Tackle. The Abraham Lincoln Brigade and the League of American Writers and the Screen Writers Guild and Albert Einstein. Our Fed friends are interested in them all.

James Evergood talked: yes, no, I don't believe so, I don't remember, perhaps. We sit here and think of Papa. Have they visited him in Cuba? Did his *cojones* retreat into his body? Did they ask him about James Evergood? Did they sit by the pool or did they go out on the boat? Did he discover, as we have, what a useful, cowardly, base word is *perhaps*? Perhaps. Comrade Stalin did not let our Russian comrades when they returned home reply *perhaps*. It is probable that they began—first gave way—with *perhaps* and then remembered, with the help of a friendly Fed and an unfriendly one, how they plotted to turn over the Socialist Motherland to the Nazis. How civilized is the United States of America! They sat in jail. We sit here and the next time it will be in New Haven.

"I don't think it's a good idea if we come here again," the pleasant
one explained. He winked and we winced, and yet we shook hands.
"I'll give you a ring and you come to our office. You'll think of some
excuse."

The Tackle remained unfriendly to the end. He did not shake
hands; we were spared that. "You got a lot of homework to do," he
said.

Comrade Stalin will help us. He was a great mentor, a great
teacher, a great patriot, a great lousy son of a bitch. Comrade Stalin—
dinner.

Seth thought: how did he get out of it? The next entry, two days
later, began, *Spring is inexorable*, and he was back to the first person
singular. He must read it again. There were things he did not understand and others that seemed funny: Those FBI agents acted out roles
so laughable that in his mind they became the cops of the Mack
Sennett comedies he had seen in revival at art houses. He had to sort
that out. But not the fear, he knew about fear. His father wrote in his
journal to keep it under control. That was his Librium. All this made
his father real and small, like himself: he was no longer a God to apos-
trophize. He shuddered with the thrill.

He held the notebook open with his hand and read between his
spread fingers the sentence that began *James Evergood talked*. He
thought: he must have gone to New Haven and I shall go to Vermont
to balance the scales. I'll do it for him. He closed the notebook; he
would not read any more now. He had made his decision and he would
have to bear the suspense for now of not learning more, in order to
remain true to his resolve.

Gary called him. He stood beyond the French windows smiling,
with his arms held out as if he might fly. Seth placed the notebook in
the center drawer and closed it quickly. He thought: shall I tell Gary?

"What a place, what a place!" Gary said. "The Jews think they
know how to live, but it's you WASPs who really do!"

Chapter 9

In a moment, while he was sitting on the patio with Gary, the headaches began again. Like tiny explosions. He felt first the knot at the back of his neck tightening, and then the pain that gathered there flash through his head to his eyes. He closed them, and the tension disappeared until the knot began to tauten again. He thought: amphetamine will take it away. He should go upstairs and take one, but he preferred to listen to Gary speculate whether Fidel's talk of putting Che's hands on display in Havana meant that the Cuban revolution was hardening in the same way as the Russian. Better these ills we know of than the ones that are bound to come when I'm alone upstairs. It pleased him that he was thinking like Gary.

"I see that you smile at my fears," Gary said. "Lying there like an indolent bourgeois in a Chekhov play. But it's the hardening process we have to watch out for. In ourselves too. You could say that I was worrying about it all along and it took being cuckolded—"

"Ho-ho, as you say," Seth interrupted.

"Seth, I can't stand it that Trudy let Mackey fuck her!" He leaned forward, his elbows on his knees, and closed his eyes hard. "I can't stand it. And with an old man too." He made a fist of his right hand and struck his knee with it. He began, unaccountably, to laugh. "I have such a nice, clean, circumcised cock!"

Seth laughed too. The headache had not resumed for a little while. He remembered his recollection of his father naked in the beach shower. His father's penis had seemed startlingly long, his scrotum full. In time his became like that but his body had not grown. He thought: John Keats.

"You know, I was inside looking at my father's journals," he said, to distract Gary, "and I remembered seeing my father naked. He was soaping his cock and pulling the skin back to get it clean."

Gary's eyebrows went up. "No shit!" he said. "I've never seen my father's. My God, I firmly believe he doesn't have a cock." He laughed, grateful to Seth for changing the subject. "Not a nice Jewish father like him."

Gary threw him a cigarette, then the matches, and they stretched their legs and smoked. After a while, Seth asked, "Gary, why are we doing it?"

Gary looked at him from under his brows, and his face became serious. "Vermont?" he said.

Seth nodded. "It could be dangerous. We're taking a risk." He drew on his cigarette. "And yet we didn't discuss it. I just said yes and I was thinking, Did I do it because I didn't want you think I was chicken? Is that why you said yes too?"

Gary scratched his head like a puzzled boy. "You think we shouldn't do it?"

"No, no, it's too late for that," Seth said, and felt the knot beginning to form. "We can't let them down. I was just talking, buddy."

"It seems unreal here, doesn't it?" Gary said, and looked around at the flower bed along one side of the patio, the bushes in bloom at the ends of the lawn, and the wall of cedars. "Too nice, too engaging, like Beethoven for Lenin."

Seth put a hand to the back of his neck. "I mean, is it as serious a struggle? Is it going to get anywhere? Look at those kids who got caught yesterday. They'll go to jail, that's all. I ask myself, are we helping them to play games?"

"Do you mean, are the material conditions ripe, comrade?" Gary joked. He sat up and leaned his hands on his knees. "Christ, I don't know. If you analyze the material conditions, like the Communists want you to, it's never, never going to be the right time for revolution."

Seth nodded to show he was listening, and leaned back to be prepared for the flash of pain that was bound to come.

"You know why I worry about the Cuban revolution hardening?" Gary said, not expecting an answer. "Because they never asked themselves questions before. Think of it. Some eighty guys, younger than you and me. They get together in Mexico City, live mostly together in apartments like communes, cook a lot of spaghetti for cheap meals, and do a little training like the kids who go to the rifle ranges in Connecticut. They get enough money to buy a broken-down boat from some Texan who had called it *Granma* after his grandmother, and they announce to the world that they're going to invade Cuba!"

Gary got to his feet and pointed to the cedars as if they were the island of Cuba. "They even give the date and then take off. There's a storm, they all get sick, throwing up all over the place, and they arrive two days late and at the wrong place. They come ashore in a swamp and don't know where they are. The first peasant they meet acts as their guide and later denounces them to the Batista forces. In an open cane field they're attacked by the air force and massacred. Twelve come out of it alive and in ones and twos head for the mountain that was supposed to be their rendezvous. Fidel gets there first and waits for them and they straggle up, some without shoes and without rifles. And when those twelve miserable bastards are finally all there, you know what Fidel said to them? He said, The days of the dictatorship are numbered!"

Seth clapped and Gary collapsed on his chair laughing. Seth said, "At that point in my lecture I always ask the audience, Would you take them seriously? The Cuban CP said they were adventurists and the French CP called their kids *une petite minuscule*."

"One won, the other lost," Gary said. "*Oy vey.*"

They were silent a moment. Seth felt better. Being with Gary, he thought, always did that. He said, "So that's where we are, clapping for Tinker Bell."

Gary nodded. "It's as good as dialectical materialism."

Seth made a fist and held it up. "On to Vermont."

"*Oy vey,*" Gary said.

They looked at one another like generals committed to a major engagement with raw troops. Gary snapped his fingers. "Just before I fell asleep last night I had an important thought," he announced. "I was thinking about the Fillmore and it occurred to me. John Brown was mad but he was right."

Seth nodded. He suddenly felt ashamed that he was not in the study looking through the rest of the notebook. What happened when his father went to New Haven?

"But who wants to be moldering?" Gary said. "I want to be molting." He got up and filled his lungs with air. "I want to turn into a beautiful butterfly!"

Seth got up and heard the window open and thought: Mother. It was she at her sitting room window.

Gary said, looking up, "Christ, I'm sorry. It's so beautiful here that I guess I've been making too much noise."

"Not at all," she said in a level, cool voice. "I just want to see Seth for a moment."

Seth was at the bottom of the stairs in the hall before he realized that he had responded like a guilty boy caught at play. He thought: what do I tell her? He bounded up the stairs. The sitting room door was open. She was seated her dainty escritoire.

"Really, Seth," she said. She shook her head slowly and crossed her legs and then kept her face averted. "I was here waiting."

"I'm sorry," he said. "I went out to think it over and Gary came up to talk—no, no, I didn't discuss it with him." It made him righteous and assured to be able to deny the accusation he read in her eyes. "I said I had to *think* it over. I wasn't about to talk about it."

She sighed. "Ah, then you agree?"

"About what?" he replied unthinkingly.

"Seth, Seth, what is your mind on?" she complained. "Stop darting about like a child. Mathilde has made you flighty." She held up a hand. "I'm sorry, I'm upset. I meant, do you agree the passage should be suppressed?

"I don't know," he said.

"About the FBI," she explained.

"I know, I know," he said.

She waited.

"What was so terrible?" he said. "The FBI must have made thousands of visits in those days. So they visited father too." He stopped; she too must have read: *James Evergood talked.* "There was only that one day. Were there any more?"

"All in that notebook," she said.

"Did he go to New Haven?" he asked in a low voice.

She nodded. He sat down on the edge of the chaise covered in flowered silk. "He cooperated?" he asked. He thought: it could be a book with a tragic ending, it's the times that were to blame.

"Oh Seth, why didn't you read it!" she said.

"I'm going to," he said. "Just forget about it for now."

"We can't just leave it like that," she said. "I have to know now what you mean to do. It's not right that it's all for you to decide. I'm involved."

"Right, right," he said. "Father never went to Washington, he never appeared as a witness anywhere . . . I don't think his name ever came up. I would've heard. Isn't that so?"

She nodded.

"Well, then you can't say he cooperated," he argued. "He didn't do any of the things that the others did."

"He didn't," she said with finality, then pressed her lips together and added, "He told them he would not appear anywhere in public and talk about anyone. Your father could be quite firm."

"But that's wonderful!" Seth said, and sprang to his feet. "He didn't cooperate at all."

"Seth, let's destroy that notebook," she said.

"But why! It's perfect this way," he replied. "Don't you see? A moment of weakness and then his old battling self comes to life again. He lives the rest of his life quietly—oh God, I need not have driven myself mad. I had only to read on." He sat down on the chaise gladly this time. "He fought like a true soldier for the Republic and then without ostentation, without publicity, for the same decent principles. He refused to be a stool pigeon."

His mother lit a cigarette, and when she had drawn on it, she said, "I want the notebook destroyed."

He smiled patronizingly, as she might have. "That's shortsighted," he said, sure he could make her understand. "We don't want a Pollyannaish portrait of him. All this makes him real. The important thing is he did not cooperate."

She blew out a long gust of smoke. "He made a bargain," she said. "He would tell them anything they wanted to use as they pleased but he would never repeat any of it in public."

"And they agreed?" Seth said.

"Who knows?" she said. "It was a one-sided bargain and he meant to stick to it. I'm sure he would have. You know that too, Seth. But he went to New Haven—oh, I don't know how many times. I thought it was to do research on Sarah Orne Jewett." She smoothed back her hair. "Destroy the notebook."

"Why didn't you?" he said impatiently. He almost yelled it. "I didn't have to know. It would have been very simple."

She looked at him blankly, stunned, unable to think of a reply. She shrugged, she looked at her hands, she smoothed her hair again. "I didn't think of it," she said. "I'm not used to this introspection, this questioning, not even with your father." She raised her eyebrows; she knew why now. "Those notebooks were mine. They contain all the life we led together and did not share because we are the way we are. They're all I have had to live with these last six years, but I'm through with them now—do with them what you want."

He thought: this is a maneuver. "You never told me I was his literary executor," he said. "You wanted to keep me out of his notebooks even before you read them. You always kept me out of your lives. You didn't let him be a father to me as he wanted. You. And you're still trying to control him."

"Seth, you don't know anything about life," she said, and he was surprised at her calmness. "I don't know much either, but I know what it is to be a woman. A wife, in any case. You think we get our way, that we wind our husbands around our little finger, all that nonsense. It's not like that at all." She paused and then said slowly, "We lived the life your father wanted."

He squinted to keep from crying. "You're telling me that he didn't want me either."

"Either!" she exclaimed. She lit a cigarette with the butt of the old one. "Have it your way. In a year I'll be sixty. I'm not going to teach anymore. I'm going to use the little money we've always had from Grandmother Morgan and live the way we could have if your father had not insisted on our retreating here and working as teachers. It's going to be an effort." Her chin trembled, and she stopped speaking until she had it under control. "These notebooks have kept me in thrall. I've come to believe I still have to do penance."

He was ashamed to think: she's going to spend it all. "I'm sorry," he said. "I need you to help me with this book. We're just talking now. I didn't mean to act like a child. All right?"

She pulled her chin in. "It's too painful to live over again."

"Of course, of course," he conceded. He thought: it must be worse for her than for me. But it was no good getting bogged down in that; they must come to an agreement: she might have a legal right to stop the book. "Nothing is written yet. I have not done the research. Maybe the book can stop at the end of the civil war."

"But that's when the notebooks began," she said. "There are beautiful things in them. His final philosophy of living. Why he wrote the book on Sarah Orne Jewett—the quietly observed life, intensely lived, full of epiphanies." She leaned an arm on the escritoire and gestured with the hand holding the cigarette; she was as changeable as he. "That *has* to be in."

He nodded and kept his head down. "I'll be coming here for days at a time," he said. "To read and talk with you. When I've got it worked out in my mind, we'll talk about it. The notebooks are going to remain here, we decided. Maybe it's best if we don't promise Yale anything definitely." He looked at her. "Oh, I forgot about the money. No reason not to sign whatever has to be signed. They don't know what there is and what can be held back. No reason either why they can't pay now."

"I should think so," she replied, and smiled for the first time. "How nice that I shall be having you here often."

"I think I'm going to ask for some foundation grants," he said, "in order to do it leisurely, thoroughly, the way he would have wanted." He saw the work stretch out before him—the reading of the notebooks, the correspondence, the old newspapers and books. The work of the real literary man, not the jogging journalist. There would be time to think things over, to reflect, to puzzle it all out.

Puzzle—the word zoomed out of the sentence and hung in the air buzzing at him. "Mother, why did he do it?" he said. "What did you mean that they tormented him about you?"

"Oh Seth, that's something I've made up in these six years," she said. She leaned forward from the waist and looked toward the open door to the upstairs landing. "Did you notice how he said that he would not tell anyone about the agents' visit, especially me?"

He moved to the edge of the chaise and nodded conspiratorially. "Yes," he said.

"There are a couple of places later on, too," she continued, "where I believe they talked to him about me. That's all I've had to go on."

"Yes, yes," Seth said. "One of them said it was you they should talk to because you ran around with international spies." He shook his head with amusement. "A fishing expedition."

She pressed her lips together. "No, darling, they must have had something on me. Oh, I have a theory all worked out. It's mad but no more insane than some of the things that happened in those days."

"Tell me, tell me," Seth said eagerly, happily.

"I was very active in Spain, you know, taking notables around." She lit a new cigarette and held up a hand to indicate he was not to interrupt. "I also traveled to Paris and London and once I brought a slew of names to New York for a Madison Square Garden meeting. I arranged for meetings across the country and my biggest coup was lunch at the White House with Eleanor. She entertained them. We knew all sorts of people, your father and I, and I could get statements of support and promises of others to bring pressure on Cordell Hull. Grandmother Morgan had known Roosevelt's mother. Old families have lots of connections."

"They could smear the New Deal by pretending you were agents," Seth said. "But all you did was perfectly aboveboard."

She shook her head and waved a hand dismissively. "No, I also took things to people on some of those trips. Sealed envelopes to banks in Paris. Once to leave one—forgetfully, would you believe it!—at my table at the Café de la Paix while I went off to the ladies'. Things like that. They all had to do with buying arms from international shady types. Who cares! What wouldn't we have done for the Republic!"

"Of course, of course," Seth said.

"I also brought messages back," she said. "Sometimes from men who I felt must be from the Soviet embassy in Paris. Though why that was I can't for the life of me understand. There were plenty of Russians in Madrid. I was told that time that it had to do with the arrangements for sending Spanish children to Russia. Maybe they didn't trust the people they had in Spain. You know, Seth, all of them, all, were called back and executed. Except Ehrenburg. He was a charming, sophisticated man. I liked him enormously and it's meanness for people to make him out a villain simply because he survived. Your father and I survived the McCarthy period—that doesn't make us . . ."

"It doesn't, it doesn't," Seth said. "You didn't finger anyone."

"No, we didn't, did we? Whatever your father told the FBI, he would not testify against anyone." She was silent a moment chewing her lips. "He wouldn't. And the talking he did was only because he wanted to spare me. I am certain of that. I was upset when I said that he made me lead a life I didn't want. He was a dear man. He didn't want to see me called to Washington before the television cameras."

"What would you have done?" Seth said.

"I would have died of fright—and shame," she replied. She shook her head thinking about it and then smiled at him. "It's one thing to be adventurous and something else to be exposed to vulgar publicity."

All this was too interesting, Seth thought, to give up for the book. How could he write about it without turning his father into a stool pigeon? And shaming his mother. And himself. Writers have to be ruthlessly truthful. "But it can't have been that they hoped to trump up a case that you were a spy," he said. "You weren't acting against U.S. interests—you didn't break any of our laws."

"It was all very scary then," she replied. "I didn't know anything about those visits of the FBI, but I remember how I felt. It seemed that every day someone you knew was called to Washington. Each time I believed that they were one step closer to us."

He had believed in that fear when he read the journal, but he couldn't now. He could not believe that Grandmother Morgan's granddaughter was vulnerable. Not to people like Joe McCarthy, the descendant, no doubt, of a cleaning woman. Those $150-a-week FBI agents should have been beneath his father too.

"I know, I know," she said, and he was startled that she seemed to speak to his unasked questions. "I've thought and thought about it and I've read all the books they've been lately publishing about those terrible days. They just used me to threaten him with. What they really wanted was a case against some of the veterans of the Lincoln Brigade. They were Communists and they were probably working up a spy case against them. Your father didn't really know them. He volunteered in Paris, with all those prominent men—Malraux, the German writers. The Lincoln Brigade people were just—well, you know, ordinary fellows recruited by the Communist party here. But your father balked at being used against them."

"Like a good soldier," Seth said. "You see, there's nothing to be ashamed of."

"Oh, he had only contempt for them," she replied. He never talked about such people but I knew how he felt about everyone who had any faith in the Russians. Even during the war, when everyone had second thoughts again, he didn't. He could have worked for the OSS, but he stayed right here. He hated Hitler but he would not write cant about the war." She sighed. "I thought he would never write again."

"My God, what a sad life," Seth said involuntarily. "The more I think about it. . . . Father had a sad life. I don't want to be like that."

"And you won't, dear, you have some Morgan in you." She looked at him and her blue eyes filled with mischief. "Your father's family was pure New England and there must have been a recessive gene there that skipped several generations and came out in him. I used to tease him about it, how he went back to the old orthodoxy—there is no redemption and we are all damned." She chuckled. "But with the Morgans there was a dash of southern, thank God. Grandmother Morgan gave us a touch of romanticism and that's why we want life to be more fun than it usually is."

She got up, refreshed and ready to go downstairs.

He looked up at her. "You don't really believe in genes, do you?" he asked.

She put a hand on his head. "Wait till you get to be old," she said affectionately. "You'll be convinced, as those computer people say, that it's the input that counts." She leaned down and kissed the top of his head. "You and I, we'll save your father from his morbidness. We won't use his journals against him, will we?"

He nodded, suffused with warmth. She gave him what he always wanted. At last. He stood and she wound an arm around him.

"And so you're going off on an adventure?" she said. "I'm so glad you told me." She squeezed his waist. "You knew that I would approve. See what I mean by genes? She cupped his face with one hand. "Be careful, but have a good time."

He was happy, happy. He winked at her.

She took his arm—he thought fleetingly of Mathilde and told him she had to get dinner started and walked him to the landing. "And your Jewish friend is a perfect cohort," she said as she left him. "Curious, isn't it? We too knew the most unexpected people in Spain."

Chapter 10

In the morning, after his mother drove off in her Volvo to school, Seth got ready slowly, feeling enveloped in soothing good wishes, the result of taking a Seconal in the middle of the night and his mother's approval of his trip. Also, Mathilde's concern. She had called in the evening, after they left the dining room for coffee near the small, odorous apple-log fire in the living room. Mathilde had put Pablo to bed and she switched, after she informed him of this, to a tone of voice that signaled she was speaking in code. "I just thought of something, Seth," she said loudly. "If there's any *problem*, you can always say he was a hitchhiker." He chuckled and said, "Good girl," and went back to the living room, happy that having told her about his trip had worked—she was thinking of him, not worrying about herself.

The man from Yale and his wife and Calvin's headmaster, who came alone, listened to Gary tell about his interview with Chou En-lai. They were deferential whenever he or Seth spoke, and Gary never forgot his formal committee manner. Later, when they stopped on the landing before going to their separate bedrooms, Seth and Gary allowed the cocktails, wine, and cognac to have their effect. They had a laughing fit. They scurried when they heard Seth's mother in the hall downstairs, and Seth was so sleepy that he did not bother to get into pajamas, nor to pursue the notion, as he had promised himself during dinner, that his mother and Calvin's headmaster might be having an affair.

He went to sleep naked and woke two hours later from a dream of seeing his father and mother in bed in sexual embrace. Ho-ho, what does that mean, he thought, and remembered there would be no shrink to tell it to. It did not bother him, and he lay on his back thinking about the book he would write until he discovered he was wide awake. He went to the bathroom and urinated and heard Gary snoring in his room beyond the door. A Seconal might make him sleep the morning, but he took one, anyway, and to his surprise he slept dreamlessly and woke before Gary. He felt so good that he took only a vitamin pill before he went down to breakfast.

After his mother left, while Gary was upstairs, he went to his father's study, as if that had been the dream and he had to check. He opened the center drawer. The notebook was there. The key was still in the bottom double drawer of the nearest file. His mother had touched nothing: she had really meant it when she said it was all his. He pulled open the file drawer, and wondered if he might take the first group of notebooks to read on the trip.

Gary spoke to him from the doorway and he wheeled around, feeling anxious for the first time in many hours. "Take nothing you wouldn't want to lose," Gary said.

"Sure, sure," he said quickly.

"I'm clean—no pot," Gary said, and threw his arms out as if he were ready to be searched. "What about you?"

Seth shook his head. He thought of his pills. He started to ask Gary about them but changed his mind. He had prescriptions for them at home. "I'm ready," he said.

In the car, Gary said, "The next time you stop for gas I pay. And let's get a road map of New England. I've got to look up the place."

"OK, boss," Seth replied, and looked at Gary and laughed. He was not afraid. He tried to recall why he had been, how he had hoped to avoid this trip, and thought of the day his father had set off for Madrid. It was mother's story. They were in Paris that July, and in another week would leave for the south. Amelie had already been hired, but his father was in the habit, afternoons, of taking him to La Rotonde to drink and chat with friends after his day's stint. Seth was harnessed in a stylish leather leash, for he had only just learned to walk. His father would tie the leash to one of the chairs and thus not worry during the conversations at the café—"Those great dialogues!" his mother said— that Seth would stray far. He was with Sartre that afternoon when Malraux arrived with the news of the uprising in Madrid.

Father got up and said, "I'm going."

"Ah, you journalists," Sartre said.

Father handed the leash to him. "Not to report," father replied, "but to fight. I count on you to take the boy to Trick." He went directly to Gare Austerlitz and boarded the afternoon train for Madrid. Seth could not hear the name Austerlitz, whatever the context, without feeling a tightening of his throat: it was not Napoleon's battle but his father's. When he first told Mathilde the story, she commented, "It sounds like a scene from a movie," and he became furious with her. Later, depending on his mood, he would sometimes think about it critically, realistically. Could it have happened that way? Why people as famous as Sartre and Malraux? Today it returned to him only in his mother's voice, with that deliberate articulation which made it seem both exact and dramatic. He could not remember when he began to add the detail that his father, who was always undemonstrative, had kissed him on both cheeks. "That's why I remember it," he would add triumphantly, "because he kissed me on both cheeks!"

Gary said, "What's this—a revolt of the rank and file?" He pointed to a filling station in the town. "Just chauffeur it in there," he said in mock command. He got out while the tank was being filled, and went to the rack of maps in the office. He returned in time to stop Seth from paying for the gas with a charge card. He explained as soon as they drove off. "We pay for everything in cash. No records."

"OK, boss," Seth repeated. "Where do we go now?"

"Oh, fuck the secrecy," Gary said. "I'll tell you what they told me. We head for a town called Hollowell, we go through it and leave it on Route 3 and stop at the first rest stop on it. No big rest stop, no Howard Johnson's, just a place to park, with a garbage can and an outhouse."

"We go in the outhouse?" Seth said.

"Smart ass," Gary replied. "Someone comes up to us and says, Have you been driving all day? And there my story ends. What did they tell you?"

"Say pretty please," Seth commanded.

"Oh, my God!" Gary said. "That's what my mother would say to me. It used to make me want to puke. It still does."

"Keep our bags in the back seat," Seth said. "Leave the trunk unlocked and don't look in it. Leave it unlocked all the time and that way we can say we didn't know that there was anything in it but the spare."

"Is that all?" Gary asked.

Seth nodded. "Is that all?"

"Yeah," Gary said. He leaned his head on the backrest. "Christ, how prosaic."

"What did you expect?" Seth said.

"Well, at least some background music going, humm-humm-humm-ha!" Gary said, with one hand up as if holding a baton. "And I've been scared shitless all along for this. I thought you'd been given the climactic lowdown. That's funny—climactic lowdown. Mixed metaphor or something. Oh yes, we should make it there by five o'clock, three hours before sundown. Now, that sounds more exciting, right?"

They got a flat soon after Northampton, and at first Seth thought something had gone wrong with the steering. Gary had no idea why Seth pulled in at the side of road, but he got out when Seth did.

"Look at that," Seth said. "I've never changed a tire on this car."

Gary stared at it. "When the car began to wobble," he said, "I thought it was psychosomatic and would go away." He followed Seth back to the trunk and stood by while he found the tools and removed the spare. "Tell me what to do, buddy," he kept saying. "What are you doing now?" He crouched when Seth crouched, looked puzzled when Seth hesitated, stood back when Seth told him to, and he was jubilant when Seth told him he could now place the old tire in the trunk. He said cheerfully, "Christ, this kind of thing makes me feel like an intellectual cripple. I don't mean I'm intellectually crippled—you know what I mean."

Seth said, "We must get the spare fixed. We can't take a chance of getting another flat, not afterwards." He was pleased with himself, and swerved back onto the highway. "We'll stop at the first filling station. We've got plenty of time."

"Oh no," Gary said. "At this I'm the expert. Let's go east or west, far from this highway, and not leave tracks. Or they'll be able to follow us with bloodhounds."

They lost an hour and a half. They stopped in a village with a block-long shopping street. They ate sandwiches at the drugstore while a young man fixed the tire at the filling station, which also issued hunting licenses. The young man expected to leave for the army soon and was looking forward to it. At the lunch counter Gary tried to engage the woman who served them in talk about the war, but she shrugged and said, "I guess they'll fix it up one of these days." They walked up and down the street and stood at a short bridge over a small stream. The rocks in the bed made the water gurgle and sparkle. Gary said sadly, "You notice what a big hardware store they have for a town this size?"

Seth nodded. He wished there were time to follow the banks of the stream. "It's nice, isn't it?" he said to Gary, and did not realize that to Gary this village was a puzzle. Seth wondered if in time he would, like his father, settle away from the city and each spring set the poles for the peas.

In the afternoon, before they were due to leave the interstate highway, they stopped to eat again. They went to a Howard Johnson's right on the highway because they did not want to lose more time and because, as Gary said, at Howard Johnson's they would be just statistics. "They don't remember people," he said. "Just how many hot dogs they sold."

Seth brought the road map from the car, and when he saw that they were no more than an hour and a half away, he had to put a hand on his knee below the table to keep his leg from twitching. He thought of asking Gary if he could hear background music now, but instead said, "Well, the coffee isn't bad."

In Hollowell there was a supermarket, a lumberyard, a diner, a general store called Partridge's Department Store, and three filling stations, one of which did body work and was surrounded on three sides by a patchwork quilt of rusting cars. They did not have to ask or search for Route 3; it was a continuation of Main Street, and five miles beyond, on their side of the road, was the rest stop. A long gas truck took up half the parking space. It was four-thirty.

"There's nobody in the truck," Gary said.

Seth replied, "He must be using the facilities," and got out and walked around the truck and returned to the car. "Nobody in the truck, all right," he reported.

"I guess we wait," Gary said. He opened the door on his side, and added, "How do you look natural in a place like this?"

Seth nodded toward the outhouse. "You act like you're waiting your turn."

As if on cue, a fat, preoccupied man came out of it and looked at them. He did not look friendly, but when he passed them on the way to his truck he paused and smiled and reached into his shirt pocket for a cigarette. "Howdy," he said, and indicated he wanted to light his cigarette. "My light is on the dashboard of the monster."

Seth struck a match for him and then took out a cigarette for himself.

The truck driver said, "If you're thinking of using that one-holer, I'd give it a minute to air out." He laughed, his voice rising surprisingly high. "I've been driving all day, you know how it is."

Gary exclaimed, "You been driving all day!"

Seth stared.

"That's what I get paid for," the driver said.

"Oh," Gary said; then ventured, "We've been driving all day too."

The truck driver looked beyond Gary, and Seth and Gary turned to look too. A pickup truck came slowly from the opposite direction, almost stopped completely, and then turned into the rest stop. There were two young men in it; the one driving was nearest to them, and he had long hair, streaked blond and held by a rubber band at the back of the neck.

The truck driver muttered, "No matter where the fuck you go you run into hippies." He shook his head, took a drag on his cigarette, and said, "See you."

They watched him hoist himself into the truck, and did not look at the pickup. It seemed to Seth that the gas truck would never leave. Even when its engine filled the rest stop with noise, it took a long time for it to turn into the road heading for Hollowell. It stayed in sight forever.

Without speaking, Seth and Gary decided that they should not look at the kids in the pickup until the gas truck was gone. Maybe it's not them, Seth thought, maybe they'll never show up.

Seth lit another cigarette, and this time Gary took a light from him. As he lowered his head to the flame their eyes met. Seth had never seen so controlled an expression on Gary's face. In unison they leaned back against the car and half turned to look at the pickup. The driver was crouched over the wheel. His passenger got out and left his door open. He wore dungarees and a wool hunting shirt and farmer's boots. His black moustache was like Gary's and his hair too did not cover his ears. He walked toward them with deliberation, almost as if he hoped not to reach them too soon. He held an unlit cigarette in one hand, and Seth thought: he only wants a light too.

The young man put the cigarette in his mouth when only a few feet away, and said, "Have you been driving all day?"

"Yes," Gary said, and held out his cigarette for him to take a light from it.

The fellow first lit his cigarette carefully, and as he returned Gary's he smiled. He was younger than the two of them. His teeth were brilliant, his eyes black, and he looked from Gary to Seth and held the smile all the while. Then he stuck out his hand, first to Gary, gripped Gary's palm, holding up his thumb for the second movement when the thumbs come together with the fingers of each hand enveloping the other's thumb; then down again palms together for the normal handshake. He went through it once more with Seth. He half turned toward the pickup, and the driver jumped out at that moment. He wore coveralls over a long-sleeved union suit, and he half skipped toward them.

Gary laughed. "So what happens now?" he said, holding out his hand to go through the revolutionary ritual with the blond boy. But the blond boy fumbled it and turned pink with embarrassment and looked from Gary to Seth and finally said, "Gosh."

The boy suddenly moved to Seth's side and put an arm on Seth's shoulder, then flushed again and removed the arm. Seth knew what had happened to the boy: he had thought Seth was his own age because Seth was small, and realized after he had touched him that Seth was older. The young man with the black moustache also responded, in his way, to Seth's height; he took for granted that Gary was in charge. Seth moved forward their orbit to show that he was to be included. He glanced back paternally at the blond boy to urge him forward too, and saw that the boy's jaw hung slightly open and that he looked at them as if in the presence of beings whose brilliance and authority blinded him. He blinked when Seth looked back at him, and moved farther away.

"It's very simple," the young man with the moustache said. He looked at the road before continuing. "You two will go in the truck with the brother here. I'll take your car and you'll find it back here tomorrow morning at eight. That's all there's to it."

Gary looked surprised. "You're taking the car and we won't see it until tomorrow morning?"

The young man nodded. "It's a simple operation."

Seth looked at the road and said in a low voice, "What about the stuff? Are you getting it or are we?"

"I believe it will be in the car tomorrow," he replied. He smiled widely again and held the smile as if to let them see his teeth. He added, "Heavy."

Gary pulled at his red moustache with his lower lip and nodded. "OK," he said finally.

Seth put up a hand for attention. "And where do we take it?"

"Yes," Gary said quickly.

The young man said, "You'll find out about that tomorrow morning." He winked. "I don't know about that myself. Not now, anyway."

Seth nodded. He thought: what happens to us? He said to the young man, "The registration is in the glove compartment."

Before he replied, the young man looked toward the blond boy. The boy flushed, and with his hands in his coverall straps drifted toward the pickup. Then the other one said to Seth, "We're not going to use the registration. If something happens, we'll let them think, you know, that it's a stolen car."

Seth nodded, and the young man continued in a low voice. "You can trust this brother and the people at the farm. The brother here walked away because nobody knows more than they need to know. At the farm they won't talk about it either. They don't really know, they just expect a couple of brothers to crash tonight. You dig?"

This time Gary nodded too.

The young man added, "I mean, it would be, you know, OK with them if they knew. But they don't know." He touched his moustache with two fingers, smoothing it reflectively. "No, a couple know. In case—but they'll let you know only in case."

Gary rubbed his hands together happily. "So we'll sleep at your farm tonight!" He threw out his arms and breathed deeply. "Great."

The young man looked at the highway and then explained, "It's not my farm. It's a collective—hey, I'm taking too long."

They walked with him to the car and removed the two bags from the back seat. Seth said, "The trunk's unlocked. We just had the spare fixed because we had a flat but the other tires were checked and they should be OK."

"Wait," the young man said, and got into the driver's seat. He looked at the dashboard. "What else?"

"It's an automatic," Seth said. "The emergency is there on your left. You release it with your hand. The key is in the ignition. I guess that's it." He stepped back to let the young man close the car door, and he almost laughed at the pang he felt to see his car in someone else's hands.

A car passed on the road and they all involuntarily studied it as it went by. The young man said, "I'm going to stay here until you leave in the truck."

"Oh," Gary said.

Seth did not know how to say good-bye. "I guess we'll go now," he said. He nodded and Gary again joined him in nodding.

The young man said without smiling, "All power to the people."

"Right on," Gary said, and led Seth toward the pickup. The blond boy crossed them on his way to Seth's car, and Seth looked back and saw him bend and stick his head inside the driver's window. The back of his head, with its waggling ponytail, obstructed Seth's view of the young man behind the wheel, and it moved as if the blond boy were kissing the driver. The idea made Seth laugh; it must be last-minute instructions they were whispering. When got to the pickup, he was not sure what he had seen and he looked again, but the boy's head was out of the car and he was giving the driver the clenched fist salute. The driver held his left arm out of the car and also made a fist, for them as well as for the boy. Seth nudged Gary, and the two made fists and glanced quickly at the road. Seth thought: a revolutionary tableau. He turned to Gary to tell him, but he saw it was a serious moment and suddenly his throat tightened and the blond boy skipped toward them hazily in Seth's watered vision.

Behind the wheel of the pickup, the boy became confident, grew visibly mature, Seth thought. Sitting next to him, Seth first noticed that the coveralls and the white union suit underwear he wore were clean and the boy smelled fresh, but the hand on the gearshift was rough and brown, streaked with the dye of farm work. As they moved out of the rest stop on first gear, the three of them leaned forward to take a last look at the young man in the car.

Gary stuck his head out the window and kept looking back. "I'd feel better," he said, "if he had at least started up the car to see if it was all right."

"No problem," Seth said. "There's nothing to driving that car."

"Oh, he's into everything mechanical," the blond boy said. "He repairs this truck and our bus and the rototiller. The family depends on him for that. He won't have any trouble, gosh no." When he turned and saw both Gary and Seth listening carefully, he blushed. "Jack's teaching me," he added. "We're going to put in the plumbing."

"Jack?" Gary said.

Seth saw the boy gulp for breath, and realized that he should not have given the other's name. "My name's Dudley," the boy said to cover up his error. When his flush subsided, he said, "When I make a boo-boo, Jack—he calls me Dud. Oh gosh, I guess it's all right. You're going to meet all the other persons in Hampton's Family."

This time it was Seth who responded. "Hampton's Family?"

"The collective, but it's not decided like," Dudley replied. "One of the women had a baby this winter and she called him Fred Hampton for, you know, Fred Hampton. And we're his family because we're into that, you know, no nuclear family, and some of us call the farm Hampton's Family but it's not decided yet. We are just trying it out because it's pretty authoritarian like just to impose a name. Let it grow and get roots and then maybe it's a name, right?—if it comes natural."

"That's sweet," Gary said.

The boy was pleased and this time smiled without blushing. His teeth were small and even. "Before that one of the brothers who used to be a Trot called it Workers of the World, Disperse. But it was more of a joke ha-ha than a name. Though two or three persons were calling it Disperse pretty regularly."

Seth thought: I can take it easy. Twelve hours or more of nothing to do. That is, nothing to worry about. Whoever had planned it was a good psychologist: a division of labor that gave everyone just enough to be responsible for. He felt like clapping the boy on the back and Gary too. He looked over at Gary and saw he smiled beatifically. He nudged him. Gary looked at him and nodded as if he too had come to the same conclusion.

"Nice rolling hills," Gary said.

"Smell the air," Seth said, and thought he would not need any of his pills. Until tomorrow morning. "Do we have a long way to go?"

Dudley replied, "Twenty miles from where we met you. In the country that's like, you know, next door. Oh, I love the country, man, I love it."

Seth looked at him paternally. He could not be more than eighteen or nineteen. "Did you live in the country before?" he asked him.

"I'm from Larchmont," Dudley replied. "But I was making the scene in the Village. That was wonderful too. I needed it for my head, you know. But I'm into survival now and the body, because rapping about it one day in the park I saw, I mean I really saw, that you have to be a whole person to be into politics. I don't put down anybody's trip because I've been on trips myself, but I'm not on any trip anymore. I'm just here."

There seemed nothing to say. Dudley turned off the county road onto a narrower town road.

"I see farms," Gary said, "but no town."

Dudley blushed. "I bypassed our town," he said. "Jack's instructions. Not because of you but so less people see you like. Our town is called South Manchuria. It's got a general store, a library, a lumber-yard, and a grammar school. And a few houses close together. Neat."

"Pretty far from everything," Gary said. "How can you be politically involved?"

Dudley nodded, and then again and again, thinking the question over seriously. Seth worried for him: Gary's question, he thought, was unfair. Dudley licked his lips. "We have rapped a lot about that," he finally said "Gosh, I wish you had asked Jack that. I get spaced out listening to him about that. Connie too. Me, I get the vibes, the feeling. . . ."

"You don't want to speak for others, is that it?" Seth said.

"That's it, that's it," he said to Seth, and he looked at him as if Seth were on his wavelength. He leaned a little toward him so that their

shoulders touched. "Right on," he added. "I want to be with everybody. We're building the new society, like Connie says."

Gary relented. "That sounds OK," he said.

"It was too much of a head thing in the Village," Dudley said. He
licked his lips again, thinking that over. "I tell you what, it was like the
vegetable garden. When I came here, gosh, a year and a half ago, I said
I want that. I want to grow vegetables, but Barry was doing that and it
was his thing. So I started another plot. We could use it and I turned
up the ground and I even got to rapping about it at the general store.
Except I wouldn't use chemical fertilizers and there was the old chick-
en house full of good manure until I began to worry maybe they had
used antibiotics with the chickens."

He stopped.

"Go on," Seth said.

"Well, it got to be a head thing," Dudley said. "I planted nine
kinds of lettuce and peas and snow peas and cabbages and tomatoes. I
was reading garden books and the rest of the time I was out there
watching the seedlings grow. It was beautiful, man, I was on a nature
high. Then Barry—he was the old Trot. I mean he was a Trot once.
Barry said, 'Your garden is a metaphor, you're making it into a private
thing for communism.' He said I was making it into a vision in my
head. It was taking the place of vegetables to eat. The next time I went
out to the garden I understood Barry. I mean those vegetables were
getting to be like poetry. I wasn't letting them be, just *be* themselves.
So I switched to working with Jack and now I rototill the gardens in
the spring and fall and I'm trying not to keep it to myself. Because first
of all they're vegetables to eat and get into your body to survive.

"Wow," Dudley added. "I've really laid a rap on you."

Going uphill, the town road turned to gravel, with now and then a
patch of tar. Seth leaned a hand on the dashboard to steady himself.
"They never fix it," Dudley explained, "because we're the only house
on it, and we don't want to cause the town any expenditures."

First the chicken house came into view. A long two-story wooden
building. Some of the top windows were knocked out and re-covered
with plastic, now golden in the afternoon sun. When they got close to
it the road leveled and turned, and they were able to see the house on
the other side of the road on a knoll that looked down the chicken

house. The house was two stories too, except for the wing that connected it to a barn. Two dormer windows at the front stared down at them, and all of the structures were of weathered clapboard. They were brightened by new cedar shingles on the huge barn roof and by the three children on the grass by the road waving at them.

"Whose kids?" Gary asked.

"We are eleven persons in the collective," Dudley replied. "Eleven plus four children. Fred Hampton can't walk yet."

He stopped the truck on the graveled turnaround in front of the house, and Seth saw, on Gary's side, the view from the house. The land sloped steeply behind the chicken house. About a half mile away was a small pond, like a cup brimming in the valley. The hills rose wooded beyond it, and in the soft light of the late afternoon were blue and black with evergreens. Gary jumped out and faced the view, his arms up waving at it. "World, world," he called. "I cannot hold thee close enough!"

He crossed the road toward the chicken house, and Seth went around the front of the truck to follow Dudley. Dudley crouched and hugged the half-naked youngsters. A girl in a granny dress, who looked about six, tried to reach him over the younger ones. "Duddy, Duddy, you came back," she said.

He reached out and pulled her to himself and the three became a bouquet in his arms. One of the infants reached around him and tugged at his ponytail. "Ouch, ouch," he said laughing. "Where's Connie? Where's Melanie?"

The six-year-old said, "Dinner duties."

"And the others?" Dudley asked.

She shrugged. "We were waiting for you to ride on the truck."

Dudley did not reply. He got up with one of the younger ones in his arms. A girl. She leaned her head on his shoulder, glad to have him to herself.

Seth said, "Is she yours?" She was blond, her hair streaked like his.

Dudley turned to him and blinked, his jaw half open with surprise.

"She's not?" Seth said.

Dudley shook his head and squeezed the child a little. "I'm not into that yet," he said. "One of these days. Right now, I'm gay."

Dudley did not look away from Seth, and miraculously did not blush. He leaned his head down to be on a level with the little girl's, and the two looked into Seth's eyes and smiled. Their gaze held him. He could think of nothing to do or say but simply smile back.

Chapter 11

Seth took his valise and Gary's from the back of the pickup truck, eager to see the inside of the house, and stopped himself from calling Gary. He thought: how nice the country is, you can let Gary roam at will, he won't get lost in traffic or be unable to find you when he's ready. He walked toward the house, following Dudley and his little troop, and felt himself expand with this freedom. The bags were foolish and inappropriate; they should have known that, and yet he was sure that no one would mind: they would think it was his thing. He looked back, wishing he could tell Gary this, and saw him come out of the wide door of the chicken house.

"Wait, wait," Gary called, breaking into a skipping run. When he caught up, he said, "You know what, it doesn't stink. It's like a country perfume, perfectly natural!"

Seth turned to him and lowered his voice. "Isn't this great? It's like an idyllic intermission."

"Pun," Gary said.

Seth thought: nothing will surprise me. And was surprised by the kitchen. Dudley led them directly to it by the side door. Its walls were startlingly white and clean and on the ceiling were painted red and orange flowers. The room was the width of the house, and against the far wall stood a large wood stove, polished black, its chrome shining. A girl in dungarees, her brown hair held, like Dudley's, in a ponytail, stood at it. She said, "Hi," and was echoed by another girl who sat at a long wooden table next to the door. She was measuring unpolished rice into a bowl, and her black hair seemed blacker for its Afro and the background of the white plaster wall.

"Hi," Gary said. "We didn't know or we'd have brought something to contribute to dinner."

"Yes," Seth said, looking from one girl to the other. "Sorry."

The girl at the table said, "We might put you to washing dishes," and nodded mischievously toward the corner where the sink stood.

"A pump!" Seth said.

The girls and Dudley looked at him and smiled. The six-year-old said, "You want me to teach you how it works? You prime it!"

"Where's Connie?" Dudley asked.

The girl at the stove replied, "Upstairs, feeding Fred Hampton."

"Oh, these are Jack's friends," Dudley said. He blushed. "Gosh, I don't know your names."

"Seth," Seth said. Then added, nodding toward Gary, "Gary."

"Right on," the girl at the stove said.

"We know," the girl measuring rice said. "You're staying tonight."

Seth smiled. Gary said, "If it's all right."

Dudley answered, "Oh sure, I mean." The girl at the table laughed. And there seemed nothing more to say. The girl at the stove crouched and opened the door of the oven with a clank. The smell of roasting chicken became strong. The other girl said, "I won't start the rice yet." She looked at Dudley, and he started and said to Gary and Seth, "Oh, come with me."

The girl at the table asked, "Shall I make biscuits?"

"Wait for me!" Gary said. "I'll be right back. I want you to teach me."

He hurried and then stopped at the door to the front hall where Dudley was leading them. On the door was a large poster-size painter's cardboard. At its top, in large hand-drawn letters, it said: RULES. There followed a long numbered list in a neat script written with an osmiroid pen. At the bottom, in larger letters that filled the whole width of the cardboard, a postscript announced: *No One Is To Enforce These Rules.*

Gary said, "Oh, I love that. It's beautiful Bakunin."

"And lovely Luxembourg," Seth added.

Dudley smiled at them as if to say that he did not have to know in order to enjoy their talk. "It's not up to date," he said. "It doesn't cover the chicken house. Chuck and Dotty are going to make a new one but we want to rap about some new ideas first and anyway they are too busy with the T-shirts now. They make silk-screen decorated shirts and we send them to the Village to sell. They're our cash crop."

Gary called from the front end of the hall: "What's this?"

He was looking into a room off the hall, and before Seth reached him, he turned and looked into the room across from it. "They're both the same!" Gary exclaimed.

The ceiling of each room was painted black, two of the walls mauve, two brown. There was no furniture. Along the outside walls were built-in storage cabinets the height of window seats and stained deep brown. Except for a pathway in front of the cabinets the rest of the floor was taken up by what looked like a huge mattress covered by India-print cottons sewn together. Blankets and pillows were neatly piled along the inner wall. On the storage cabinets below each window lay slim pillows for sitting.

"Wow!" Gary said. "Who makes up the bed?"

"I make up this one," Dudley said, "and Melanie the other one across the hall." He walked into the passageway between the mattress and storage cabinets. "It's a small house and we figured this was the best way to use up the space."

"What about upstairs?" Gary asked.

Seth did not ask. Things would explain themselves, he thought. It was another world, and it was no use being rational about it.

"The three rooms upstairs are for the children and the sick," Dudley said. "Two rooms for the children and one for whoever is sick."

Seth thought: they all sleep together then.

"The children don't mind?" Gary said, but Seth could see, as Gary stared at the long mattress, that he was thinking about the adults.

"Well . . ." Dudley said, and stopped to think it over. "Sometimes they come down in the middle of the night. We don't chase them back." He opened the top of two storage cabinets. "You can put your things in this one," he said to Gary. "It's Jack's." To Seth he said, "This is mine. You can use it."

A young man with a beard—he was closer in age to Seth than to Dudley—stood in the doorway. "Hi," he said. "I'm the king of the chicken house and I take a bath every day!"

"Ho-ho," Gary said.

Dudley told him Gary and Seth were Jack's friends. "I'm showing them around," he added.

"I heard, I heard," the fellow said. He pulled on his beard, looked down, and then decided to get in the conversation. "About the kids, some of us feel they should all sleep down here too and then the rooms upstairs could be used for like seminars or to write, not just the barns. But more important there is such a thing as infant sexuality, right?"

They joined him in the hall. "Gosh," Dudley said.

The chicken-house king shook their hands and kept a hand on Gary's shoulder. "I mean, after all, that's what we're into," he said, grinning and shrugging as if he only half meant it. "We are all trying to become like children again. Get rid of our hang-ups, get polymorphous."

"Polymorphous without the perverse," Gary said.

The fellow clapped him on the back. "You get the idea! You're together, man."

It was then Seth saw the girl at the top of the narrow steep farmhouse staircase. She was barefoot and her movements were noiseless. She wore a long cotton dress, dark brown with tiny yellow flowers. As she walked down, her face came out of the shadows. Her hair was black and loose, and her tanned face was slightly flushed, as if she had recently blushed and the thought that caused it was still on her mind. But it was her eyes that held Seth. They were brown and almond shaped, and the thick lashes that framed them seemed needed to hold in the clear liquid in which they swam. If they overflow, Seth thought, there would be placid, happy tears.

"Connie," Dudley said, tenderly but also vying for her attention. "Is Fred Hampton all right?"

She smiled and nodded slowly and looked at Gary and then at Seth. She continued looking at Seth. "Hello," she said.

She has been nursing him, Seth thought, and almost put out a hand to touch her. He saw that Dudley felt the same impulse; he had taken her hand. She let Dudley hold it, and Seth was surprised to feel envy.

She took her hand away to brush back her hair. "Freddy is sleeping now," she said; her voice was low, uninflected, but not because of boredom or weariness. Seth waited for her to say more. "And now I'm going to make the salad," she added, and he heard the common sense in the flatness of the vowels like an echo of a world he had known.

"Christ!" Gary exclaimed. "I forgot about the biscuits. I'm going to help with the biscuits." He turned and skipped toward the kitchen and called back, "I want to do everything!"

The chicken-house king followed laughing. "You will, man, you will. You want to come with me to the chicken house? Sundown is the best time to gather eggs."

Connie spoke in a low voice that carried only to Seth. "You're Seth Evergood," she said. "I've read your book."

"Gosh," Dudley said, reluctantly excusing himself. "I'm going to give the kids a ride in the truck."

Connie stepped down from the bottom step of the stairs, and Seth saw that she was not as tall as he had thought. No more than an inch taller than he. It was her dress and her broad shoulders that had deceived him, and he felt like drawing her to him. He thought: vanity, vanity, I'm attracted because she knows who I am. He followed her to the kitchen, unconsciously trying to glide noiselessly like her, and to make out as she walked ahead of him what her body was like under the long, full dress.

The girl at the stove said, "Connie, the salad, you said you'd make a salad. But what is there?"

There were two new persons in the kitchen. A girl and a boy. Seth decided they were the ones who print the T-shirts, but he did not go over to them at the long harvest table. He wanted to stay with Connie.

"There's watercress at the stream, remember," Connie said. "And new radishes in the garden and the romaine is now tall enough to pick the leaves separately." She walked to the wall where the pots and utensils were hung, and Seth watched her brown, strong arm reach for a deep colander.

"Can I help?" he said.

She nodded slowly as she had to Dudley. "Oh yes," she said. "You can help me pick. Anyway, I want to talk to you." She smiled to show him she meant his book, and Seth decided, because she had been discreet, that she was one of the ones who surely knew what Gary and he were doing here.

"Aren't you going to put something on your feet?" he asked as they went out the kitchen door.

She shook her head. She stood a moment on the granite step and looked toward the fields. Then said, "The way to the stream is all grass and the vegetable garden is right behind the barn."

He thought of taking the colander from her, but there was nothing girlish about her and she did not seem to expect it. She sighed, and stepped off the granite step and walked along the house and barn. "I can never get over the sight of this place at sundown. That's when we saw it the first time. Jack and I discovered it."

"Jack?" he said involuntarily.

"You met him," she said. "He took your car."

He nodded, and thought about her and Jack. He recalled Jack's brilliant smile, his thick black moustache. Was he Fred Hampton's father? But he had decided that he would take things as they came. This was an interlude. He shook himself as if that was not a nice thought, and saw she was pointing to the vegetable garden.

"Half an acre," she said. "You'd be surprised how many people half an acre can feed. We learned that from the Nearings."

"The Nearings?" he said. "Oh yes, *Living the Good Life.*"

"It sounds corny, doesn't it? But it's true," she said. She looked at the garden as she talked. "Four of us went to visit them at their farm in Maine, and they let us stay and learn. He was eighty-six then and she was near seventy and they live from their garden and have plenty left over."

"They're socialists," he said, as if answering some unspoken criticism.

"First, the watercress," she replied, and swung the colander toward the horizon where the field sloped down and its end could not be seen. "Then we'll come back here. There's still more than an hour of daylight and that's the sign for dinner—when it's dark." She swung a foot to step off the path and walk on the grass and he watched it make its arc. The foot was brown and wide and the big toe round and separate from the others. She saw him, and said, "No fear, I can walk almost anywhere like this. We're a clean commune. We're a mess in many ways but you're not going to step on dog shit or glass here."

"Wait then," he said and crouched and then sat on the grass. He took off his shoes and socks. "I'll leave them here." He stood and flung them toward the barn. "God, it already feels great!"

She smiled and he noticed, as he had not in the semidarkness of the house, that her teeth were large and crowded her mouth, making her lips full in repose. He thought: she is sensual, and immediately said, "You're nice."

She walked ahead, and when he was at her side, she said, "Well, I admire you. Your book taught me a lot. Three or four of us read it and we rapped about it a whole evening. How long since you've been in Paris?"

"A year," he said. "I'm interested in the good old U.S.A. now." He spread his toes and pushed forward to let the tall blades of grass run between them. "Ummm, that's nice. It's good to get away like this."

"I guess it is getting away for you," she said. "Now, for me the country means politics. In a funny way. My parents both lost their jobs during the McCarthy period and they went back to my mother's folks in the country. Kentucky. Father farmed for several years and I was terribly happy. That's how I thought of this when things got so heavy in the city."

He was going to ask her about that but remembered he had decided to let things come as they would. "Can I carry that?" he said, pointing to the colander.

"OK," she said, "if you like." She handed it to him and swung her arms and then unselfconsciously brought both hands to her breasts. She held a hand to each, supported them a moment, and then moved her fingers, lightly feeling them. She explained, "I have more than the baby can use."

Before he could answer, she pointed to the trees at the bottom of the slope. "The stream is there," she said. "Dudley calls it Dippedy Doo. That's because it starts out of some rocks higher up and dips and turns as it goes by." She smiled, and he realized that her smile created suspense for him. "It's just a little stream, no more than three feet wide, but it never goes dry."

"And it starts on your property?" he said.

"We think so but we don't really know," she said. "And we like to believe that we don't care."

It was this irony that made him think of her age for the first time. He asked.

"I'm twenty-six," she said. "I've been on my own since I was eighteen and that's a long time." She stopped and looked back at him.

The bottom of his feet felt tender and she looked down at them as if she suspected. They were a few yards from the maples and birches, and the grass was thinning out. "From here on there are rocks but the ground is wet and that's nice. First, as I was saying, I went off in search of the Beats to write poetry." She gave him her hand, and then took it away. "No, you walk behind me and step where I step."

"Ahhh, ahhh," he exhaled as soon as he stepped on wet soil. He heard the gurgle of water and realized that the wet rocky bed was the stream: despite what Connie had told him, he had been expecting a river. He sat on a boulder and drew up his feet to its smooth sides. "If you squint," he said to her, "it's as big as the Mississippi."

She sat on a smaller rock below him, hitched her dress at her knees, and placed her feet in the water. It covered them and they looked, as the water passed over them, wavering their outline, like the other rocks in the bed.

"Where's the watercress?" Seth asked.

"Right here," she said, and leaned down and touched the deep green plants along the edge. "They're a gift, like dandelion greens and sour grass and berries." She pulled one and dipped it in the water and passed it up to him. "We encourage them a little, though. In the fall we sweep away the leaves around here so they won't smother them."

He chewed and could not describe to himself the new taste. They had the familiar tartness, the edge he expected from its intense green, but they were not bitter, they were sweet. "It's gourmet cooking," he said.

She leaned her elbows on her knees and, half turning, said, "Was the French CP as bad as you said?"

He nodded. It did not surprise him, how she moved from one subject to the other. He did not think, as his mother would have, that she was flighty. It was her maturity—maybe her new maternity—that made her accept and pass on each thought as it came to her. Naturalness, that's what it was. He did not feel challenged or argued with or expected to perform. He did not feel held to any course. He thought: I do not want to think; and chuckled because he had not once in thought called up his notebook. It was in his jacket in Dudley's storage cabinet and he thought of it as a foolishness he would not again indulge.

Her eyes opened slightly when he chuckled, but she did not ask him what had moved him. She said, "My parents were in the CP and it's still their touchstone but they're nice people. I can't imagine them supporting goon squads in the May uprising."

He nodded. "Rank-and-file members in France are like that too," he said. He got up and said, "Is it all right if I step right in?" and thought: I'm talking just like her.

"Everything's all right," she said. She reached up and took the colander from him and began to pick the watercress. "Your feet look very happy."

He looked down at them. "Too white," he said.

Inside him, and he thought of it as emanating from his chest and not his head, the feeling was born that some thing was going to happen. The water, at first cool, made his feet cold, and the sensation traveled up his legs, making the thin hairs on them rise. He stepped back to the other side of the stream and the mud now warmed his feet. He crouched and began to pick the watercress on his side of the stream. When he handed her the first bunch, he saw beyond her the field they had crossed and the roof of the barn sitting on it at the top. Above the roof the sky was pink.

"Beautiful," she said, and slowly tossed her head until her long hair fell behind her shoulders. Her eyes seemed filled to the brim.

"You can't see what I see," Seth said.

"I see the sunset itself," she said. "You see the reflection."

He looked over his shoulder. The horizon was red and orange and gold, and halfway up the sky the colors turned mauve and blue. He got up and walked to her side and then crouched again. "Did you hear my knees when I bent down?" he asked. "They went thuck, thuck."

"Sit up on the rock and stretch them," she said. She held up the colander and shook it a little to make the watercress settle. "I'll pick just a little more."

He sat on the rock and held out his hands and shook them to dry. Then he stretched his legs and felt the muscles tense in his calves and thighs. He let his head droop forward and just before he closed his eyes he saw his chest, outlined under the turtleneck pullover, rising and falling with his breathing. He opened his eyes again and saw that his nipples must have tightened; they were tiny buds on his chest. He smiled: they were so proudly inconsequential.

"The edge of your dress is wet," he said, but she did not look around. The dress was pulled tight across her shoulders and upper back. She was wide there. He could not tell about her waist; the dress loosened again as it fell from her back and tauntened around her buttocks because it was caught under her knees in her hunkering position. The buttocks were small but rounded perfectly and the dress was pulled between them. "You don't care?" he said, though he did not want her to move.

She shook her head, half straightened, and exhaled loudly all at once. She did not turn to him until she had sat again on the rock below his knees. "It's full," she said and put the colander away from her.

Seth looked down at her and said, "But we have more things to carry from the vegetable garden." He noticed that her lashes were like fans from this angle and that her nose seemed wider and flatter.

"I'll carry them in my skirt," she replied, and looked down at herself as if to check on what he saw of her. She brought one hand to her breast. "Oh, damn," she said. "I'm dripping," and without looking at him, pulled the top of the dress away from her body with one hand and slid off the rock to kneel at the water's edge. All in one motion, it seemed to Seth, though she did not hurry. One hand lifted her skirt above her knees and then, with her back to him, she hiked it up to her neck and clamped down her chin to catch the dress.

Seth saw the bowed head determinedly keeping the dress up and her arms reaching into the stream and, out of his sight, bringing water cupped in her hands to her breasts. "Oh, oh," she exclaimed each time. Her strong back was outlined against the dress with every gasp of her body. Then she laughed and the sound was unexpected: he was delighted that it was high and uncontrolled like a young girl's.

She lifted her head and let the dress fall as she got up. "Cool water sometimes helps," she said, standing before him. "Like cold showers with boys."

As he watched, the dress absorbed the water on her breasts and clung to them. They were pointed and firm and high on her chest. The nipples stood out so distinctly that they seemed to yearn to get beyond the fabric. This made him smile. He raised his eyes to hers and lifted an arm off the ground without thinking and held it in the air palm outward as if there were no intervening space between it and the breast it wished to cup. She closed her eyes and swayed a little. He felt his penis struggling with his shorts and pants to find room for its tumescence, and he sat up abruptly, awakened and feeling foolish.

Legs apart, he leaned a hand on each knee to get up, but she was suddenly before him, kneeling between his legs. She put a hand on each of his bare feet and drew one up his left leg, sliding the hand under the cloth, and smiled to herself. Her hand was cool and moist and sent a series of shivers up his body. He giggled. She lay her head on one of his knees and he felt the pressure of her breast against his leg. Her eyes closed and he placed a hand on her hair. It was thick and substantial like the weight of her body and he slowly ran it between his fingers and held it as he had wished to clutch the grass with his toes. She did not move and he did not want to. His breath came easily but slowly and there were long pauses when his body was suspended and sustained by the air about them: it did not breathe and push and occupy space but was all feeling and immanence.

This pleasure was her doing. He was flooded with gratefulness. He studied her to learn her secret. Her eyes were still closed. Lightly, tentatively, he touched first the bridge of her nose, then let his finger slide into the hollow of her eye and follow the dark thick fringe of her lashes. They were real. Thick hair that tickled his fingertip, moist like grass around a pond. He leaned his head forward and she lifted hers and parted her lips in the beginnings of a smile. He bent farther and his lips reached her hair. From it and from her dress arose the smell of sun and soap, and in a moment too the heavy, sweet odor of her maternity and the wetness of the stream. With his head on hers they were folded into one another.

He felt her move, her hands press on his thighs, and he lifted his head, afraid she was getting up. He did not stop her: all this had been a gift and he would not force it to persist. She pulled herself forward with her hands grasping his thighs, and she lay her head on his groin and kept her arms along his thighs, her hands reaching around to the small of his back. His sheltered penis stretched along the bone of her jaw, throbbed a second and became still. He hid one hand under her hair and his fingers moved up her neck and then down to her back under the fabric of her dress. The tips of his fingers touched her shoulder blade and he remembered Amelie saying when he was a boy,

These are your wings from the time you were an angel and flew down to us.

She withdrew one hand from his back and, holding her head up a little, pulled the front of his shirt out of his pants. He watched her lips kiss the thin line of hair flowing to his navel and then move down and close over it. The tip of her tongue burrowed, darting in and out. He laughed. He did not want to; he did not want to interrupt her. It was his body that laughed and it felt right, as everything had that happened between them. Her eyes looked up at him. They were misty but her wide mouth opened mischievously and she showed him the tip of her tongue. She used it like a brush to draw a line along the crease of his stomach, while her hand came down to open his belt. He drew in his breath to make it easier for her to draw it open. The ends of his belt fell to the sides like a gate pushed wide. It was going to happen. He held his arms to his sides and his hands pressed on the boulder and his body lifted, offering itself. He kept his head down, his eyes open, watching her hands work at the clasp and the zipper, her face momentarily intent but thoughtless like his own.

She smiled when she saw his plaid boxer shorts. She reached a brown, squarish hand inside, grasped the root of his penis and gently drew it out so that its head alone was in the air. He gasped. She took her hand away and it stood out of the shorts pink and white like a new shoot. She half closed her eyes and studied it. The air laved it and it throbbed, and he had to restrain himself from laughing. With forefinger and thumb she touched the head of his penis and drew back the foreskin just enough to uncover the slit at the end of the light red emerging bulb. A drop of liquid formed in the slit and slowly dropped to her thumb and she quickly enveloped his penis in both hands and placed her head on them like a child in a storybook going to sleep. He brought his knees together to hold her to him but still propped himself up with his hands spread on the boulder. Ah, this, this, this.

He closed his eyes a moment and opened them immediately. He had to see her; he did not want her to be just a weight on his legs and his groin. She must have known, for she unfolded her hands and reached up to the elastic of his shorts. He watched her green-stained fingers ease them down and saw his body lift again to let her pull them below his buttocks. They caught at his knees. She looked up at him and he bent forward and placed his lips on hers. They were moist and warm and tasted of watercress. She held her hands to his face to keep it still and, half standing over him, dipped her tongue into his mouth as if he were a vessel. He shook his legs free of his clothes and she stood and bent from the waist and put them on the grass to one side. He saw the veined underside of his penis and sighed as the air cooled his legs, feeling all the more naked because his chest and neck were still in his shirt.

He waited for her to take off her dress—he knew she wore nothing underneath—but she did not. She knelt again, never looking up from his groin, and one hand moved across his belly straightening out the blond curls of his pubic hair. She drew back her head and looked at it critically and then with both hands she brushed the hair up again and again until she was satisfied that it formed a halo.

"Ah Connie," he said, and felt he had told her about his life.

She looked up, her eyes enormous, her heavy lips curled at the corners, and said flatly, "You have a perfect cock." It throbbed and his body moved forward, offering itself. He saw only the top of her head. Her black hair was a tent over his groin. His heart stopped. He felt her lips, then her tongue. It entered the sack of his foreskin, its tip pushing and turning under it and her teeth nibbling at the edges and pulling it back. He smiled to himself; he knew now why men always laughed nervously at the peeling of a banana. One of her brown hands moved from his pale thigh and disappeared, like a small woodland animal, under the tent of her hair. It held his scrotum and his exclamation turned into a moan which stopped when her mouth encircled the head of his penis. Neither moved. From her mouth waves of heat traveled through his body. He felt his breath ebbing as a function his body no longer required: the life that sustained him entered along the cord of his penis from this squat bundle pinned between his knees.

Her tongue slid along the underside of his penis. He contracted. He bent over her head, his hands down her back. "I'll come, I'll come," he exclaimed, and he brought his hands up around her head but did not pull her away.

She lay her face on its side on his thigh. The head of his penis was still held by her lips. With one hand she brushed back the hair lying like a veil on her face, catching it behind her ear, and the movement freed his penis. It sprang up and she smiled and gazed up at him. She kept a hand on his scrotum and gently, playfully, she pulled and cupped it. He bent his head and kissed her lips. They were wet, form-less, and will-less, and from them emanated the odor of heat. His hand moved under her dress and held a tight, round breast. She moaned and then her tongue darted into his mouth. His fingers became wet with her milk and he kept his hand still and felt her heartbeat in his pulse.

He laid his head on top of hers and with half-closed eyes saw, foreshortened as in a tapestry, the clean, white parting of her hair, the stream, the wet ground with their footprints, the colander and his plaid shorts. His erect penis was held by his legs and he felt it too looked blindly at the scene.

She said, "We have to get back. The radishes and lettuce."

"Oh Connie," he said, and tightened his arms.

"We have the whole night," she said.

He kissed her again. This time his tongue was in her mouth. She pulled back and said, "Oh no, we have to do something about it." She got back on her knees, pushed his legs aside with her hands and delib-erately moved down—he saw her mouth open, her nostrils flare, before her hair fell forward—and took his penis in her mouth. Her tongue moved up and down. Seth watched as if it were all now hap-pening at regular speed and he propped his hands again on the rock and began to move his waist until his legs trembled and his chest pant-ed. "Oh God, oh God," he called and then could say no more because his breath failed him.

She stopped before he came. She stood and pulled her dress up and then walked awkwardly, legs outspread on either side of his, until she stood over his glistening penis. She reached down with one hand and held it straight up, and the dress fell and covered their joining. She slowly sat on him and when she had taken in all his penis and he felt her buttocks on his thighs he began to come, quietly, a slow flow like the milk of her breasts. Her eyes were wide open, looking inward, and her hands lay on his chest. When his breath came easily again, she closed her eyes for the first time and he felt his penis squeezed and drawn.

In a moment she smiled. "How am I going to get up?" she asked, and did it without stumbling. She stepped toward the stream and then looked at him for a last survey. He still leaned back on his hands and he spread his legs a little as if to let her see better. She pulled her dress up over her head and threw it higher up, where the grass was thick. Her body was evenly brown though not as dark as her face and forearms. Her pubic hair was thick and black, and he put a hand to his crotch as he watched her. She squatted over the stream and cupped water with both hands and washed herself.

He stood, and felt the ache on his buttocks where they had pressed against the boulder. He walked to the stream and squatted facing her. He began to wash himself and they laughed, looking into each other's eyes. He reached out and put his hand on her mound, and then fingered the cool, tiny penis of a clitoris. She did not move until he took his hand away. He dried himself with his plaid shorts and put on his pants without them. He had never felt this good, this free. He thought: boxer shorts of the world, throw in the towel; and looked up toward the house thinking of Gary. He folded the shorts carefully and stuck them in the back pocket of his pants. He turned to look for her. It has happened, he thought, I love her for it.

She had dressed and picked up the colander and was retrieving some of the watercress that had fallen out. No, I love *her,* he corrected himself, and felt his penis begin to rise again. "Come," he said and put an arm around her to help her walk up the slope. She looked at him calmly, interestedly, as when they had walked away from the farmhouse, and her face was still wet with the water from the stream.

"That was nice," she said.

"I love you," he replied.

"Of course." She smiled and this time her large teeth showed. "Now for the vegetable garden."

"You don't believe me," he said.

"On the contrary." She handed him the colander and shook her dress free from her body, airing it. She took back the colander and said lightly, "I love you too."

Chapter 12

They were all in the kitchen when Seth and Connie returned. The chicken-house king sat at the end of the bench nearest the door bent over a guitar, and he struck it to announce their entrance. Everyone laughed. Gary said, "Let us now sing of bucolic pleasures!"

Connie stopped at the head of the table and placed a hand on the shoulder of a young man with a goatee who had not been around earlier. He turned his head and kissed her fingers. She asked, "Should I check on Fred Hampton?"

A new girl with hair combed loose like Connie's said eagerly, "I went up and looked at him, Connie. He's asleep."

Connie puckered her lips and sent her a kiss. "Then I'll make the salad," she said, and went to the sink and dumped the radishes and romaine in it. Without looking at Seth, she held out a hand for the colander.

As he walked across the room to give it to her, he felt everyone watching him. He checked; they were. He thought: they do not appraise, they accept. But there was also an eagerness in the air he did not understand. He looked from one to the other and each time he saw a new face he nodded and some said, "Hi," and others, "Right on." He made a round of the table greeting them and ended with Dudley, whom he tapped on the shoulder like an old friend. Dudley reached up and handed him a lit joint. "Your turn," he said, and blushed.

"Homegrown and great," Gary called. "You don't have to look so apologetic, Dudley."

Dudley giggled, then bit his lips. "I didn't know Seth was a writer," he said, and flushed even more.

"Dudley writes poetry," Melanie, the girl with the Afro, explained. She sat next to Gary and he held an arm around her.

Seth drew on the joint and he lifted the hand holding his shoes and socks, upward as if he were taking off. "Who's next?" he asked, and saw that on the other side of the table another joint was being passed.

With uncustomary boldness Dudley said, "We've got to keep it moving." He took it and passed it on to the girl next to him. "A rule of the family."

Seth skipped across the room to take his shoes to the storage cabinet. He called back, "Remember, I follow Dudley!"

In the front room he placed his socks inside the cabinet. Not the shoes, because Dudley kept his things so neat and clean. He sat them in front of the cabinet and then remembered his shorts. He took them out and unfolded them and shook them out, wondering where he should hang them to dry. He heard Gary laugh, and looked up. Gary stood in the doorway, supporting himself with one hand on the side of it. Then he threw both arms out and came to him laughing and hugged him, squeezing hard. "Oh, buddy," he said.

They held one another by the elbows in a huddle and looked into each other's faces. Gary's eyes were open wide and he nodded and nodded as if Seth were telling him a long story. Seth said, "I've never had such a good time buddy, never, never."

"You're going to sleep in this room, huh?" Gary said.

Seth pinned his shorts between the lid of the cabinet and the top and let them hang outside it. He fluffed them a little and giggled. Gary grabbed his arm and shook him. "Got them wet, eh, my boy!" he said.

"And you?" Seth said.

"Me?" Gary said. "I too am deep in country matters—ho-ho! I kneaded my first batch of biscuits."

"I mean, are you sleeping in this room?" Seth said.

"I sleep wherever Melanie sleeps," Gary said. He danced back and forth in the narrow passage between the mattress and the cabinets. "I sleep wherever my Melanie sleeps," he sang. He held a hand out to Seth as if Seth were receding from him. "My God, that *is* good pot!"

Seth felt his first pang of anxiety. "I'm worried about tomorrow morning," he said soberly. "Maybe I shouldn't smoke. We've got to be there at eight and I have to drive."

"It's all arranged, it's all arranged," Gary replied, and gripped Seth's arm to steady himself. "The chicken-house king gets up at daybreak to feed them. He'll wake us. Anyway, see"—he waved a hand at the windows of the room—no curtains. Everybody wakes up with the sun." He grabbed Seth's elbows again and looked closely into his face. "And everybody goes to bed when it's dark."

"It's an interlude," Seth said. "It's a grand interlude." He saw Connie's face from his position on the boulder, his penis in her mouth, and wished she were with him now. He said, "They're good kids, they're leading a good life."

"Let's get back to that pot," Gary said, leading him back. He stopped in the hallway and looked seriously at Seth. "You worried about the driving?"

"Not really," Seth said. "Pot has never had any effect on me."

Gary walked alongside him, an arm on his shoulder. "You know what these kids are going to do this summer and fall?" he said. "They're going to distribute their extra vegetables free to their neighbors! This year they doubled their planting, which means they'll have lots left over. Tomatoes, cucumbers, green peppers in the summer. And other stuff in the fall. Rutabagas, you know what that is?— turnips!"

Seth pulled him back a moment. "Gary, do you know who Fred Hampton's father is?" he asked.

Gary's eyes opened wide. He sucked on his moustache with his lower lip. He shook his head. "I never got to asking about the children," he said. He winked exaggeratedly. "I learned long ago that children are the result of copulation."

In the kitchen two hands went up, a joint in each, when they entered. "Last drag," one of the boys called. "Food's on."

Gary went back to Melanie, across the table from Seth, for whom a place had been saved between Connie and Dudley. The three children moved from lap to lap and they ate what they liked from the wooden bowl that happened to be there. Except from the bowl with stuffing, which was kept out of their reach. Everyone ate directly from it and passed it on. A mixture of chicken livers, rice, onions and nuts. When it reached Seth, he took two spoonfuls, and the boy with the goatee across the table said, "Spiced with hash."

"You're kidding!" Seth said, and looked at Connie.

She nodded and took the bowl and passed it on without eating from it. She put a hand to one breast in explanation.

Seth was puzzled. "You don't like it?" he said.

She looked at him from the corners of her eyes, a sidelong glance that excited him. "It would get passed on to Fred Hampton," she said.

Melanie said, "Are you sure about that, Connie?"

Connie smiled, then shrugged. "I don't know," she said. "But acid does for certain. Maybe not hash."

The boy with the goatee again passed the bowl to their side of the table. "I guarantee it," he said. "Right, Dudley?"

Dudley turned a pink face to Seth and gave him the bowl.

"I love how Dudley blushes," the boy with the goatee said. He giggled. "I just love it." There was a burst of laughter from the other end of the table. "Oh shit, I missed that!" the boy said. He called to Gary, "What was that? I didn't hear."

"Respect the table, my grandfather used to say," Gary replied. "No cross conversations. In fact, no conversations. Eating is a serious matter. First a blessing, then you chew each mouthful fifteen times."

A girl whom Seth had not met until now said in a high wistful voice, "Well, maybe there is something to that. We ought to think about it." Like the boy with the goatee she wore a sweatshirt spattered with colors, and Seth figured they were the two who made the silk-screen painted T-shirts. "Maybe we ought to have something like that when we eat. Such as hold hands and be quiet a moment. Quakers do that and they're not bad. We don't have to think of God. We could think of people in the Movement, brothers in jail, brothers who have blown their minds."

"Beautiful, beautiful," said the king of the chicken house. "Dotty, that is beautiful."

Connie leaned on Seth with her shoulder, and whispered, "He is the most gentle person. He takes care of the chickens but he won't kill them. He won't even go near the chicken house the day Jack and I slaughter them and put them away in the freezer. We have to do it a big batch at a time, so he won't have to go through the experience often."

The boy with the goatee waited until he had everyone's attention. He announced, "I got a better idea—we hold cocks and cunts and think about balling!"

Dudley giggled. "What's new about that!" he said.

The boy pointed at Dudley. "Don't dare blush. There you go!"

Connie spoke in Seth's ear. "When Dudley giggles, I know the hash has taken effect."

Seth heard it from far away and he placed a hand on her leg and it seemed to melt into it. A thought approached and fizzled, approached again and finally stuck. "Electricity," he said. "A freezer. You have electricity." He laughed and held on to her leg and leaned against her.

Across the table Gary licked the bowl of stuffing, which was now empty. The light outside had turned blue and Seth saw him outlined against the window, turning the bowl and cleaning its edge with his tongue. "Round about the caldron go," Gary said, and looked at Melanie, offering the bowl to her. "Double, double, give up the struggle." Melanie swayed and pushed it away.

Gary stretched his arm across the table and offered the bowl to Seth. "And now about the caldron sing," he called in a high voice, "like elves and fairies in a ring!"

The king of the chicken house strummed his guitar. "Great, man," he said. "Let's sing."

"Elves and fairies," cooed the boy with the goatee.

"Shhh," Connie whispered. One of the children had fallen asleep on her lap. The little boy dozed on the girl with the spattered sweatshirt. The six-year-old had wedged herself between Dudley and Barry, the gardener, and her head lay on Dudley's shoulder. She complained, "I don't want to go to sleep." Connie repeated, "Shhh."

They were quiet. The room was dark in the far corners. Once in a while a string of the guitar was plucked. A light flared across from Seth, and he watched it like a conflagration on the horizon. It went out, and the boy with the goatee seemed to be writing in the air with the lit end of the joint. Another conflagration, another disembodied orange tip in the dark. "By the itching of my thumbs," Gary whispered, and stopped to catch the lit joint and then added, "Something wicked this way comes."

Both reached Seth simultaneously, from opposite directions. He drew on one, passed it on, and then the other and passed it on. It was almost totally dark, and he looked quickly at Connie to recall her face. The child was still in her arms, and she looked at him as if he were another charge. He placed his head on her free shoulder and it was so huge and comforting that he thought of getting on her lap but could not untangle his legs. "Isn't that funny!" he said. He thought: I must remember that for my notebook, that pot makes my penis so big that it tangles with my legs. The thing I must accomplish is to teach all three to stand and walk, and then teach others. We would not be so frail then but stand sturdily and walk quick: that is what we are all struggling for. I must remember. The voices of the others boomed and whispered but in the long silences the thought returned and he was sure he would remember. He leaned his elbows on the table and waited for another pause to announce it to the brothers and sisters, but it was too subtle. He would have to write it down, and when the joint reached him again, he drew on it slowly, carefully, and knew he had hit on an original thought.

"No lights," someone said far away. "No lights."

"That which hath made them drunk," Gary said, "hath made me bold, my Melanie mine."

Seth turned to Connie. "You have a freezer," he said. "That's what I wanted to remember."

He saw the glint of her teeth in the dark. "Shhhh," she said.

"It's important," he replied. "Electrification. Why do you have a wood stove? Uneven development."

Her hair brushed against his face. "I'm going to take this one upstairs," she said. "Dudley can tell you." She tried to get up but the bench held her in.

Seth stood up and said, "Wait," to the joint that Dudley held toward him. "Connie has to get out," he said. His head was clear, his limbs his own. He stepped over the bench and took the child from her. His hand covered the child's soft buttocks. Infant sexuality, he thought, and quickly said, "Shouldn't I put on the lights?"

She whispered, "No, we all know our way in the dark."

He put his mouth to her ear. "When do I see you again?"

"You'll see me," she said in her common-sense voice, and took the child back in her arms.

The girl in the paint-spattered shirt carried the boy, and Barry the gardener, whom Seth had yet to hear speak, picked up the six-year-old. He was huge and Seth reached a hand to check and yes,

Barry's shoulder was a good foot higher than his. Seth heard his deep voice say, "You will see us all later."

"Connie?" Dudley whispered. "Can I come?"

"Three's enough," she said, then added in an amused voice, "You tell Seth about the electricity."

"Oh yes, oh yes, gosh," Dudley said. He and Seth were alone at their side of the table. He passed Seth the joint and then straddled the bench. "We can smoke by ourselves." He giggled. "Isn't it funny about the electrical equipment?"

Seth straddled the bench too, faced Dudley, and drew on the joint. While he held the smoke, Dudley leaned forward and sucked on the joint without taking it in his hand. Seth felt his rough hand on his wrist steadying it. "Now, your turn," Dudley said, and he leaned back on the bench on his elbows, his back almost touching it while holding the smoke in. When his turn came again, his body sprang forward from the waist to a sitting position.

Seth said, "I didn't know the bench was a seesaw."

"It's my fault," Dudley said. "I'll stay still." He gripped Seth's wrist again. "I'll show you how to make it last. We'll share the smoke. OK, you open your mouth like a fish. Have you done it?"

"Uh-huh," Seth said, his mouth open and a giggling rising in his chest. Before he could laugh, he felt Dudley's nose touching his and their upper lips meeting. Warm, sweet air blew into his mouth and nostrils. He inhaled.

Dudley moved his face back. "You forgot to exhale," he said.

"Hey, Dudley," Seth said. "What about the electricity?"

The guitar strummed. Gary's voice boomed in Seth's ears. It said, "Sirrah, a word with you!" Then Dudley's, farther away: ". . . next day the delivery truck came right up and unloaded a washer, a dryer, two freezers, an electric can opener, a refrigerator, an electric carver, an electric mixer. Electric, electric, everything like from a Larchmont home. So I wrote and thanked them because like they thought that's what we needed." He leaned forward and took a drag from the joint. "OK, open your mouth and don't forget to send it back."

This time Dudley's mouth encircled his own. All the smoke went into his mouth. It felt hot. He drew away. "I love Connie, Dudley," he said. "I love her." He leaned an arm on the table and thought about that. Dudley would understand all that happened at the stream, but he had to get it right so that he would see the significance of it. He said slowly, spacing each word, "I love Connie."

"That's really together," Dudley said. "I love Connie. I love that you like love Connie. Gosh, Connie is the mother, she is."

A clatter of the bowls. Gary's body lay across the table. "Never seek to tell thy love," he said. "Sirrah, a word with you."

Dudley said, "That's funny."

"Gary, buddy, what're you doing?" Seth said.

"There's one thing I got to be doing," Gary said. "Multiple choice. What does drink provoke? Does it provoke nose painting or sleep or urine?"

The boy with the goatee dragged him back to their side. "You got to piss? It's very easy. You walk out on the grass and pick a spot you want to bless."

"Lechery," said Gary. "It also provokes lechery, but right now I got to piss."

They all decided to go out with Gary. Dudley said he would come out later. It was his turn to clear. Seth walked alone toward the kitchen door where the others were leaving. He thrust his legs forward through the thick air, twirling his arms to thin it out and make some space for his body to move ahead. He bumped into the king of the chicken house.

"Where's Connie?" Seth asked him.

"Putting the kids to bed with Barry and Dotty," he said. He placed an arm around Seth's waist and helped him step down from the door onto the granite slab outside. "Whoops. Don't you worry, Connie will come back. The balling is later."

Seth thought of a long eighteenth-century ballroom with chandeliers and sconces along the walls. Glittering crystals. Couples dancing. A sprung floor that rocked with you.

"See the stars," Seth said. It was lighter outside and the figures of the others skipping down the short slope from the house were clear and vivid. He headed for Gary. He was far away and when he caught up, he said, "See the stars on the Mediterranean?"

Gary urinated. "Seth, buddy, I'm glad you came up," he said. "I just thought of something and nobody to tell it to. Ready?" He threw his head back and sang, "Nor shall my sword sleep in my hand—" He laughed. "Not tonight!" Then he sang again, "Nor shall my sword in sleep my hand. ... ."

Seth began to urinate next to him. "Till we have built Jerusalem in England's—"

"Vermont's," Gary corrected.

"In Vermont's green and pleasant land!"

"You can't really sing Ver*mont*," Gary said. "You have sing *Ver*mont." He turned to Seth and asked, "Are you going to put yours back in?"

Seth said, "I don't recognize the quote."

"It's an original, buddy," Gary replied. "I mean, I was going to zipper up just now and I realized, what the hell I don't have to. Think of that, my boy—we don't have to zipper up at all!"

"I love Connie, Gary," Seth said. He lowered his hand and held it around his sack and remembered. He must tell Gary how it had been. "I'm not wearing any shorts, buddy," he explained. "I love her."

"I love her, too," Gary said. He held out his arms and then threw one around Seth's shoulders. "Which one is she? She's not Melanie? Oh, oh, oh. They're the same and separate, the same and separate— that's it."

"Look at the stars," Seth said.

"To be thus is nothing," Gary said to them, "but to be safely thus—ahhh!"

"Maybe we can come back," Gary continued before Seth could reply. "I want to live this way, building Jerusalem." He held his arms up again. "Jerusalem!"

Seth felt himself rise. If Gary were not holding him down and he could twirl his arms he could fly higher. No, it was not that. He needed to run down the slope and then he would have the impetus to sustain himself in the dark air. He must first start with long hops. He thought: the secret is we have always tried it against the wind when it's the wind that would carry us the way it bathed me by the stream my cock rising. His notebook, he must write that down.

He crashed into the boy with the goatee. The boy peered into his face. "Have you pissed?" he asked. "Don't piss yet."

"I don't think there's any left," Seth said, and looked down at himself and wondered.

"Too late, too late," Gary said. "We have cast our seed on the ground. Waterborne, that is."

The boy explained that Dudley was taking the leftovers to the compost heaps and that it was the custom to piss on the heaps to help them rot. The boy added, "We don't let just anybody piss on our compost." They followed him around the barn, their arms about one another, and the boy kept repeating, "Urea is urine," and Gary laughed each time and asked, "Are you sure? In Cuba they're spending a lot of money to build a factory to manufacture urea. I have to tell Fidel."

"I bet you know Fidel!" the boy said. "Don't say anything about him until we're inside in the rapping room."

Dudley came toward them carrying a large wooden bowl. Behind him the two girls, the chicken-house king, and two boys that Seth had yet to talk to. "It's all over," Melanie called, and flung her arms around Gary.

"Wait, wait," the boy with the goatee said. They watched him run to the first of the compost heaps by the vegetable garden. He climbed up the sides, which were made of slim tree trunks laid upon one another, like a stepladder. At the top he steadied himself. They saw the black outline of his body against the sky and then the stream of urine catching the light. "Right on!" Melanie yelled.

"In another hour," said one of the boys, "the moon will be shining."

The girl who had cooked the meal put an arm around him. "Dyno," she said. "You're going to give us a rap on the stars?"

"Why the inconstant moon?" Gary asked. "You always know when it's going to be there."

The boy with the goatee stopped them. He held an arm through Seth's and tried to bring Gary to him too for his announcement. He called to the others, "Gary has been in Cuba, he knows Fidel—"

"And Chou and Ben Bella and Nkrumah," Seth added.

In the awed quiet that followed, the chicken-house king said, "No shit?"

The boy with the goatee regained his voice. "So we'll postpone the rap about the stars because we've got Gary only for one night."

"Around a fire," Melanie said, so they made a line outside the barn door while one of the boys passed out logs for each to carry in.

Seth stood next to the chicken-house king and the boy with the goatee, arms held out to receive his logs. "Where are we going to make the fire?" Seth said. "I didn't see a fireplace."

"In the rapping room," the chicken-house king said. "You were in the one across the hall."

The boy with the goatee giggled. "That's the ballroom."

Seth remembered his resolution: no questions.

The boy with the goatee added, "After sundown the family develops class lines. There are the talkers and there are the fuckers."

The chicken-house king shook his head. He did not agree. "Not everyone talks but everyone fucks. One way or the other."

"Or the other or the other," the boy with the goatee said.

Seth thought of Connie. Where would they go? No questions, he told himself again. He laughed and the others joined him. Barefoot like this, out in the night, everyone young—every thought was permissible, everything was play. Nothing had to be said, as in the days when he ran at hide-and-seek with the children of the cooks and handymen during the time with Amelie in France. He remembered the hash and the pot. He laughed again. The joke was on him: it had had its effect. He knew why: he was happy.

The dark was now his friend. The silver-birch logs in his arms were startlingly white, but they did not assail his eyeballs like electric lights. The house was darker still, but he did not stumble, nor did the others. Natural light, he said to himself, natural light. He would never have a headache again. He had only to switch off the lights. He put his two logs in the bin next to the fireplace, and he looked around. Melanie arranged the kindling and the others sat on the mattresses while the boy with the goatee stood by a pile of pillows at the window and distributed them. Each time he called a name he flung a pillow. "Seth!" he said with special emphasis. Seth caught it and hugged it and thought of Connie.

He went out to the hall and stood at the bottom of the stairs. He walked up halfway and stopped. The three came down, Connie last. He had not forgotten her face: her wide mouth, her flat nose, her almond-shaped eyes. Dotty's and Barry's presence was like that of ministering angels: he put his arms around Connie before she descended the last step. His head fell between her breasts and he pushed up his chin and kissed the hollow of her neck.

Dotty went on, but Barry stood by quietly as he had done during dinner. He was a tall, protective palace guard standing watch. Connie stepped down and kept one of her feet on top of Seth's. He lifted his slightly to feel the pressure of hers on his instep. He pressed himself against her thigh.

"Is everyone in?" she asked.

Seth told her what they had done. He wanted to ask her to go into the other room with him. He didn't. He looked into her eyes and waited.

"I want to hear him," Connie said. "But first maybe we can step outside." She looked at Barry too and spoke for him. "We always do."

He thought: but isn't Jack . . . and stopped himself. Barry walked behind them, the sound of his boots becoming the presence that his huge bulk standing quietly had been. In the kitchen Dudley wiped the table in semidarkness. "Connie!" he said, and threw the rag in the sink and joined them.

They sat on the granite slab which was the step for the kitchen door, and together they looked down the slope to the chicken house. The gravel road was like a light brush stroke in a monochrome. Connie sighed. Barry reached into his workshirt and extracted a joint. When he drew on it, he held it out to Seth without speaking.

"My mother and her friends always used to complain about putting the children to bed," Connie said. "I remember once her going inside after bringing me a glass of water and saying to some people who were there for a meeting, 'It's the last straw, I've had it.' I must have been a pest. But I love putting our children to bed. They're so clinging, so warm."

Dudley passed the joint back. "Like puppies," he said.

"After a while I went to bed like a good girl," Connie said. She leaned her elbows on her knees and her face on her hands. "I don't think they knew I masturbated myself to sleep."

I should be shocked, Seth thought. He drew on the joint for wisdom. This is why I love her, he reflected, because she talks the way a man does, because I don't have to open doors for her, because . . . He laid a hand on her back and ran a finger down her spine. "That's nice," she said.

Dudley leaned forward until his face was next to hers across Seth's knees. "Did you really, Connie?" he asked.

"Didn't you?" she replied.

"Gosh, yes," he said.

His ponytail was alive and Seth reached for it and held it still.

"I keep telling you, Dudley," Connie said, "that girls are very much like boys."

Seth gave up Dudley's ponytail and with both hands reached for Connie's long black mane. He held it like a rope and then laid his face on her back. Behind him Barry sat like Buddha. Barry looked down on him and smiled without parting his lips and Seth felt that he had been photographed. In Barry's mind the picture would stay forever and he, Seth, would always be looking at Buddha worshipfully while lying on the pillow of his beloved's back. Buddha's hand came toward him in the arc of blessing, and Seth drew on the joint he discovered between its fingers in a moment of revelation. He slowly sat up again with the joint attached to the hand still between his lips and drew on it yearningly, as if the life of Buddha's huge body thus flowed into his own. Buddha's mouth moved and there was no sound, but Seth knew that it said I love you. He said it for Connie too and Seth looked with divided eyes toward her and the bulk of her body squatted at the stream. Buddha nodded and gave him permission to place his hand on her mound and lave it with sweet water.

Connie propped a hand on his knee, and he saw that they were no longer at the stream. Barry gave him the joint once more. Connie leaned across his knee toward Dudley and placed a kiss lightly on his nose. Seth giggled. "That's funny," he said.

"If you boys are finished," Connie said, getting up, "I want to go inside and hear Gary." She held out both hands to Seth and he took them and she pulled him up. "And you, too, you have to talk about France."

He floated up toward her and met her body sooner than he had expected. "And love," he said. "Love."

"Gosh, Connie, I dig Seth," Dudley said. "I really dig him."

"What about you, Barry?" Connie asked. "You like Seth?"

Seth turned to him too. He wanted to be his brother.

Barry slowly nodded and released in Seth a flow of love that took in this whole house and its sloping fields. "I was in awe of him," Barry said in a deep voice that was like an emanation, "but he is like a little boy and he belongs."

"To us," Connie added, keeping an arm around Seth.

Seth giggled. "I don't think I can walk," he said. "But I can fly!" He looked from one to the others. He did not have to think with them. With them there were no walls: they flowed into one another. And the house too. He had floated through and out of it during this perfect life. He could feel his way in it with his own light and now be discovered himself alert and happy and loving of everyone around the fire in the rapping room. The pot, of course, but it was more than that. There was Gary, his red hair flaming like the logs in the fireplace, and his eloquence was a gift they all gave him. He thought of James Evergood: Father, father, you needed these sisters and brothers to help you with your decision.

"The Centenary Column," Gary said. "But you have to hear it in Spanish. *La Columna del Centenario!* You hear how grand it sounds? The Cubans give these resounding names to the things they do—"

Melanie asked, "Did you cut cane?"

"I did, I did," Gary said. "*El Trabajo Voluntario!* Hear that? But when you get into the back of one of those trucks all crowded in with all those people from the city, black and white and oh beautiful in-between, and no distinctions. When you go out with them it's not awesome. They're joking and singing and talking and reminiscing about what lousy cane cutters they once were. And predicting we'll all be dead beat when we come back. I was used only to meeting big shots, you know, on trips for the committee, but in Cuba there are no big shots. I remember this little chick, she said, 'I'll help you get into the truck on the way back.' And Christ if she didn't!"

"Beautiful," Dotty said.

"But *La Columna del Centenario,*" Gary continued, "out in Camagüey in the middle of Cuba where in the old days people only thought about getting away to Havana, out there some forty thousand kids are living voluntarily in the countryside—like you—and they work at anything in agriculture that they are assigned to. They started doing that in 1968, one hundred years after the first revolutionary uprisings. That's why the big resounding title. But they're not marching along the way it sounds. They live in small camps, one hundred and fifty, three hundred to each. Communes really. Right?"

"Right on," one of the boys murmured.

"And did you sit around and rap with them too?" Dotty asked.

The boy with the goatee laughed. "They got a rapping room too!"

"Out in the fields," Gary replied. "Let me tell you. I drove out with some army guy to visit some camps and we came to one midday and the camp commandant was not there, so a fellow working out in the office suggested we try to find him in the cane fields. And off we went. We got off the dirt road and headed to a spot where the cane was being cut. It was the lunch break and everyone was under the shade of one big tree or of the truck that brought them there. They don't cut cane between one and three because the sun is so hot then. So they have classes. 'What is a peninsula?' asked the kid who was the teacher. He had a small blackboard, about two by three, propped up against the tree trunk. 'What is a peninsula?' he asked."

"No shit, what do they want to know for?" the boy with the goatee asked.

"That's their thing," Dudley called out to him. "Gosh," he added.

"'Well,' one guy said, 'it's where the land sticks out,' and he went over to the blackboard and drew it. Wow. Everybody laughed because it looked like something else. It looked like a cock. Then another guy got up and he said, 'A peninsula is a body of land surrounded by water on three sides.' You know what happened? They applauded. They clapped the brother on the back. One more victory. And me—you know what happened to me? I've been through college, I have a Ph.D. I have the greatest bourgeois education you can get. I cried."

"Beautiful, beautiful," Dudley said.

"And when Seth and I got here today," Gary said, "and I saw this place and the spread you put out for us, I thought that. A peninsula is a body of land surrounded by water on three sides. So, class, what is a peninsula?"

Melanie threw her arms around him. The boy with the goatee withdrew a stick from the fire and lit a joint with its burning end. He offered it first to Gary. "A peninsula is . . ." he began.

Seth called out, "I love you, I love you."

Chapter 13

Hours later, sitting alone on the granite slab step of the kitchen door, Seth felt that the chill before dawn, which made him shiver and contract and hug himself, was an emanation of his desolation. His intelligence made no connection with his feelings. He covered his face with his hands and withdrew them quickly, because he was drawn back into the dark from which he had escaped. The even, gray light dispelled the mystery of the night, but it had no warmth and no direction. He thought: it is the sun, like the mind, that gives intelligence to the day. I must wait. The drugged sleep will evaporate and then I will know what has happened to me. Not know but make sense of it. He did know. It was as clear in outline as the chicken house and the edge of the barn and the sloping fields were to his eyes now. The hands he had drawn away from his face, even the clothes he had managed to find in the dark, told him with their odors the bodies he had known, that had known his. Sharply, distinctly, his own arose from them, acrid with fear and shame.

He had loved them all. They had freed him. Sitting behind Connie, hugging her with his legs, he had mused while Gary talked; he had leaned his head on her shoulder from behind as if looking at the fire over a wall. Sometimes he had to look away; it was too bright. These times he lifted her curtain of black smooth hair and placed his lips on her neck and inhaled the musky, trapped air. He whispered, "I am a mollusk, I am going to cling forever."

His legs surrounded hers and his arms crossed each other at her waist. She permitted this the way a mother does a sleepy child. Sometimes she leaned an elbow on his knee. This mixture of tolerance and indifference and acceptance was delicious. He let a hand drop down between her crossed legs, and she did not take it away. Only when she joined in the discussion and had to straighten her neck and sit up did he move back his head and listen with the others. Dudley or Barry, sitting on either side behind him, passed him a joint then, and he held the smoke in his lungs while she spoke. Her flat, commonsensical, commanding voice passed through his body on its way to the others. He thought: I am your vessel and your vassal.

She said, "Everyone here wants to be simple like that. That is why we are here. Some of us have tried—oh, many things. Right, people? We wanted to discard all the trappings of the American middle-class civilization. America with a *k*. We decided we couldn't do it in the city. All the plastic shit clings to everybody there, workers and middle class. Maybe not the blacks, not them, they always know where it's at. But we couldn't change the color of our skin. So by a process of elimination we came to the country, not because it's poetic but because it's real."

The chicken-house king picked up where she paused.

Melanie said, "Wait, Connie didn't finish."

"Everybody speaks," Connie said, shaking her head and pointing to him and then listening with interest.

Dudley whispered to Seth, "Did you hear Connie? That's what I was trying to tell you." He huddled closer to Seth to take the joint that Barry passed. "It's not a metaphor, it's real." He held the smoke and then said, "When Connie talks like that I really get together. Look." He took one of Seth's hands and placed it at his crotch.

Dudley's erection made Seth giggle. It was small, almost smothered by the coarse cloth of his coveralls. Seth squeezed and twisted it all in one motion and giggled again.

"Gosh, that hurt," Dudley said.

Seth rested his face on Connie's back and said, "Sorry, Dudley, I was just fooling."

Dudley lay back on the mattress. "No, I deserved it. I was a bad boy," he said. "Are you going to punish me too, Barry?"

Through half-closed eyes Seth watched Barry slowly nod with the whole upper part of his body. Barry smoothed a crooked joint and lit it from the tiny butt of the other and flicked the butt into the fireplace without getting up. With one hand on Dudley's ponytail, he gently lifted Dudley's head off the mattress and placed the joint between his lips. "Groovy," Dudley sighed. He drew from it and let his head come down on Barry's lap. Barry stretched his long arm and held the joint at Seth's mouth and turned into Buddha.

Seth thought: Barry Buddha Barracuda. He opened his mouth and lifted his head off Connie's back to tell him but instead he giggled. He should tell Gary. Gary would understand.

From far away Gary said, "But what about politics? All that is great, but where's the political involvement?"

Connie's back straightened. "All that is the foundation of our politics," she said, and Seth's head fell off her shoulder. He felt Barry's large hand spread out like a fan support him in the hollow between his shoulder blades. It held him like a strong pillar. The hand slid around him until it was Barry's whole arm on which he rested. Slowly, gently, Barry let him come down to lie on the mattress, and he pillowed his head on Dudley's thigh. Seth looked at the reflection of the flames scurrying on the black ceiling. They responded to the sound of Connie's voice.

"We'll spread like a stain," she said. "A dot here, a dot there, where the people make their own food and their own economy and their own babies. The blacks and the Third World people take over their own communities. No pigs there, no capitalist economic relations. In the Third World the guerrillas are doing the same. The stains spread. Slowly—it takes a long time to make a world revolution. You know how the Chinese did it. You read *Fanshen*. They organized every blade of grass, they held the regions, they reclaimed the soil, they taught the farmers to plant and harvest together, then to pool their farming tools and destroy the fences. In that way everybody counts, every blade of grass."

Seth felt the movement on the mattress, the exhalations and the murmurs. It was applause for Connie. The boy with the goatee called, "What do you say, Gary?" Seth brought his outstretched legs together and felt his knees push into the taut, firm flesh of Connie's thighs. "Connie, Connie," he said to himself, and saw Barry's hand, holding the joint, descend to his mouth. He took the butt between his lips and the hand covered his face a moment before retrieving the joint. It was warm and smelled of the soil and it moved down to his throat and cupped it and stroked it to help him inhale and hold the smoke. He brought up his own hand and it was so small against Barry's that he laughed and let it go.

Seth heard Gary's voice pick up the melody, rise above the murmurs in a new key. "I say it is beautiful, for I believe a leaf of grass is no less than the journeywork of the stars," he recited, and Seth saw the shadow of Gary's rising body on the ceiling. It spread its arms. "Take my leaves, America, take them south and take them north. Make welcome for them everywhere, for they are your own offspring. Surround them east and west, for they would surround you. And your precedents, connect lovingly with them, for they connect lovingly with you."

"No presidents," Dudley murmured. "Everybody's equal."

Connie stood. There was something wrong. Barry stirred. Then a girl's voice called, "Take him to Connie. Let him kiss her hands, for they're really together."

Connie shook her head. Her long hair flew up like a twirling skirt. Seth saw that wide smile, the flash of her teeth. She sat down on the mattress and placed her hands on his feet and leaned back on his upraised knees as if on a throne. She kept shaking her head as they brought Gary to her. He crawled the last two steps. She laughed. He bowed his head at her feet. "Oh woman," he said. "They are your offspring."

Barry grunted. Dudley sighed. Dotty called, "Beautiful, beautiful, Connie!"

Seth wished to be in front of her bowing too, but her back was against his knees and she still held his feet and he did not want to remove himself from her. Beyond her shoulders he saw the red halo of Gary's hair and his eager, avid expression. Gary put an arm around Melanie and another around the boy with the goatee. They knelt beside him holding him up. Gary threw back his head and spoke to everyone but ended with his face looking into Connie's. Seth remembered that look, and he closed his eyes to recall where he had seen it. On my own face, he thought.

"I have perceived that to be with those I like is enough," Gary said. "To stop in company with the rest at evening is enough. To be surrounded by beautiful, curious, breathing, laughing flesh is enough!"

"Oh man," said the boy with the goatee.

Gary put a hand on the boy's mouth to stop him. "There is something in staying close to men and women and looking on them, and in the contact and odor of them, that pleases the soul well. All things please the soul but these tease, seize, ease, please the soul most of all!"

Barry's descending hand brought Seth the answer. "American Lit One!" he called. He drew on the joint and stared wide-eyed at the ceiling while he held the smoke. The tall grass bent with the wind of the fire. He exhaled. He knew: a woman waits for me.

Gary called, "Where is Seth, what is he?" His head swiveled looking for him. His body wobbled trying to crawl to him. "Buddy, buddy, buddy, we are on the long march to take Richmond. Cut. Shot of soldiers, their boots on the steps. Cut. Shot of baby carriage, the future endangered. Cut. Shot of soldiers, rifles at their waists, bayonets at the ready."

"Eisenstein," Seth called, and closed his eyes again.

"There he is!" Gary said, and pointed Seth out. "Oh, that was the unkindest cut of all."

Connie held a hand to Gary's chest and he looked down at it and moved his chest from side to side and she involuntarily caressed him. "Open your eyes, Seth," he said, smiling at Connie, "for mine have seen the glory of the coming of the Lord. Ho-ho."

Connie raised a forefinger to her lips. She smiled. She looked back at Seth. He seemed blissfully asleep, his head still on Dudley's leg and his knees open. As Gary and Connie watched, Seth's knees slowly straightened and he sighed. Dudley was half awake, and Barry sat above him and Seth smoking the last of a joint. Connie kept her finger to her lips and a hand on Gary's chest.

Gary whispered, "Oh, Chickamauga."

Connie looked at Barry. With a movement of her head she told him to take Seth to the other room. Barry pinched the butt and threw it over the heads of those kneeling around them into the fireplace. They were all silent, and they watched Barry carefully, easily, pick up Seth in both arms. Dudley got up too and wobbled a moment and then went ahead, opening the way for Barry. The boy with the goatee giggled, and Connie said, "Shhhh."

Gary waved a hand. "Good night, sweet prince," he said.

In the other room the light of the moon fell on Seth's face as Barry passed by the first window. Seth said, "Connie . . ." Barry stopped and hummed in his ear to reassure him. Dudley went ahead to the far corner on the mattress and pulled back the covers. Barry kept him cradled until he laid him down. He removed his arm from under his knees last. Seth murmured, "Connie?" Barry again hummed in his ear. Dudley knelt at Seth's feet. In a moment Barry looked at him and nodded, and Dudley began to undress Seth. He folded Seth's pants carefully and put them away in the storage cabinet. When he returned to the corner, Barry was pulling the turtleneck shirt over Seth's head. Seth half sat up. "Where is everybody?" he asked clearly, then closed his eyes. "What's that?"

"What?" Dudley asked.

"The bright light," Seth murmured, his eyes still closed. "Who put it on? Connie?"

"The moon," Barry said.

Barry's voice was a deep rumble and Seth moved his head to Barry's shoulder to be nearer its protection. "It hurts," he complained. Then: "I'm cold."

"We'll get under the covers," Dudley said.

They covered him and then took off their own clothes. They stood in front of him while doing so to keep the moon from shining in his eyes. Dudley got under the covers first. "Gosh, I'm cold too," he said. "Hurry, Barry." Barry folded his dungarees and his workshirt, and the mattress trembled as he walked to the storage cabinet. Dudley turned on his side toward Seth. "Are your feet cold?" he whispered. "You can rub them on mine."

Barry returned with a lit joint. He sat next to Seth and brought up the covers to his own waist. Seth opened his eyes, and this time the bright rectangle of light stopped below his collar. "Where's Connie?" he asked. Barry handed him the joint and he put it to his lips and inhaled. The room, long and black and silver, turned into a still shot.

When he withdrew the joint, he could not understand why Dudley said, "She's rapping. She told us to bring you here."

Barry did not reach for the joint, and Seth drew on it again and it heated his chest and he knew he had not done wrong. "Oh Connie," he murmured, "is this right?"

Dudley took the joint. "This is where Connie sleeps," he said. "She'll come here later."

Seth looked at Barry. Barry nodded and that made things right. Seth tried to nod too but his head only rolled to the side. At eye level he saw the grass on Barry's chest brooding warmly in the afternoon sun. He walked on it with outspread hands over and over the undulating fields, catching it between his fingers. He explained, "My feet are cold."

Dudley giggled. "I'll rub them, that's what brothers are for," he said. He disappeared under the covers, and the sound of his laughing came from far away.

Seth watched the moving bedclothes and pulled up his feet to avoid the rising waves and his knees formed a mountain in the waters. He turned to Barry and Barry smiled and Seth felt the water on his instep and on his ankles. It was warm. They were Dudley's fingers, and the transformation made him giggle and turn once more to Barry. Barry smiled and now handed him the joint, and at Seth's shoulder two feet appeared. They were cold and he leaned over on Barry's chest to get away from them, but they did not matter, for he was warm now; the heat radiated from his chest and his legs, waves that climbed and receded, and he hung on to the floating timber of Barry's arms and moved his waist to lower it into the water and opened his legs to receive it. His sigh filled the room. Wet, wet, wet, the warmth lapping at his groin. He swelled and moved, circling and pulling away, and each time he entered the water it sucked him in and held him suspended. He reached down to free his limb, but before he could reach it, he felt the underbrush growing on Dudley's flesh. It teased his palm and his fingers moved away like a school of fish and twined around the twig that rose above the bush. It was smooth and sharp and he looked up to tell Barry, but he only sighed and his mouth hung open. The twig throbbed in his hand and the round O in the middle of Barry's beard descended, exhaling smoke until it surrounded him. He inhaled to take the smoke and sweetly, shyly, a little fish swam between his lips.

Seth opened his eyes. He was wide awake. Barry's eyes were an inch away, closed, and his tongue was fully inside Seth's mouth. Seth thought: I am compromised. This is Dudley's cock in my hand and his mouth eating mine and this prong at my side can only be Barry's hard-on. He eased his head back and tried to see beyond the fringes of Barry's beard. Barry's tongue licked his chin. They were alone in the room, but he was not certain. He remained still and felt the grip of Dudley's hands on his buttocks and his mouth clamped on his penis. He moved his head to the side, and this time saw the whole room. No one. He quickly, curiously, lowered his free hand and gripped Barry's penis. The head alone seemed to fill his hand. He squeezed. Barry's mouth moved to his ear. "Seth, my little boy," he murmured, and his deep voice sent vibrations through his body. "My little son."

Suffocation and fright. He kicked his legs and the bedclothes flew away. He felt immediately the sharp thrill of the cool air and the movement of Dudley's mouth. So this is it, he thought; the subject of all the jokes. Cocksuckers, asshole buddies, queers. He let go of their penises, and Dudley moved quickly between his legs and from a kneeling position took in one motion the whole of his penis in his mouth. Barry kissed him again and his tongue felt for Seth's. He pulled his back and thought: it is they who are doing this. I am the recipient. He had never witnessed such obeisance and greed, and he responded with a momentary pity and tenderness that made him reach for Barry's cock again. I am in command, he thought, they are in my power. He squeezed Barry hard and lifted his legs to Dudley's shoulders and clamped his head between them. He heard his voice say harshly, "Suck it, suck it, suck it!" and he pushed his pelvis forward, forcing himself into Dudley. Barry's mouth left his and Seth felt his beard on his chest and then his teeth biting his nipple. He pushed and withdrew, pushed and withdrew. "I'm coming!" he warned, but he held the head between his legs cruelly, punishing it. "I'm coming!" In a spasm of kindness he opened his legs to free him at the last moment, but Dudley did not move away. His hands lifted him closer and in the moment that Seth lost control he felt Dudley's finger invade him. He gasped and began to thrash and ejaculate, thinking alternately and at once: he's swallowing me, he's violating me, feeling violence and submission, powerful and caught; clanging and clashing until all his responses merged into a bruising ecstasy in which he levitated and pleaded and moaned and called, demanding it not to end. When his body felt the mattress again, they turned into his angels and slaves once more. Dudley's head remained at his crotch, holding his soft penis in his mouth, and Barry's arms held him gently, cradling his head on his shoulder. Seth's body twitched at intervals and in the pauses he wished himself into sleep.

Connie said, "Here, here, this one's for you." Her hand, at the back of his neck, brought him toward her breast. Behind him, closing him in, the huge wall of Barry's body, his penis between his legs and extending beyond them, so that it lay under his own. In the moonlit side of her body Dudley sucked at her other breast. Seth tasted the sweetish milk on his tongue and understood the gurgling smacking noises from Dudley. Beyond his moans, movement. He lifted his head and saw Connie looking down smiling at him, shaking her head to show she could not move. "Connie," he murmured, and saw above her the boy with the goatee standing naked, watching and slowly masturbating. He closed his eyes and took her nipple in his mouth again while she rubbed his head and sighed. Mine, mine, he thought, and moved his body on top of hers and felt Barry's penis slip away. He pushed at Dudley's body with his own, but his head remained on her breast until with one hand he lifted it away.

"Connie!" Dudley protested.

"Children, children," she said.

Her legs would not yield. She returned his head to her breast. She moaned and he knew it was a command. He sucked and got a knee between her legs and pushed forward but found he was soft. He lifted and felt hands on his buttocks kneading and searching. He tightened and fell to the side and a small soft body held him from behind, nipples writing on his back. "Sweetie, sweetie," a girl's voice said, and he remembered her paint-spattered shirt. Her hands came around him and stroked him and he saw Dudley climb back to Connie's breasts and he began to cry and feel his penis lengthen. "Big, big," the girl said and he remembered her name and said, "Cunty, Cunty," and cried again at his error. On all fours, the moonlight silvering his back, Dudley looked like a young goat swinging his lowered head from one breast to the other. Behind him Barry positioned himself and moved forward on his knees. Seth called, "Dudley," to warn him and knew as he said his name that this was a ritual and he rolled away not to see it.

The girl now faced him and she moved her body to his and spoke, but he heard only the voices of the others. No words, only sounds.

Grunts and piteous moans and angry urgings. The girl stroked and he held on to her and listened. "Here, here," he finally heard her say and felt himself enter her. "Don't move," she said and he closed his eyes and nodded because he did not want to, anyway, only to listen to the sounds. Her body began a weaving motion clamping and releasing and her legs climbing and stretching and she spoke into his ear softly, "Cunt, fuck, shit, cunt, fuck, shit!" He remained rigid, unmoving and unmoved, and listened to the storm at his back for the sound that Connie had denied him at the stream. He isolated her voice and it led the others. "Boys, boys," she moaned, and the pain flashed from the back of his neck to his temples and he closed his eyes tighter and tighter until he heard her break into a scream. The pain exploded in his head and he sobbed in unison with the dying sounds. The girl gripped him harder and her voice rose in agony. "Cunt, fuck, shit!" she repeated hotly until the words turned into a whimper and she began to cry too.

She moved away from him and lay at his side not touching. He looked up at the ceiling and his erection was a sharp pain that he felt he would carry forever unreleased. He thought: it was not love, I am a fool, it was not love, I am a fool.

The girl at his side said, "I need some grass," and got up and crawled away. In a moment the boy with the goatee approached on his knees and asked, "How was she? Did you come?" Seth brought up an arm and covered his face. The boy did not go away but placed a hand on Seth's erection. It hurt and Seth lifted a leg and positioned the foot on the boy's body and pushed. The boy called, "Hey!" and crawled back laughing and this time Seth kicked hard with both feet until he went away. When he felt himself alone he opened his eyes and remembered the nightmares in which his mind caught up with the runaway anxiety and told him just as the dream became unbearable that none of these things had happened. He forced himself to look. The moon had changed and shone aslant the room and lit up only the far corner beyond him. The three lay together, asleep.

"Here," the girl said, extending a joint.

He shook his head and did not look at her sitting up next to him.

"You're like me," she said. "You get disgusted when it's all over." She put the joint in his mouth. "Now, sit up. You'll feel better."

He made the effort and they sat in the middle of their unoccupied mattress and faced the windows with their knees drawn up. She lit his joint with hers and he smoked it as if it were a cigarette. Its extra harshness simply made his mind clearer.

"At first, everyone would stay with me afterwards," the girl said. "And they still will. But I'm trying to work out of that. I want to help others."

Like me, he thought. In the dark front corner someone was reaching his climax. She did not seem to hear it and he said nothing. His penis lay limp and calm between his legs. He talked to his psychiatrist: Doc, you wouldn't let me get on your lap, so I got on Barry's and I held his cock in my hands. A big cock, bigger than mine. He heard himself saying it in a light, joking voice, and decided, Yes, that's all that happened. Why was I so scared? A night of balling, that's all. The shrink replied, That was not it, it was Connie—you were looking for romantic love and a blow job and romantic love is dead. He looked around and the wavering rectangle of light framed Connie's face and Barry's lying next to hers. Her mouth was open and she snored.

The girl at his side said, "Why did you push the brother away? He needed help."

He giggled. He thought: after all this I can still be embarrassed. Finally, he said in a small voice, "I was tired."

"Help him," she said. She looked ahead at the shadows between the windows and made a hissing noise. "Chuck," she called, and the boy with the goatee got off the storage cabinet there and walked slowly toward them. He held a hand around his erect penis and waited at the edge of the mattress. "Come here," the girl said, and tapped the mattress in front of Seth.

"I'm sorry," Seth said when the boy got to them.

"Give him a drag," the girl said, and Seth lifted his hand and the boy took the joint from him. The girl said, "Now, do him."

Just the other side of Seth's knees the penis appeared disembodied. Seth stared at it, and it seemed to emerge from the dark, joined to nothing. The girl at his side moved closer and he placed his hand around it. It slithered back and forth in his hand and he felt then the body behind it pushing and withdrawing and breathing hard. "Great, great," the boy said and Seth opened and squeezed his hand to his rhythm. The boy pushed forward against Seth's knees and he opened them and the boy got closer. The boy grabbed Seth's shoulder and his penis touched Seth's cheek and, in a panic, Seth let go of it and pushed at his groin. He fell back on the mattress and the boy's knees descended on his chest and pinned him down. The boy searched for Seth's hand. "I don't want head, man, I want you to lie still, still. . . ." he said and his voice disappeared with his panting and his hand stopped searching for Seth's. "I'm coming!" he suddenly called. The first wet spurt hit Seth and he closed his eyes and clamped his mouth and waited. The knees released him. The boy and girl held each other close, lying full length alongside him. Seth pulled at the bedclothes to clean his face, but they would not give. He turned his head down into them and wiped his face.

They made no move when he crawled away. He stood up in the passageway between the mattresses and the cabinets and was surprised that his penis was erect again. He took his clothes from Dudley's cabinet and made his way around the front of the room. He kept his head down and to one side, not wanting to see the bodies at the first mattress. A hand reached up and caught him. "Is this a dagger I see before me?" Gary asked.

The girls with him giggled. "It's your buddy you've been rapping about," Melanie said.

Gary let him go. "Seth?" he said, as if he hoped it were not he.

"He came looking for you, I bet," Melanie said.

Seth held the clothes in front of himself, and Gary said, "Go on, buddy, go take a leak."

In the hallway, while putting on his clothes, Seth heard Gary argue with the girls. "You don't understand, he *is* my friend," he said. "I love him, I trust him with my life and he trusts me with his. Don't ask me any more about that, you know why we're here. He is my buddy and I don't have to ball him to love him."

"But wouldn't you like to?" Melanie insisted.

Seth listened for Gary's reply. There was the noise of a tussle. Then Gary laughed. "Hmmm, I'll have to think about that," he said.

He urinated a few steps from the kitchen door, wishing they were already leaving and afraid to get away from the house. The water issuing from him made him feel cleansed and better, but when he sat on the stone slab at the door the light came up and he smelled on his fingers and arms the acrid odors of the night. He needed his jacket where the pills were, but he did not dare return to the room. He could wash at the sink. The door creaked when he opened it, and he paused a moment to listen. The kitchen had been cleared. There was a basin in the sink, and he tried the pump and it caught without priming. There was a yellow, rough soap on an abalone shell, and he pulled off his shirt and washed with the cold water. No towel. He dried himself with his shirt and went back to the stone slab. He shivered and clamped his jaws to hold still but felt better. Between the corner of the house and the chicken house an orange glow had begun while he was in the kitchen. He thought: *Red sky at morning, sailors take warning.*

He wished he were back in Connecticut writing his book. That was his real work. If I had come here alone, he said to himself, I could walk away right now and no one would know. These kids don't matter. As far as they are concerned nothing happened. And nothing did happen. Gary was not with me, he doesn't know. It was they who served me, I did nothing. If we're stopped on the way back, I can say I know nothing about it. He asked me to drive him up here after I had gone to visit my parents' home and they can check that I had real business to do there. Well, I drove him here as a favor and since it was late they told us we could spend the night and asked to borrow my car, which I had no reason to refuse. No reason at all. Gary will back me up in all this. It was really the way it happened. Why should two suffer? I never saw it, my bag was in the back seat. I shall take an amphetamine.

He heard the noise of the pump, then a man's voice mumbling, and he moved quickly to the edge of the granite slab and sank his head to his knees. He did not want to talk to anyone. Then another voice, and the kitchen door opened and someone stepped out. It was the chicken-house king. His fingers lightly tapped Seth's head. "Hi," he said, and went on. He stopped a few feet away to urinate and called back, "I get to see the sunrise every morning. Look." Seth lifted his head: it was going to be all right, no one was going to talk about it, of course. "I started coffee on the stove," the fellow added, and went on to the chicken house. Seth was alone. He thought: but he didn't know anything, he was not in the room with me. He brought his head to his knees again. He waited for the other person in the kitchen to come out.

Gary said, "Now I know what my father meant about the good times he had in the army. He'd say, I got screwed, stewed, and tattooed, but he had no idea of the ramifications or resonances—ho-ho! Or did he?" He sat on the step next to Seth. Seth did not look up, and he put a hand on Seth's hair and ruffled it a little. "Hey, buddy, you shouldn't have left so quickly back there. I thought of a great thing to say while shaking hands with your big whang—oh, what suspension of disbelief is this I read before me!" He laughed and got up and walked to the grass. He urinated and looked back at Seth. "Are you OK, Seth?" he asked.

Seth shrugged. He cleared his throat. "I'll be fine," he replied.

"We can have coffee soon, thank God," Gary said, and came back and sat with him again. "I'm worn out. I wish we could stay another night, but I'm not so sure . . ." He cocked his head and looked at Seth, and when Seth finally guardedly returned his gaze, he slowly winked. "Still, it was great, wasn't it?"

"Oh, sure," Seth said.

"They're not exactly emotions to be recollected in tranquillity, eh?" Gary said. He rubbed his chest ostentatiously, then Seth's back. "Did you get buggered?"

Seth looked away as if he had been slapped, and felt the color rush to his face.

Gary smiled. "So that's why Dudley blushes all the time!" he said.

Seth shook his head hard. "Come on," he protested. He frowned and looked down, afraid he might cry.

"Listen, you could say I technically was," Gary said, and leaned over and nudged Seth. "Technically. There I was, on my knees investigating a sweet little clitoris, when—bang!—something entered my nether orifice. Ho-ho! I flew across the room. Unattached, needless to say. But can you say I'm a virgin now? We had a discussion about it— had it happened or not? To be or not to be? That's why I'm not so sure about coming back. I flew across the room because it was a pain in the ass. Next time it might prove a pleasure."

Seth pretended to look at the sunrise; he wanted Gary to stop that kind of talk, but it had made him feel better. "I was too stoned to know what happened," he said, and then looked toward Gary, avoiding his eyes. "Well, not too much," he added. He shrugged. "I don't know that one can talk rationally about what happens in bed," he said, and thought: it's all right, I'm OK.

Gary got up. "Hey, I smell the coffee," he said. He gave Seth his hand to help him up. "Now, I don't know about that. Why can't one bring reason to bear on sex? You take buggering, it makes sense. What more direct way to get to the prostate? A super short circuit! And when it comes to receiving or giving a blow job—"

"Let's have coffee," Seth said impatiently.

"Well, it's very curious about the flesh. Everything human is natural to it," Gary said. He held his head. "Oy, oy, I guess we'd better have coffee."

Seth held the door open for him, and saw him look at the landscape. "Dear native regions," Gary recited. "I foretell from what I feel at this farewell—"

"God damn it, Gary," Seth said. He trembled with irritation. He thought: he's disgusting, he gets buggered and wants to talk about it. There was movement inside the kitchen and he remembered Connie and wished he could get away. No, thank God for Gary, he wanted him at his side. "Come on," he said, less harshly.

"A little Wordsworth never did anyone harm," Gary said. "I wonder what he would've said about all this. Oh hell, he knew Byron and Coleridge. Byron, that's my revolutionary. Or did Wordsworth know him? He came later, right?" He looked at Seth with a preoccupied squint. "Trudy would know. God damn Trudy, maybe I'm just getting even with her. Oh my, Seth, there's so much to talk about!"

Chapter 14

Seth had no time to improvise or be prepared. Connie stood naked at the sink, washing her breasts. "Ho-ho," Gary said, but she did not turn around until she was through. She smiled and pointed to the cupboard above the sink. "Mugs," she said, and she walked past the table serenely on her way to the hall. At the doorway she turned her head and said, "I'm going up to Fred Hampton now, but don't leave without seeing me. Remember that."

Gary took two mugs from the cupboard and brought them to the table. He looked to see that she was gone and then said to Seth, "Wow." He leaned down and whispered, "She's terrific, but I couldn't make her come. Did you?"

"We'd better think about what we have to do," Seth said, as if he had not heard. He thought: *she's sick.* He got up and brought coffee from the stove. "We have to shave and put on some respectable clothes." He looked around for sugar and milk. The sugar turned out to be in the cupboard with the mugs. He remembered Dudley's talk about the electrical equipment, and opened the door to the summer kitchen to look for milk. There were two deep freezers and a large refrigerator lined up along the inner wall.

"Wow!" Gary said over his shoulder. He read the labels on three boxes across from the refrigerator and saw they contained the dishwasher, clothes washer, and dryer. "Nothing like the simple life," Gary said. In the kitchen he drank his coffee silently.

Seth took his wristwatch from his pants pocket, wound it, and strapped it on his wrist. "It's six-thirty," he said. "I figure we have to leave here at seven-thirty at the latest." He saw the kettle on the floor next to the stove, and he filled it at the pump and placed it on top. "That's for shaving," he said. "When you finish your coffee, go and get your bag. I'll get mine now."

There were several lumps under the bedclothes, but Seth did not look at them. He did not want to wake anyone. He did not want to see them again, and anyway, they needed the kitchen to themselves as long as possible. Gary was still at the table when he returned with his bag. Seth frowned. He did not want him there when he took his pills.

Gary looked up eagerly to share what he had been thinking. "There's a kind of cultural lag. No plumbing, but they've got all that stuff in there."

"Go get your bag, buddy," Seth replied. He sat at the table and lit a cigarette. He figured when he finished smoking it should be time to start shaving. "Go on," he said.

When Gary left, he took his jacket from the valise and reached for his pills. They were not in the pocket where he had left them. Wait, he said to himself, don't get excited. He held the jacket up with one hand and with the other went through each pocket of the jacket twice, the second time to feel if there were any holes. He stood up and dug both hands in his pants pockets. The pillbox. It lay in the valise; it must have fallen out of the jacket. He picked it up hurriedly, to take the pills while he was still alone in the kitchen. It was empty.

He thought: I'm defenseless, I'll never make it home, I'll never make it. He looked through the valise and his hands began to shake. He sat down and waited. When he felt calmer, he drank the rest of his coffee, and slowly, one by one, to get himself under control, he took out the razor, the blades, the shaving cream, the lotion, and the deodorant and sat them on the table. He read the labels to help himself think. Someone took them. Who? Where's Gary?

He heard a noise and turned with a start. "How's the coffee?" the chicken-house king asked. He went to the stove, and Seth took his shaving equipment to the sink. I'm OK now, he said to himself, but what about later? "Do you have any aspirins?" he asked.

The chicken-house king shook his head. "We have herb teas," he said. "They're better. Want me to make you some camomile?"

Seth said no. They could stop somewhere and buy high-potency vitamins. When do the stores open? A couple of vitamins could give him energy, but for the others he needed a prescription. Stay calm, he said to himself, do not think about it. Take a Librium. He turned to his valise before he realized that these too were gone. He thought: *I'm an addict.* If only he could tell them he had to have the pills. One of them must have taken them. I need them, I need them, he said to himself.

"A mirror! A mirror!" Gary called. All the others seemed to have come to the kitchen with him. "Brothers and sisters, stand aside and see the great transformation act. All the world's a stage. See Brother Seth and Brother Gary play respectable middle-class types! Brother Seth—" He placed the hand mirror above the sink and stopped smiling when he saw the grim look on Seth's face. "I'm sorry, I'm a pain in the ass."

The hot water and the lather helped. He kept his back to them; they sat at the table drinking coffee and listening to Gary. At intervals he had to place his hands in the basin of hot water. It warmed and soothed him. When he turned around, he kept his head down and he took all his things to the valise and then went off to the front room with it. He rubbed the after shave lotion on his chest and face and slowly dressed. He put on a shirt and tie and a clean pair of slacks. He shook out his jacket and put it on and sat on the storage cabinet to smoke and wait for Gary. The bedclothes were twisted and pulled away from the mattresses. If he did not have to drive the car with its cargo to New York, if he could just sit quietly somewhere, he would be all right. Gary did not come to the front room. From what Seth could hear he was undressing and dressing in their presence. "Ho-ho," Gary exclaimed once in a while. Maybe someday he would think all this was funny. He shook his head to himself. Not now. What if the car was not at the rest stop? What if they had caught Jack with it and the things?

"Seth!" Gary yelled from the kitchen.

Dudley appeared at the door. "Seth—" he said and then stared at him. "Gosh. You look like my father." He looked down and blushed. "We're ready to go," he added, and looked at Seth again and smiled. "Gosh."

Seth jumped off the cabinet and picked up his valise. The motion made him feel dizzy and he had to stand still a moment. "Dudley . . ." he began, thinking to ask him for help.

Dudley replied, "Seth," and started toward him with his arms out to embrace him.

"Seth!" Gary called, and this helped propel Seth past Dudley without appearing to avoid him. Dudley placed a hand on his back and Seth hurried toward the kitchen to break the contact. There was a burst of laughter from those inside. They raised their fists. Seth automatically smiled as if he were on a lecture platform. He felt dizzy still. He was going to fall. He let go of the valise. He could not fall. They were all around him, the three girls kissing him and the boys hugging him, and they moved with him and Gary and there were always arms about them and if he stumbled and gasped for breath it was natural and cause for more laughter. At the truck they moved back a little from the two. Seth held on to the door handle and the feeling of gladness and purpose that he always experienced at departures gave him the energy to open the door and climb inside.

There was quiet. Gary stood outside holding the door open. "Hey, I'm sad," he said to the others. "Hence, loathed melancholy!" Seth saw him apart for the first time. He wore a tie and shirt and his hair was wet and slicked down. He raised his hand and said, "Here's Connie."

She came toward them wearing a long dress and holding Fred Hampton naked in her arms. She walked slowly and the others fell back some more. Seth thought: *she's acting all the time.* She moved her head to keep her long hair away from her face, and Seth looked away and said in a weak voice, "Come on, Gary, let's go."

Gary did not move. She came up to the truck and turned to look at the others behind her. Fred Hampton was asleep. Seth looked at him quickly. He had black hair. He thought: *I don't care who his father is.*

"Seth, Gary," she said in a low voice. She waited for their attention. Seth heard her say flatly, as if disdaining dramatics, "Drive your car to the only parking garage on Thompson just before Houston. Uptown from Houston. You park it there after five o'clock today or after five o'clock tomorrow. At no other time. You say, I've been driving all day, Ed. And he says, Are you leaving it overnight, Mr. Hoover? If the attendant doesn't say that, don't park it there. Come back when there's another on duty. But don't worry, he'll be there today and tomorrow, after five."

She moved Fred Hampton to her left arm and held out her right hand to Gary and then stepped closer and held it out to Seth. He meant to act imperturbable and lean over coolly and shake her hand, but he was afraid any move would bring on the dizziness. He hesitated. "Will you be able to drive all right?" she asked. "You're not looking well."

"Ho-ho!" Gary said, and started to laugh. She turned a serious, questioning face to him, but it had no effect on Gary. He winked. Then added, "It's just his city costume—you've never seen him in it. The distinguished journalist!"

Because he stepped back in order to gesture, Gary was not hit by the stream of urine that suddenly left Fred Hampton. It just missed him. It formed a clear, sparkling parabola and spattered against the window of the truck until Connie put her hand at the source and deflected it onto herself. "A fountain!" Gary exclaimed, and everyone laughed and rushed up to the truck and Seth had to make no explanation about how he felt. Dudley and Gary got in on either side of him and he had only to smile and nod. "Come back, come back," they yelled over the noise of the engine and Gary held his head out the window and blew kisses and Seth nodded some more and thought: *never, never.*

He leaned his head back against the seat and closed his eyes and felt each move of the truck in his bones. He longed to be home. The long bathtub, the chaise in his study, Mathilde dissolving the aspirins in sugared water. His real work awaited him. In his ear Gary whispered, "Thompson up from Houston. We've been driving all day, Ed. Remember that." His stomach contracted and the saliva at the back of his throat tasted sour. The truck bounced over a high bump and he opened his eyes, afraid he might vomit. Gary's face was close to his, studying him. He said, "Lean back and rest, buddy, you've got a long drive ahead." Dudley hunched over the wheel and his ponytail bobbed with the truck and the breeze coming in the window. Seth closed his eyes again. They were on the gravel road now. Maybe he could make it.

An image from a newsreel he had seen when he was a boy. He saw the flattened, strained face of the man. The lead runner in a hurdle race. White shorts and white wooden hurdles, legs and arms pumping, blurred flashes of figures behind him, shadows he had outrun. Each time he came to a hurdle the arms stopped and the legs lifted and spread forward and aft, flying for an instant and then pumping again until, as if pulled by strings, they rose above another hurdle. Again and again and then the noise of cheering from the screen and around him. He too. A long view and there was the runner, far ahead, only a clear stretch of track to go. He took a deep breath, lifted his arms and expanded his chest to meet with pride the glittering ribbon now in sight.

He opened his eyes. "What if the car isn't there?"

"Gosh," Dudley said.

"Nay, nay, it will be there," Gary said. "As sure as Hamlet's ghost." He leaned an arm on the window and let the breeze hit his face. "And then we shall smite the sledded Polacks on the ice and drive straight to New York."

He had to wish that the car would be there. He sat forward and looked ahead. Still, if something were to happen, it was better that it happen to the others. It made a better story. He had simply lent the car, that's all. Would they believe him? He had no choice. He leaned back again. Like his father, he had no choice. He could see the track clear beyond this hurdle and he had to keep going. If he did not make it, there must be some way to recover. He looked at Gary. Gary would understand that it was right that he should be saved. He would remain true later, the way his father had. Of course, of course, that was the way it had happened to father. It had no importance; it was his later life that counted. Or his earlier. There was no reason to use the incident in the book.

He heard Dudley and Gary talk across him. "And will you really come back, Gary?" Dudley asked.

"For a visit," Gary said. "Not for good. Everyone has his job to do. Mine is in the city."

"Oh sure," Dudley agreed. "Everybody's got to do his thing." He blushed. "We're all making the revolution, right?"

Seth moved his head to look at Gary, and Gary avoided him. He sighed. "Well, Dudley," Gary finally said. "We're sort of like the ladies auxiliary."

Seth did not have the energy to laugh. He said, "You bastard."

Gary covered his face with one hand and laughed behind it. It sounded as if he were gasping for breath. "That's not a put-down," he

said. "They also serve who—we *are* a kind of adjunct, not even advis-
ers. The blacks and Puerto Ricans won't listen to whites. They call it
equality and all that but they mean to be the leaders. They know they
are. It's not a subjective thing, it's a historical fact about white
America. No class, no historical force exists in our country to make
the revolution, except them. White revolutionaries in America are like
shooting stars. Beautiful, they light up the sky. But they don't make a
constellation."

"Now, class, let's do a close examination of the text," Seth said.
His head lay back on the seat turned toward Gary. He tried not to think
of what Dudley made of all this. "You're saying we're fools to be on
this fool's errand."

"No, no!" Gary argued. He was happy they had found a subject.
He half turned in his seat, his back to the landscape, and faced Seth.
"Let history go its way, we've got to do what we can. I'm not so sure
about historical forces, anyway. Historical forces are mostly hindsight.
We're something new. We're in the same boat with them but we're
nowhere near the wheel and we can only paddle with our hands."

"Ho-ho, buddy," Seth said bitterly. "Mixed metaphors."

"No, no, mixed metaforces," Gary replied. He bounced in his seat.
"Oh, super! Did you hear—mixed metaforces!"

Seth closed his eyes and placed a hand on his stomach. It felt tender and sore. Gary's jostling had made it feel like the center of his
being. He opened his eyes and said with a simplicity he had never
before achieved, "I'm scared, Gary."

"Scared?" Gary said. "But why—" He stopped, then said, "Oh
that. Should I be too? Come on, you're putting me on. You told me it's
just a little errand."

Seth gave up. He made an effort to smile. "I was just trying out
the idea."

"OK, let's really examine this errand," Gary said. "We're picking
up something—we don't quite know what—from we don't know
where or whom and taking it to others we don't know either. That's
our job. Right, Dudley?"

Dudley turned toward him and said, "Gosh."

"That's us, the ladies auxiliary holding bazaars, folding bandages,
knitting sweaters, to raise funds," Gary continued. "But we're in the

boat, nevertheless, we're in the boat, thank God. And the kids are making the best of it—that's my revelation. Not the best of the bourgeois world. That only happens in Balzac's novels. Not the world of the corporations and the expense accounts, nor of the sweetness and grandeur of power. Novels depict that to be significant, but it's not life, it's literary manipulation in order to demonstrate what little boys are made of. You can't live by that. Let us sink into insignificance —that's real life!"

This time Seth turned to Dudley and asked him, "Is that right?"

Dudley opened and closed his mouth. "I've got to talk to Connie and Jack about that," he said. Thinking about it, he let the truck slow down and he had to shift gears "Gosh, I think we'll have to rap about it in Hampton's Family tonight."

"No fair, no fair," Gary said to Seth. "I was speaking metaphorically. I'll start all over again. The committee got involved for a while with introducing the Panthers to people with money to raise those enormous bails. Parties with richies on the East Side. The first Panther from the New York group came to a Fifth Avenue penthouse. He'd been out of jail less than a week. Trudy took one look at him when he got up to speak and she whispered to me, 'Not counting the overcoat, he's wearing at least three hundred dollars of expensive mod.' It blew my mind. Quick, thinking like a social worker, I told myself, deprived background, TV consumer aspirations, all that shit. But the fact is the Panthers are involved with power and with the bourgeois world. Even to knock it down you've got to deal with its symbols. You've got to dress the part."

"But—" Seth began.

"Wait, wait," Gary insisted. "I'm not knocking the Panthers for using our funds to dress like slick cats. My point is about the kids. They are creating centers of resistance to the bourgeois world. Making the best of it is living a little communism now. It's a matter of the soul and consciousness, not history. Those who can and will shall break the power of the bourgeois state, but the kids shall be there with their communes to remind the leaders what it's all about. Now, isn't that a grand and glorious role to play?"

"In the clear light of morning," Seth said, "it all sounds insane and you most of all."

Gary looked at him with concern. "Ah Seth, buddy, you're not feeling good."

The truck stopped. Dudley looked left and right, and turned onto the paved highway. Any moment now. The truck took the new road smoothly. Seth thought: if it's like this my stomach and nerves can take it. He sat up and wondered whether it was the road or the suspense that made him feel more alert. He turned to Gary and said for his benefit only, "We're all niggers now."

They had driven a long while, it seemed to Seth, before Gary spoke again. "In time—oh, in much time—after many defeats, the grandchildren of this generation will look back and think calmly about us. The way we do about Bakunin. They'll see that the revolutionaries today aren't grubby or bohemian or sex maniacs, but sainted fools. I love them."

Seth stared ahead and saw, as if zooming out of the road that carried them to the rest stop, the fearful possibility that made everything and everyone suspect. Without turning, for even Dudley and Gary fell into its maw and it was too late to test them, he asked, "How do we know we are not in the hands of provocateurs?"

Dudley too was more alert. "What's that?" he asked eagerly. "What are provo . . .?"

"Police agents," Gary explained. "Agents who set up a situation to go wrong."

Dudley shook his head vigorously. "There are no pigs in Hampton's Family, gosh no. Nobody gets to be a brother without dropping acid as a test. Connie and Jack stay with them and talk to them." He shook his head again and squinted as if there were more to say but he could not now remember.

"That's all?" Seth said.

"Well, yes," Dudley said. "No, if we're not satisfied, they have to take a second trip."

Gary asked, "And did anyone have to go through it twice?"

Dudley flushed. "Me." He looked at Gary and hunched his shoulders. "I didn't talk at all the first time. It was so groovy taking a trip with the brothers and sisters I loved. Not like when I was making the scene in the Village and I wanted to stand on Second Avenue and stop traffic and talk and talk—there it is."

The rest stop. Seth looked at his car, his dear familiar car, as if he had been gone a lifetime. It was dustier and shabbier, but it was back, like a cat that had strayed. Jack was not in it, and he and Gary turned to Dudley and said so simultaneously as the truck slowly turned into the stop.

Dudley shook his head again. "Jack was not supposed to be here," he said. "He gets back to Hampton's Family on his own. I just drop you off and keep going." He looked back at the highway. "I'm going to Hollowell and buying chicken wire at the hardware store. You know, so I can say I drove into town to buy something." He sighed with the effort of so much talk.

"We'd better get out," Gary said. He opened the door and jumped down. Seth moved over carefully before getting out. He felt light-headed, but he was not dizzy: the pleasure of getting away. He jumped down and stood still a moment to steady himself. If only he had an amphetamine.

"Wait!" Dudley said. He moved across the seat to the open door and held out his arms to them and grabbed Seth's head first. "I love you," he said, and before Seth could move kissed him on the lips.

"Oh, what the hell," Gary said, and leaned forward and kissed Dudley. He backed off and added as farewell, "You're a good boy, Dudley."

Dudley closed the door and looked at them with bright, happy eyes. "Oh, I forgot. If you see me in Hollowell when you drive through, we are supposed to act as if we don't know each other." He took a deep breath and tried to remember if there was anything else he had forgotten. "Gosh, I feel funny about that, acting like, man, you're not my brothers."

Gary looked at the highway. "Better go now before anyone comes by."

Dudley scrambled back behind the wheel, and Seth turned back to his car. I'm going to make it, he thought, and opened the door by the driver's seat. He turned and yelled, "The bags!"

"Christ!" Gary exclaimed, and ran to the truck, stopping it before it got on to the highway.

Seth watched him and thought: *we're mad, we're all mad.* No car had gone by while they were there and he wished hard that Gary would hurry. He thought of the speech Gary had made in the truck, and said to himself, *They're not sainted fools, these revolutionaries, they're madmen.* He would look at the road no more and instead slowly let himself drop into the driver's seat. The gas tank was full and the speedometer showed it had been driven 450 miles. All night. Canada? Gary ran around the front of the car with the two bags, smiling at him through the dusty windshield, and opened the door to the back seat and threw the bags in. As he placed a hand on the handle of the front door, he exclaimed, "Oh Christ, don't start it!"

Seth saw Gary crouch and look at the front of the car and he knew another tire had gone. The truck was on the highway. There was no calling it back. He leaned his head on the wheel and waited.

"It's flatter than hell," Gary said.

When Seth looked up, Gary was standing with his hands on his hips staring at the tire as if by looking he were doing his part. It seemed to Seth that in opening the door and getting out of the car he was using up all his energy. His legs trembled as he walked around the front hood. It's an omen, he thought, we won't get away. The tire was down to the rim. He automatically squatted to look at it. It had sustained a deep cut. "God knows where it was driven," he said, and leaned a hand on the tire to keep himself from falling forward.

"Well, at least this time I know where the jack is and how to put it together," Gary said. He walked to the trunk of the car and added, "And the spare should be in—"

"Gary!" Seth called.

Gary removed his hand quickly from the hood of the trunk. He needed no explanation. They stared at one another across the length of the car. They breathed in unison. Finally, Seth stood up without taking his eyes from Gary. He nodded, and Gary responded with an almost imperceptible smile, as intimate as a lover's. Gary said, "We have to look, buddy."

With deliberation Gary pushed at the catch, and the top of the trunk came up, hiding him from Seth. Seth turned toward the highway to keep watch. It was then he first saw the state police car turning into the rest stop, too late to tell Gary to close the trunk.

"Gary!" he called, and hurried to him. He had thought: I must tell Gary now to protect me, to say I know nothing, but instead found himself at Gary's side, pulling at his arm, whispering intensely, "I'll swear you know nothing—it's my car, you know nothing."

Gary did not listen to him. He had heard the noise of the car and stared at it as it pulled alongside. A blond, red-faced trooper looked at them with a frightening smile, and said. "You're in trouble, gentlemen."

"I—I . . ." Seth began, and saw that the policeman's smile was a real smile. "We've got a flat." He looked quickly to the highway. No other police cars. He looked back at the trooper and saw he was alone. He thought: we must close the trunk. He made a motion with his hand to get the top down but Gary's arm held it up stiffly. There were two flat wooden crates inside, one on top of the other. When he pulled his eyes away, the trooper was out of his car.

"I saw it as I turned in," the trooper said, looking at the front of their car. "You must've cut it on a country road."

Gary came to life. "Yes, I was just getting the jack out of the trunk," he said. Seth saw him realize that the trunk should be closed. He started to bring the top down and then stopped. "Terrible way to start the day," he added.

"You got a spare in there?" the trooper said.

"Sure, sure," Seth said, standing by Gary, blocking the trooper's view of the trunk.

"We'll be all right," Gary said. "Just change the tire, that's all."

"I'll give you a hand," the trooper said respectfully, and moved to the trunk. "You're not dressed for the job and I'm an old hand at this." He looked inside the trunk, picked up a wrench and began to remove the spare. "Good thing you were loaded down," he said, nodding toward the crates. "It must've helped you keep it under control when it went off."

"Yeah," Gary said happily. "Here's the jack."

Seth felt the blood returning to his extremities. It brought back his trembling and his weakness. He would not have been able to change the tire, he thought, and it was no use to stop the trooper now, he might become suspicious. "Officer, it's very kind of you," he said weakly.

The trooper turned his head toward him and smiled. "It's just a little service for visitors to our state," he said.

Seth let Gary be the trooper's assistant. When they began to jack up the front of the car, he moved away from them and tasted the acrid saliva in his throat. He walked through the grass wet with dew until he reached the nearest tree. He leaned a hand against it and, while supporting himself thus, vomited into the tall weeds. Behind him he could hear Gary talking to the trooper, and when he finished, he felt well, as if he had just awakened from a good sleep. John Brown was mad too, he remembered Gary say, but he was right. He turned and saw Gary awkwardly rolling the old tire to the trunk. He recalled what he had said to Gary when the trooper pulled in, and he looked at him now as if he were his own, his beloved child. I'm not bad, he thought, I'm not bad, after all, and did not wish, as had become usual with him, that he could tell this to his shrink.

When he got back to the car, Gary was trying to persuade the trooper to take a five-dollar bill. The trooper wiped his hands on a large red handkerchief and shook his head. "I tell you what you can do," he said. "You're going to need a spare. That one's shot. If you're going back through Hollowell, get it at Charlie Eaton's garage. You can't miss it. Charlie's my brother-in-law. Tell him Roger sent you."

"It's a deal," Gary said, and they all shook hands.

They watched him drive out of the rest stop heading away from the town, and when he was gone, Gary threw up his arms and yelled, "Only in America! Only in America, buddy!" He danced to the back of the car and waited for Seth to come and look inside before he closed the trunk. Seth did not join him. He opened the door to the driver's seat and shook his head at Gary. He sat behind the wheel and thought, he is my buddy, even if I never see him again after this he is my buddy, but this is not for me: I am my father's son.

Gary jumped into the front seat. He put his hands on Seth's shoulders, brought his face close, and exclaimed, "Say not the struggle naught availeth!" He leaned back and gave Seth the go-ahead. "We'll stop somewhere and have a great breakfast and then—New York!"

"Yes," Seth replied. "New York." He reached in his pocket. "The key!" he said. "I don't have the key!"

"There it is," Gary said. "In the ignition. No one steals anything in these parts. And no matter how we try we'll never be niggers to them. Especially in these duds."

"New York," Seth repeated, and as he reached to turn the key, he thought: I am free. He experienced one final revelation, as mysterious and unforeseen as a dream, the sensation that they rose with their car to their destination. In Hollowell, Dudley came out of the hardware store and heard the explosion. He looked up at the sky for the jet from the air base fifty miles away that must have caused it. He shook his head and frowned. Someday there will be communes all over the world, and no more sonic booms.